HOWLING WOMEN

HOWLING WOMEN

SHELBY HINTE

Library of Congress Control Number: 2024947229
ISBN 979-8-9851070-8 (paperback)
ISBN 978-8-9851070-9-8 (ebook)

First Printing, 2025

Cover design and interior layout by David Wojciechowski
Cover art by Challenger99/Shutterstock.com
and Login/Shutterstock.com

LEFTOVER Books
Rochester, New York
leftoverbooks.com

"There are always logical explanations for the loss of one's mind in the desert… Isn't that what passion is — bodies broken open through change?"
— Terry Tempest Williams

"I was looking for love in all the wrong places / Looking for love in too many faces / Searching their eyes, looking for traces / Of what I'm dreamin' of"
— Johnny Lee

"I'll be alright, as long as there's light from a neon moon"
— Brooks & Dunn

ONE.

I left my husband the same day I left my boyfriend. Goodbye, California. Goodbye, life I thought I wanted. Hello, New Mexico. Hello, place I thought I'd never return to. The so-called land of enchantment. Though, to me, it has always just been the place where bad things happen. It's nicer to imagine it was some desert enchantment that brought me here rather than the more likely truth—that the state itself is a type of succubus. Those mystical vortexes as real as anything else, sucking people in, making it impossible to ever truly leave. I didn't use to believe in all that—vortexes, magic, fate—but now I am not so sure. Here I am, back where I started, unable to leave. This isn't a metaphor. I'm literally not allowed to leave. That's how it works when you're awaiting trial. When you're out on bail. When you've shot a man.

Not everyone thinks it's a good idea to go writing all this down. At least, my lawyer doesn't think it's a good idea. I've only talked to the man a couple times, mostly on the phone, but he thinks I'd be better off keeping my mouth shut. I get the sense he's not into the touchy-feely stuff like my therapist. It's funny to say that. *My therapist.* I may have spent more than a decade in California, a place where practicing forms of self-care is basically a personality, but I'd never once gotten close to acquiescing to the idea that sharing your private life with a stranger made you healthier. I guess this is just another way I never truly escaped my upbringing. Where I'm from, cheap beer and a dim-lit bar are all the therapy a person needs.

Technically, *my therapist* is a chemical dependency counselor. Court-mandated. She goes by Dr. Camille (no last name to speak of). I'm not sure if she's actually a doctor or if it's a term of endearment from the other employees at the probation department. Her office is across the hall from where I pee in a cup twice a week to prove I haven't been drinking or using drugs. Also court-mandated.

Under normal circumstances, I would be all for keeping my mouth shut. This never would have happened if I'd kept my secret a secret. It was opening my mouth to Howling Woman that got me here in the first place. She's the one who found his address. The one who suggested we get in her pickup truck and drive south to pay him a little visit. The one who brought the gun. For my part, she wouldn't have thought to look him up if it weren't for me coming undone.

In the end, it was me that shot him, though. That would likely be all that mattered in the eye of the law. That's the problem with the law in general. It's always trying to assign blame like such a thing that can be done. The law doesn't care about the story. And the story is bigger than just the shooting. It goes back to our upbringings—mine and Howling Woman's. It goes back to shitty stepfathers, mothers that let bad things happen to their children, and growing up in homes where you drink away your feelings before they ever reach the surface. Maybe it isn't useful to go that far back. Dredging up the past hasn't brought me anything but trouble, but it's hard to imagine this story frozen in the present moment. Hard not to imagine that everything before now played a role in me getting here. Maybe my whole life was building up to this moment.

TWO.

The week I left my husband was one of those weeks that feels like a million years. I'd had an abortion only a few days prior to getting on a plane for New Mexico. I hadn't told anyone about it. That's the normal protocol for secret abortions resulting from extramarital affairs. The way I see it, if you are cheating on your husband and you get knocked up and you don't know for certain who the father is, you only have three options to choose from: One, you confess—pray for forgiveness and spend a lifetime atoning to your partner with no guarantee that they won't eventually come to their senses and leave your ass. Two, you end the affair in secret, play pretend, raise the baby with your husband, never letting on that you stay up at night wondering who the father is and fear one day you will be found for the fraud you are—your whole life a lie, and by proxy, your spouse's life too. Three, terminate the pregnancy, terminate the marriage, and get the hell out of dodge.

I went with option three. I took a Lyft to and from the clinic while David was at work. Spent a day in bed playing sick and planning my escape. On the day I left, my husband didn't even say goodbye on his way to work. Of course, David had no idea his whole life was about to change, that when he'd get home, he'd find a note on the counter from me that read, *I don't love you anymore. I'm sorry. I hope you find happiness with someone else. Please don't try to find me.*

It wasn't an easy thing to do, but it was easier than the alternatives. I cried the whole drive to the airport. Part of me was mourning my marriage, but the other part was mourning that I hadn't become the type of woman I hoped California and college would turn me into: a woman who read books and went to art museums and had a man that reached out to hold her hand in a room full of people.

Not long after David and I were married, we took a trip up north with his mother to stay in a cottage and feel close to nature. It was something his family did, taking weekend trips to rural places where the locals lived in trailer parks tucked behind giant conifers out of sight from tourists. Before we made it to the cottage side of town that was neatly pruned for tourists, David pulled off the side of the road to get gas at a dilapidated white station. There wasn't a single car in the lot that had a matching set of tires. In the fuel port next to us, a white woman with a large belly and peroxide blonde hair smoked a cigarette and yelled at her son to share his hot Cheetos with his baby sister. Near the trash cans, an emaciated man with no shirt and pants sagging low enough that you could see his pubic hair drank from a tall can of Steel Reserve. His skin was sun-leathered and he swayed back and forth like his mass was too small to hold itself up against the elements.

David's mother, a woman, who, like David, was a vegan and worked as a professor at Berkeley, went into the store to pay for the gas. After we'd filled up, the three of us safely inside our Prius, David's mother looked out the window as we drove away. She shook her head watching the gas station disappear behind us.

"How depressing," she said, "Everyone there looks like they walked straight off the pages of *The Grapes of Wrath*."

David nodded his head in agreement. I sat in the back, watching their heads nod in tandem, wondering what they would say if they ever saw where I'd grown up. They'd met me as a bookish college student far from home. I worked hard to uphold that image.

As far as my boyfriend went, I sent him a text message the morning I left.

I can't do this anymore. Sorry.

Until now, I never referred to Avery as my boyfriend. I didn't have a word for him before I left. He was just the man I was sleeping with behind David's back.

I'd graduated nearly a year and been married to David for two when I met Avery. I was waitressing at a "gastropub" in Oakland called Merritt Tavern and was unsure of how to transition into the next phase of my life. My job paid my way through college, but I never imagined I'd be there so long after graduation. In my imagination, I always had some vague picture of living a literary life. When I closed my eyes, I would see myself in a black turtleneck, a chignon hairdo, a glass of wine in hand as I enjoyed a party in a room full of books with elegantly dressed people who'd never lived in a trailer or ate boxed mac and cheese even a single day in their life. Sometimes I would see myself reading in a library or writing in a country house with walls made entirely of built-in bookshelves. The problem was, I didn't know how to get from my real life to that imagined one. College and academics had for so long been about separating myself from where I'd come from that I don't think I really got to the part of the story where I formed another tangible ambition. I needed a bridge from college life to real life, but I didn't know how to build it.

Then came Avery—a forty-six-year-old busser with zero ambition who liked to call me his little whore when he fucked me. Sometimes he'd spit on my face when he came like something out of a Mary Gaitskill story.

Avery was my Al Pacino to Michelle Pfeiffer's Johnny in *Frankie and Johnny*. Only he wasn't as obsessed with me. He never looked at me with doe-eyes and said, "Everything I want is in this room." My affair with Avery came more from having finished college and finding that I was still a waitress, that I didn't know how to be someone whose life had any type of meaning. When I was younger, I thought that movie was so romantic. I wanted a man to want me as badly as Johnny wanted Frankie. Now I see that film for what is, a lonely waitress unable to recover from the abuse of her former boyfriend, begging Johnny to leave her alone before submitting to his demands for affection. A waitress and a cook, together in love, ostensibly aspiring for nothing more.

But Avery didn't want me like Johnny wanted Frankie.

I understand, was all he texted back after I told him I couldn't do it anymore.

That was it. No goodbye or desperate appeal for me to love him back. Why is it that no one loves anyone like they do in the movies? It's not that I wanted a long goodbye or anything, but it'd be nice to imagine that the thought of losing me could make a man believe his world was ending. I was leaving my home and marriage. I'd terminated my pregnancy without ever really considering whether I wanted to be a mother. For all he knew, it was his child. Of course, I hadn't told Avery I was pregnant. I'm not fit to be a mother. I'm smart enough to know this much. Anyone could see it. I'm more of the smoking by the gas pump than the pantsuit type. It's in my blood.

It'd be nice to imagine that our short affair could exist as nothing but a miniature blemish in the picture of my life. The kind of thing so inconsequential that over time you don't even notice it, but I'm not sure that's how it works. Things like that leave a stain you can't get out so easily. Even if you think you've wiped it from the surface, it's left its mark on the fibers of your life. Forever there. I'd like for my affair to be something I didn't need to bring up. The truth, though, is that I wouldn't be here if it weren't for Avery.

When I left David and Avery in California, I honestly thought I might be getting a fresh start. Thought maybe I could be different. Better. More moral. Less concerned with gaining the affection of men. Less obsessed with being seen as civilized. Thought maybe it was possible to shed the skin of who I used to be. I wasn't thinking about how I'd done that once before—eighteen years old, leaving my mother's house and the girl I'd been there. In the end, I hadn't gotten as far away from myself as I thought I had. Then again, it doesn't seem fair that the onus of change is always put on the woman. Why should I be the one to change, to become a better person, to try and be smarter than where I came from, when it's the man that lived where I came from that really ought to be the one to change? My life might look a whole lot different if I'd have thought to ask this question sooner.

THREE.

The story of how I ended up here, awaiting whatever fate a jury will give me, wouldn't make much sense if I didn't at least include something about my mother, though I imagine in court this part of the story might be considered extraneous. Hell, every detail besides who fired the gun might be considered extraneous. Funny how a life in the eyes of others can be distilled down to such a limited number of details.

"In a sensitive case like this, it's imperative we're strategic about which details we include," my lawyer says. I keep thinking about Aileen Wuornos—how at first the details made her sympathetic, but then, in the end, when the jury had heard too much, she became something else. I first learned about who she was when I was in middle school. My mother took me to see a biographical film about her in the theaters. *Monster*, it was called. We never finished watching it, though. Less than halfway through the movie, my mother grabbed my hand and pulled me up from my seat to leave. The scene on the big screen as we were walking out was a battered and restrained Charlize Theron, playing Wuornos, laid out across the front seat of a car. Half-conscious from the beating, a man sodomizes her with a pipe as he tells her to scream. Through the dark hallway leading out of the theater I could hear Theron screaming in surround sound. In reviews I read later, not one described the rape scene in detail. Like most assaults to women, they said things like "vicious" and "heinous" but how different those words sound than: *Theron's character, bloodied, beaten, restrained and half-conscious, was raped in the ass with a large metal rod as her attacker kicked and screamed at her to make some noise.* Even in Wuornos's testimony, as she tries to describe her rape, she struggles to find the language for what was done to her. At one point, she refers to rape as sex. Through tears and staggered breaths she interchanges words like anus and rectum area, constantly pausing to mumble, *I don't know what to call it*, or simply, *I don't know*. In the description of her sodomization (no pipe mentioned in the testimony, so maybe that was Hollywood), she says, "I don't know if he came—or what—or climaxed—I talk street talk, so I don't know if he did that." She shrugs, looks down, looks to the lawyer as if seeking validation that she is using the right words to describe the action correctly. Plenty of reviewers described *Monster* as a sympathetic take on the story of Wuornos. Lot of good that did her. Probably not in my best interest to draw any parallel lines between me and Wuornos. I was never a prostitute. I never went on a killing spree. Like Wuornos, and the media, I too struggle to name what happened to me, but I would never describe rape as sex. I might agree that Wuornos is a criminal, but I would never call her a monster. Maybe my own fear of what might happen to me is making me more sympathetic to her, tempted to believe that context matters, that people don't do things for no reason. What caused an action should mean something. Maybe it should even mean as much as the (re)action itself.

As far as I see it, details matter. The story of what I did wouldn't exist without the detail of returning to my mother. She still lived in New Mexico in the house we'd moved into when I was eleven. It started out as a rental, but eventually the aging landlord sold it to her. She'd never intended to buy it. It had been meant to be a temporary landing spot after she left James Dixon, my stepfather. In another life—the one before I got arrested, and really, the one before I made my way back to New Mexico—I never mentioned him. I didn't even think about him. At least, I worked hard to never think about him. With everything that happened, I guess there won't be any avoiding bringing him up. But for now, I want to talk about my mother. About what a mistake it was to return to that house of hers where she was never meant to stay.

I hadn't been back in over a decade, and I didn't know why it was the first place I'd chosen to go after leaving my husband. Maybe a simple lack of options. The front lawn was full of knee-high weeds that looked like a drying golden forest in front of the single-story adobe style home. Teal trim lined the doors and windows. On the garage she had painted what looked like a roadrunner-jack-rabbit creature in various shades of greenish brown. When I'd lived in the house it had been off-white, old, and unmemorable like all the others in the neighborhood, but it appeared my mother had gotten creative since I left.

"Where's David?" she asked from the front door as I rolled my two suitcases over the crumbling walkway.

I shook my head.

"Oh," she nodded, "You know, I always thought it best to leave everything behind."

"Maybe I should have."

She didn't lean in to hug me as I approached. She stepped aside to let me pass and I could smell the burn of vodka that permanently laminated her skin. Instinctively, I looked at my watch. Eleven forty-five in the morning. Old habits die hard, but none as hard as tracking the start time of your mother's drinking to map your movements for the day. It wasn't a fair judgment. After all, I'd had a Bloody Mary on the plane myself. Then another. And another, until I could see the discomfort palpable on the flight attendant's face, like she was about to have to cut me off but didn't want to.

"You won't believe what I have done with your old room."

I followed her down the hallway and the smells of adolescence came to me like the pillow that smothers you to death. Cigarettes and liquor. Patchouli and rose soap. Dog piss and bleach.

"I ripped up the carpet and painted a constellation on the cement."

I looked at the cracked floor of my old room. It was painted black and smudged in the places where she had stepped before it was dried. There were yellow and white polka dots splattered in no ostensible order.

"Exposed foundation is really big in Europe right now."

"Looks great."

"Let's have a drink, huh?" she said, and I thought about fighting the urge to say yes simply to refuse her indulgence, but I didn't know how to be with her without a drink. I needed something to ease into this new life, to settle down after being thrusted hundreds of miles through the air out of one life and into the next. Everything had moved so quickly. A drink could slow down time—give me a second not to feel like everything was moving too fast to grasp.

"Sure," I said, and followed her into the kitchen, relieved in some way that she was still the same woman I'd always known. The kind that could solve any problem with a drink.

The call from David came the next night. The house phone rang right as my mother was sliding two frozen pizzas into the oven for dinner. I don't even know how he found her number.

"Will you get that for me, Bean?"

"It's him." It came to me like a vision, her house phone ringing in the dim-lit kitchen, my husband on the other line, calling the wife who'd left him and blocked his number. I could see him sitting on our couch in our tidy living room, body leaned forward as if he could transport himself to where I was. I felt an urge to reach into the phone and touch him, tell him I changed my mind, I'd made a mistake, I wanted to go back to pretending I could be a wife. I could make up a semi-believable story and things could return to normal—my looming thirtieth birthday and fear of not being good enough for him the cause for my erratic disappearance. Play it off as insecurity and self-doubt. It might hurt him, but he could forgive an existential crisis if I could be doting. Eventually I might even settle into a calm, not altogether meaningless life shelving books in a library and being home in time to cook him dinner every night. He could continue on the path toward becoming a tenured professor and his world would be big enough for the both of us, big enough to consume what I'd been trying to escape the first time I'd left home.

My mother slammed the oven door shut with her hip and walked around the counter to where the phone hung on the wall. "How do you know?"

"I just do."

"California turned you *clair-ee-voy-ant-ee*?" (That's how she said it, pronunciation all wrong, the way so many words got twisted up on her tongue and came out incorrect). She wiped her hands on the front of her jeans and picked up the phone. "Vicki Barnett speaking," she said, the mock professionalism of her voice undone by a slight slur.

"Oh hi, David, and to what do I owe the pleasure of a call from my favorite son-in-law?" She winked at me like she was about to enjoy this game of telephone with the husband of mine I'd never introduced her to. I put my head in my hands and willed the conversation to end quickly. He must have been talking in his fast, ranting manner because my mother wasn't saying anything. I wanted to take the phone from her so I could hear what he was saying, if he still loved me or if I had already become a monster in his eyes. It wasn't right, that I should desire his love despite my inability to love him back. Whatever love he felt for me wasn't really for me. It was for the version of myself I'd shown to him. I loved her too—the woman I wanted to be—but the real me, the one that's capable of pointing a gun at a man and pulling the trigger, wouldn't let her live if it meant having to be erased. I know this now. David does, too. But he didn't then. Not yet, and so he thought he still loved me, that the woman he'd met still existed.

"No, I haven't heard from her. You know Sabine, she never does tell me anything." She paused, listening, and her face fell into a frown. "Well, David, I will give her a call, but I don't know how much she'll listen to me. Once that girl gets something in her mind, she sticks to it." She paused again and nodded her head as she listened, "Okay, you take care of yourself. I am sure it will all work out the way it's supposed to."

She hung up the phone and walked back around to the other side of the counter. She reached into the cabinet and pulled down an expensive looking bottle of gin and two tall glasses.

"What on earth did you do to that man, Sabine?"

"I don't want to talk about it." Her eyes scanned my face, and I shook my head. "Please?"

"Okay." She bit her lip like she was keeping herself from talking, and, for a second, I thought I saw a wave of disappointment wash over her. Maybe she'd hoped that failing at marriage would unite us in some way, that we could share battle wounds and somehow finally connect with one another, be a real-life version of the Gilmore Girls, but our problems had always been a lot less white-collar than those CW approved family dramas, and we'd never been the type of mother and daughter that had long drawn-out conversations about our feelings. In the twelve years since I'd been away, I could count on one hand the times we'd seen each other in person.

"Why don't we have a drink?" she said. We'd already been drinking—cheap Irish cream and coffee for breakfast, her signature Diet Sprite with vodka as we watched daytime television in her dark living room—but she asked it like the idea of a drink was something novel.

She pulled an ice tray from the freezer and plopped five big cubes in each of our glasses before pouring the gin in just below the rim. For a second, I wondered what it would be like to tell her everything. How I'd been unfaithful to my husband. Not just with Avery, but with other men too, in lots of little ways. Mostly flirting, some texting, never anything as far as I'd let it go with Avery, but there was something inside of me that needed too much. Why wasn't the love of one man enough? Why wasn't any of it enough?

"Cut us one of those limes, Bean."

I cut one of the limes into wide wedges that she squeezed into our glasses and stirred with her long, skinny finger. She licked her finger clean and passed me a glass.

"To forgetting exes," she said, raising her glass in a toast.

"Cheers." We clinked our glasses, and I took a long swig. "Nice gin." I turned the bottle toward me so I could see the label. It was a big cylindrical bottle with frosted glass and cursive font across the front. I wasn't used to seeing my mom with such expensive looking liquor. Her taste had always been *whatever gets the job done cheapest.*

"I stole it."

"I don't want to know."

"Some asshole from the Fork in the Road who'd been hollering at me for weeks. I finally said I'd go out with him, you know how it gets when you're feeling lonely, and he drank so much of the damn stuff that he couldn't get it up." She threw her head back and laughed.

"Seriously, mom? I really don't need to hear this."

"He was an asshole. I'm telling you." She clucked her tongue and her head swayed on her neck like a leaf in a heavy breeze. "He badgered me forever and then, when I'm finally feeling like I need a man and any old one will do, he can't even show up at the shop. Didn't even get out of bed to walk me to the door. What do I care if he thinks I'm a thief?"

"God, you are fucking crazy. You know that?"

"You know, he had one of them globe on wheels things that looks like the world, but when you open it up there's all sorts of bottles inside. Have you ever seen one of those?"

"I think so."

"Fancy Californians you know probably got plenty of shit out there like that. I snatched the fullest bottle he had right up from the world. Nice shit, too, though I'm not usually a gin drinker."

"Well at least you got something out of it."

"Sometimes, being a bitch is all a woman has to hold onto," she said, lifting her glass to mine, a toast to bitches everywhere. It was a line she'd been using since I was a kid. It was a quote from the film *Dolores Claiborne*, and she used it any time she needed to justify her erratic behavior. What was worse was that the film was an adaptation of the book which I'd never seen her read. I'd never seen her read any books for that matter, which is probably part of how I got it in my head that I could go to college and read books and somehow I wouldn't wind up like her. It was a judgmental thought. Naïve to think that I could be better than my mother if I just lived a more intellectual life than her. As if that was all it took. As if there is such a thing as being *better than* someone else. Isn't it all a matter of opinion? And really, for all the books I'd gone and read, I was still standing in my mother's kitchen, drinking her stolen gin, and cringing at her quoting a film adaptation of a book she'd never read.

When the pizzas were done, she mixed us two more drinks and I picked a movie. We ate and drank and didn't share another memorable word for the whole night. Every so often she would take our half-empty glasses back into the kitchen and return to the couch beside me with full ones. If nothing else, my mother was great at helping to anesthetize my mind.

*

I don't exactly remember going to bed. It wasn't so uncommon—blacking out before bed and then waking in a fit in the middle of the night. For some time, I had wondered if David had noticed my restless sleeping, how sometimes I'd wake in a sweaty panic in the middle of the night and the only way I could get back to sleep was by getting out of bed, walking to the kitchen, and taking a long pull from the whiskey bottle I kept tucked in the back of the oven drawer.

After the phone call from David to my mother's house, I drank glass after glass of her stolen gin. No amount of frozen pizza could soak up the level of drunk I was on my way to. We sat in the living room drinking and watching reruns of *Law & Order* and then whatever came on after it. I had no memory of standing from the couch and walking myself to bed, but I woke up there, in just my underwear, a pile of drool gluing my face to my pillow, and a hangover as bad as they come. The usual morning-after montage began, disjointed images flashing into my conscious brain until I had enough information about the day before to know the headlines of my life but not enough to understand what it all meant and how it all fit together. I recalled sitting across from my mother, her sing-songy voice on the phone with my husband, and I felt the wheel of gin and shame turning in my gut. There was no way David didn't know that I was at my mom's house. I just knew it, and it was enough to serve as an excuse for me to get the fuck out of there before he showed up banging on her door. Not that I saw him as the type to bang on doors, but she didn't know that, and it would be easier to blame my leaving—which I decided right there in my drooly mess was the next right move—on him.

It wasn't just David's phone call that told me I should get out of there. It was the whole sad mess of her house, the way even with all the lights on the place was perpetually dim, the way the swamp cooler didn't make the house cold it just turned it into damp heat, the way even through a blackout-sleep I woke in a panic I hadn't felt since childhood. I knew I had to leave. The dreams at my mother's house were more visceral than they were anywhere else. Even my honed skill of blocking subconscious thoughts out over the years wasn't a match for the way they took hold of me there, woke me with my muscles fighting to break free from the prison of my flesh. With my eyes closed in bed, all I could see was the face from my childhood, the one I'd spent most my life trying to forget. In the night, in my dreams, it was breathing its lactic, tobacco breath on me. Its body on me, so much bigger than me. I was tangled in the sheets, fighting it away, but it was too strong, and I woke with my heart pounding, throat a closed fist, gasping for air. I needed to find a place where less history clung to the walls.

*

"But you just got here," my mother said when I told her I was leaving. She was in her bathrobe pulling a generic brand of some Irish cream from the fridge as the coffee maker sputtered.

"I know, but I need to be alone for a little while."

"Where you even going?"

"I'll decide when I get there."

"Get where?"

"The bus stop."

She clucked her tongue and took a deep breath in, "You know, you've always been a difficult child, Sabine. I always could sense you didn't really love me."

"This doesn't have anything to do with you. Why do you always have to be the biggest victim in the room? Not everything I do is about you. I need a change of scenery. I need to air out my head."

"Well, if you're going to talk to me like that I don't want you here anyway. Go on and leave."

She walked out of the kitchen and down the hall, not stopping to look back at me. I heard the click of her bedroom door, and I imagined her opening her closet and sliding her clothes to reveal the shelf where she kept her bottles of vodka and Diet Sprite.

FOUR.

I hadn't planned on winding up in a bar so soon, but my getaway bus broke down on the side of the road north of Truth or Consequences, New Mexico. Shortly after, two white vans pulled up to cart us passengers off to an auto shop fifty miles away like something out of a buddy road trip movie. We were told another bus was on its way and would get us to our final destinations. It was there, outside the shop, that I first saw Yu. I hadn't ever heard of the town before. I'd stepped around back behind the shop for a cigarette and gazed around the mostly barren desert landscape. The shop was situated on a mesa that dropped off into a valley surrounded by a high, rocky mountain range. There were no other buildings around it, and I was reminded of the lonesome gas stations in horror films, the kind operated by a helpful mechanic with missing teeth and a torture chamber in his basement. It didn't look like the kind of place full of promise. There were dust devils reaching toward the sky, and the sun, even in late-spring, was a relentless thing, but in that dusty valley below was what looked like a small town. I half believed it was a mirage, and my eyes kept returning to the surrounding mountains. The peak pierced the clouds as if it could open up the sky itself. If the town below wasn't a mirage, I wondered what it would be like to live in a place whose geography formed a barrier between you and the rest of the world. I liked the idea of being cradled by mountains, away from everything else. I put out my cigarette on the bottom of my shoe and took a step toward the valley below. It was one of those moments in life where something big happens and you don't even know it. The kind of moment you look back on later and wish you would have paused to snap a mental picture of it all so you could recall exactly what you were thinking and feeling and seeing right before the moment your life changed. Now, I can't even remember what thought ran through my head as I took my first step toward Yu.

In a college writing class, I learned about plot through Freytag's pyramid. A professor drew the little line sketch of what was basically an open triangle on the board and walked us through all the parts that make a story. Silly to think that someone came up with something so elementary to depict a thing as nuanced as a story. She told us the exposition was all about setting the stage, establishing norms and desires and fears which then get disrupted by the inciting incident, and, usually as a result, a character's desires are threatened. This is how a story begins. An inciting incident disrupts normal life. The rest of the story is simply how the character responds to the inciting incident and how they move around or through it in an attempt to protect their desire or avoid their fears. In stories, the beginning is clear, but in real life it isn't so easy to identify how something begins.

If this is the story of how I got arrested, then is arriving in Yu the beginning or is the leaving that preceded it? If it's the leaving, then is it leaving my husband or my mother? If it is leaving my mother, then was the catalyst the phone call from David or the nightmares? If it was the nightmares, then I can't help but think the beginning of this story goes a lot farther back than these last few months, which makes me think it isn't actually possible to ever tell the whole story. How could you possibly fit it all in? Once you start going back in time, trying to get to the real beginning of a story, it seems inevitable that the distance you might have to travel is infinite, like before you were born, maybe before the earth was born.

It's futile to search for the beginning. The writing of this confessional is meant to be an act of honesty, but there is something inherently dishonest about trying to manipulate the events of my life into a narrative. For the purposes of this confessional, for not wanting to stop myself in my own existential tracks, leaving that bus behind, stepping into the valley toward an unknown town, was a sort of beginning, and one thing is for certain, that little town in the valley wasn't a mirage, though it reified the term *ghost town*.

Not one person was walking on the sidewalk when I first showed up. The air above the singular main road shimmered as if full of gasoline. There was a ten-foot high hand-painted sign with a dust devil burned into the wood where the dirt turned to sidewalk. The words "Welcome to Yu" were burned in a cursive arch above the dust devil and outlined in yellow paint. Yu. Never before had I heard of this town two hours north of where I'd grown up. How many other things existed that I should know about but didn't?

The first building I walked past was a closed apothecary. Its walls had peeling white paint and its facade was all windows. It displayed bundles of sage and crystals in all sizes and colors on misshapen wooden rounds. There was a gold window decal of a pentagram with fine etchings in its lines and beneath the pentagram was gold lettering that said, *True Love Begins With Self-Love.* Across from the apothecary was a country market with a faded fruit basket painted on the white door. A closed coffee shop was a little farther down the road and in front of it were raised garden beds in metal stock tanks. Near the front door was a sculpture of a giant coffee mug from what looked like broken and recycled dishware. The town was cute, quiet, oddly shut down for the middle of the day, and it seemed like the type of place that one might go to find themself, or disappear, or, at the very least, take up arts and crafts.

In the distance, I could hear voices chattering and the unmistakable sound of a jukebox and bottles clinking. A bar. That's what I needed. A drink.

I walked to the corner and looked down the street. Across the street, a man in a denim vest sang "Friends in Low Places" off-key across the street to a woman in a peach tank top and cutoffs.

"Oh, geez. Won't you shut the fuck up, Josué?" the woman said as she threw her head back and laughed a hysterical, drunk sort of laugh—the kind of laugh that meant she did *not* want Josué to shut the fuck up even though his singing was terrible.

They stood in the dirt lot next to a big adobe structure that had an enormous black lizard painted on the wall with radioactive green strokes zigzagging across its back. Above the wooden door, in thick black font was the word *Whiptail.*

My mouth salivated with the thought of a cool beer. I stepped off the sidewalk. Toward The Whiptail.

FIVE.

Inside The Whiptail, the jukebox was playing a song from my childhood that had a banjo and a woman's rasping voice that sounded as though it was being plucked by a thick, calloused finger. I pulled a heavy wooden barstool back and sat down. My eyes fluttered to adjust to the low-lit room.

"Where you comin' from?" the bartender, a tallish man, forty maybe, with a slightly round belly and a black mustache, asked as he set a coaster down on the bar top in front of me.

"South of here," I said, digging in my backpack for my wallet.

"Oh yeah?" He stretched his forefinger and thumb across his mustache, "I'd have guessed you were coming from California."

"What gave you that impression?"

"You got that…" the bartender twirled his hands in the air like he was about to unveil a letter on the board in Wheel of Fortune, "West Coast kind of swagger."

I snorted a too loud laugh and thought I must be looking better than I felt if the bartender's first and only line wasn't *What are you having?* I ran my fingers through my hair with one hand and covered the acne on my jaw with the other. It didn't matter though, it was too dark in the bar for him to see my shitty complexion, and besides, I was off men anyway. I'd made that decision on the plane leaving California. No more men, at least for now, at least until I could get my shit together. I put my hands on the bar in front of me and let my breakout flush in all its glory.

"I say something funny?"

"I never really felt like I was from California."

"Called it," he said, snapping his fingers. "And what in the hell brings you into this little mound of dirt?"

"My bus broke down."

"Ah, vortex." He snapped his fingers again.

"Vortex?"

"You know, magnets and shit?"

"And just when I thought I might have found a place to settle down in…"

"Hey, hey, hey, I didn't know you were in the market. I wouldn't have led with the vortex so soon. It's something we joke about around here." He winked. Was he flirting? Who cared? Not me. No more men. I projected too much onto them. I yearned for a kiss or touch that could change my life. It was like that with books, too, thinking if I read the right one then I would discover the answer to my problems. I know better now. There isn't one thing that can fix a person. I don't know if I knew this yet, sitting in the bar, but I knew getting him to want me wouldn't be the thing that made me hate myself less.

"You know what, I'm gonna buy you a drink. What are you having?"

"You don't have to do that."

"Hey now, before you get all weird about it, I'm not proposing marriage or anything."

"Sure," I said, wondering if accepting a drink from this bartender really was breaking my new *no men* rule, but like he said, he wasn't proposing marriage. It was only a drink. "I'll have a Fernet."

"A *For-what*?"

Of course a place like The Whiptail wouldn't have my drink of choice. When I'd moved to California and discovered that people in the service industry drank it like water, I hadn't heard of it either. It was the ideal beverage. Herbal and instantly euphoria-inducing. Those botanicals masking the scent of alcohol so you could drink around the clock, leaning in close to customers and asking if they wanted cheese on their burger without them ever catching a whiff of what you were up to when no one was looking.

"I'll just take a Jack, neat, and a Budweiser."

"Those we have." He reached into the well and grabbed the Jack Daniels. "So, where are you heading?"

"I was heading to Utah, but that plan got derailed."

"What's in Utah?"

"I don't know. I've never been, but I thought it might be nice to see those red mountains."

"What have you got against the mountains here?"

"Good question."

"This place is a lot better than Utah. Less Mormons. Practically no tourists."

"Well then maybe here is where I'm headed."

"No shit, so you're for real then?"

"I guess this place is as good as any place else I've never been."

"Hey now, the vortex might not be such a hoax," he said, looking over his shoulder at the denim-clad man who'd been outside when I got there. "Josué, Cat, would you believe it…" he turned back to me, "What's your name, sweetheart?"

"Sabine."

"Nick," he said, extending his hand out to shake mine, and then hollered to the couple, "Sabine here just moved into town."

"We're broken," the woman said, tilting the top of her empty beer bottle toward the bar.

"Another?" Nick asked.

"We have got to get out of this bar, Nick," the man said.

"How bout a little one to welcome our new neighbor?"

"A baby one," the woman said.

Nick poured them each a shot and they raised their glasses from across the bar at me. Already I felt the bubbling of newness inside of me. Raising shots to strangers like I was the kind of person that made friends without any effort at all. I've never really had a lot of friends, but making friends in bars is different than making friends anywhere else. Easier. Circumstantial. In bars, you share a common goal, and that is unifying in a way that's hard to find in well-lit places.

Nick clinked his glass with mine and I shot my whiskey back in one big swallow. Instantly I could feel the way it wrapped itself around me. The whiskey a lover whose touch might be powerful enough to erase the craving for a man's hand on my back. My body softened at the sweet heat of it on my tongue and in my throat. Yes, I thought, stopping in this bar, taking this shot, is exactly what I needed to help figure out my life.

"Welcome, sweetheart, and god damn you, Nick." Cat slammed her shot glass on the bar and pulled Josué toward the door.

"Love you too," Nick hollered as they disappeared out the door and into the sunshine beyond the bar.

Nick pulled a Budweiser from the fridge at his feet and set it down on the coaster in front of me. "I'm only fuckin' with you about the vortex. Some myth the hippies around here love to say exists in the mountains and brings in new folks. Course, its history goes back a lot longer than when the hippies showed up and made it into a spectacle. Goes back before most of us showed up, but if it ever really did have power, I'm sure us humans have gone and fucked it up like we do most things."

"Sounds about right."

"Don't worry. You're in good company here." He winked at me and then walked to the other side of the bar and reached for a bottle of wine in the ice well. He leaned close to the woman he was pouring the wine for and whispered something in her ear. She gave him a demure smile and then playfully slapped his hand. So, he was that kind of bartender. I wasn't anything special.

The bar interior was one big square inside another. The bartender was surrounded by four sides of weathered wood and the side furthest from the door had a section of bar top that was on a hinge and lifted upright so that the bartender could get in and out of his panopticon. There was a small stage with an elaborate looking light setup on the far end of the room. Every inch of the walls other than the one behind the stage were covered in an eclectic assortment of dust-covered objects. Fire hazards no doubt. Business cards and postcards. Dollar bills with people's names written on them and bar napkins with line drawings of women with anatomically impossible breasts and waists. A framed painting of a cactus with an incredibly large and dangerous looking penis. A taxidermy raccoon that looked like it had been run over and I wondered if it had happened before or after it had been stuffed. All the items overlapped one another as though the walls themselves couldn't contain the history of the place. Of course, there was a jukebox—the kind that seemed to play a never-ending rotation of sad country songs and eighties ballads.

The Whiptail was perfect. Magical even. I've been thinking a lot about those first couple minutes in Yu lately. Especially what Nick said about the vortex. I didn't believe in it at first. Not when Nick told me about it and not when Howling Woman did either. Now, I am not so sure whether some of what got me to where I'm at was out of my control. Being born to my mother, that I was genetically predisposed to chaos, and even that vortex. Not that I am saying I've been converted to being a vortex believer or anything, but is it so improbable that a magnet in a mountain was capable of wrenching something out of a body? It's easy to brush this sort of thing off, but it doesn't feel so unbelievable that us paltry humans might be vulnerable to the momentum of the earth. I wonder how that would sound to a jury. *Sorry I shot a man. The mountain made me do it.*

SIX.

I was getting drunk. I hadn't planned on it. Just one drink I'd told myself, but there I was, no longer able to keep track of how many times Nick had topped off my shot glass.

"Another?" Nick asked me, the Jack Daniels already in his grasp like he knew my type.

"Oh sure. What the hell?" I threw back the rest of my Budweiser and Nick laughed.

"You know, I think I am going to like you. Stick around long enough and we might turn out to be real good friends." He reached for a second shot glass from the shelf and set it next to mine. I loved bartenders that didn't make me drink alone.

"I'm not so sure. I've never been very good at making friends."

"I find that hard to believe."

"It's just the way it is. I probably wouldn't have ended up here if I had more friends."

"You're young. You got plenty of time to make friends."

We both shot back our whiskey and he pulled out another Budweiser from the fridge. He twisted off the cap and set the bottle down in front of me. A wave of affection for Nick washed over me in that moment. He was feeding me drinks, not looking at me like he was thinking, woah, slow down speed racer, and he thought I looked young. I didn't feel young. In a couple of months I'd be thirty and that number weighed heavy. It's not exactly that I think thirty is so old, but I felt like I looked older. I could already see fine lines crinkling around my eyes when I smiled. Twenty-nine is an unfair age in a female body. At least one like mine. There were wrinkles on my forehead and around my eyes, but I still broke out in acne on my cheeks and jawline. When I was younger, I used to try and hide it beneath thick brushes of foundation, but as I got older the heavy foundation accentuated the age lines. You couldn't win as a woman—not if you weren't a beautiful woman. Sometimes, when David would stroke my face and call me beautiful, I would look at him like he was the craziest man alive. How was it that he didn't see what I saw—a prematurely aging woman with dusty brown hair and bad skin? Before David, I'd never been in a serious relationship. There were just the men I fucked. I hadn't ever thought of myself as the kind of woman a man could commit to spending the rest of his life with. I kept waiting until the moment he'd look at me and see that I wasn't beautiful. That I wasn't anything. It's hard to imagine committing to eternity with another person when you know it's only a matter of time until they realize they couldn't possibly love a woman like you.

It doesn't give me much hope for what's to come—knowing I'm not beautiful, that I don't come from a *good* family. Aileen Wuornos wasn't beautiful. She didn't come from a good family. Surely it had something to do with the fate that befell her.

Lizzie Borden was beautiful though. Ladylike. From a good family. The defense was mindful to allude to her beauty. It doesn't matter that she remains immortalized by literature and film as a woman who murdered her family. Even children know this.

> *Lizzie Borden took an ax,*
> *Gave her mother forty whacks*
> *When she saw what she had done,*
> *She gave her father forty one.*

What does Lizzie Borden care? She got away with murder. My crime wasn't nearly as heinous as her alleged ones.

The door to The Whiptail opened, letting a streak of sunlight cut through the darkness of the bar—a reminder the day was still going on outside. An enormous guy with tattoos up to his chin, a pink leather vest on, and a Chihuahua in his arms walked in and sat down two barstools over. Nick plopped a coaster down in front of the man and poured him a drink without even having to ask what he wanted. Another regular. Nick leaned across the bar and made kissing noises at the Chihuahua and the man released her onto the bar top so Nick could pick it up. Nick carried the dog over to me and put her down on the bar in front of me. She shivered on the bar between us and looked up at Nick waiting for him to pick her back up.

"Sabine, meet Spike."

The golden Chihuahua wasn't more than four pounds. Her toes were painted Barbie pink and she wore a leather collar around her neck that was embellished with tiny silver spikes. I reached to pet her, but she scampered off down the bar back to her owner.

"Don't be offended. She's shy around strangers," the man said.

"Jesse, this is Sabine. She just moved here."

"Not exactly…"

"She's from California."

"California. That's fancy. What the hell brought you to our sweet little trash pile?"

"It's pretty random actually. My bus broke down outside of town."

"The vortex," Jesse said, shaking his head.

"Don't go scaring her off, Jesse."

"She looks like she doesn't scare too easily." Jesse gave me a coy wink. "Now, about the music, this is simply not going to cut it. Nicky, be a dear and give me some quarters, will you? This place could use a little ambiance."

He pulled a couple dollar bills from his pocket and set them on the bar in front of his drink, his heavy, silver pinkie ring made a satisfying clunking sound.

Nick snatched up the bills and counted out twelve quarters. "Don't play any of that dance shit. I'm not in the mood today, Jesse."

"Touchy, touchy, barkeep," Jesse said. He scooped Spike up into his arms and asked if I had any requests.

"Something country."

"I wouldn't have pegged you for the type."

I took a sip of my beer as Jesse and Spike walked over to the jukebox. I hadn't listened to country music since I'd been a teenager living with my mother, and now that I was out of California and back in New Mexico, I had a yearning for crying guitars and songs that told stories about drinking and cheating and hometowns and dirt roads and neon signs. David liked black metal and classical, which seemed a weird enough combination of tastes, but I found they both suited him in different ways. I hadn't listened to either genre before I'd married him, but he was a record collector and so his music tastes had been the soundtrack of our marriage. Country music never blared from the speakers of the bars or restaurants or shops I frequented in Oakland, and with the exception of a short-lived country bar near Jack London Square, the Bay Area consensus appeared to be that Country music was below urban sophistication and intellect, even in a bar.

"Hope you're in the mood for a tear-jerker," Jesse hollered from the jukebox. A mechanical noise replaced the song that had been playing as a new record was selected. The whole bar filled with a soft guitar and an angel's voice. It was one my mother played a lot when she'd first left James. The singer's voice a soft question, asking a woman, herself presumably, if she really thought the night before would last forever, if she really thought that guy hung the moon.

I pulled my beer close to my lips and closed my eyes. I could hear my mother in her bedroom, her sobs a sound I'd grown to equate with the angel's voice in the song, and even in this bar, miles away from her, I was certain I could hear her on the other side of her bedroom door with this song on repeat late into the night. It had been the only period of my life with her that I could remember her not drinking regularly. That window of time right after we'd left James Dixon.

The night before my mother left him had been an especially terrible one, but nights when my mother wasn't working at the Fork in the Road, no matter how bad it got between her and James, were still better than the ones where I prayed my door would remain shut until daylight. I spent a lot of time trying to forget this night, and I certainly never spoke of it out loud.

I remember it clearly for a couple of reasons. One being that it was the day before the Fourth of July and so they'd begun drinking from the moment they woke up. They were the kind of people I didn't know were a kind until I realized that some people didn't mix bottom-shelf Irish cream into their coffee and beer into their morning tomato juice as they counted down the hours until it was appropriate for them to prepare a proper drink. It hadn't evaded me that in some ways, I had become this kind of person, too, but because I had married a professor and lived in a nice apartment in an urban area, it was easy to pretend that my life was somehow different from theirs.

On their last day together, my mom and James had been in the backyard for most of the morning, drinking their spiked beverages and chain-smoking while I sketched portraits of my Beanie Babies onto the art pad I'd received for my eleventh birthday. As the sun settled itself into the sky the way it does in the late afternoon, they returned inside. My mother made me a bowl of mac and cheese with a hot dog cut up into little pieces and told me I could watch television. Finally, I thought, and I kissed her as a thank you. Her mouth tasted like ethanol and tobacco. I was grateful for the television so it could block out whatever sounds would come from the other side of her bedroom door. I hated when she and James were behind closed doors together. It was always either them screaming—the sharp sound of an open palm on flesh—or the wet noise their bodies made as they thrusted into one another and my mother moaned. She had an unnatural moan like the women in pornos. Later, I'd grow used to hearing the sound late into the night during the years when she was trying to erase the memory of James's touch on her bare skin. She made the same high-pitched "ah, ah, ah" sound I'd heard dozens of women make in shitty adult films where young, fake-titted actresses cried in pleasure as fat-cocked men jerked off and came on their faces.

I never moaned like that when I had sex. I grunted and panted like a dog and didn't care if it was sexy as long as I got to that place where all the pressure that had built up inside of me for my entire life became a flittering buzz that was all bursting and relaxing and softening. What my mother did wasn't the sound of female plea- sure. It was a sound to help get men off.

I squeezed a decent size glob of ketchup onto my mac and cheese and stirred it in until the noodles and hot dog bits were the color of toxic, orange slime. I muted Nickelodeon and strained my ears to hear what noises were being made down the hallway to get a sense of how the day would go. Moaning. Ew. I unmuted the televi- sion and turned it up so I couldn't hear anything but the rugrats as they made their way out of the baby gate with Tommy's screwdriver.

Before the episode finished, my mother and James emerged from the bed- room, their faces sweaty and red. My mom came and kissed my forehead and took the mostly empty bowl from the coffee table.

"*We're going out for a little bit, Bean. Don't watch too much television. Okay, sweet- heart.*"

"*Okay,*" I replied, looking around her to the glowing screen.

It was hours later when they returned from whatever bar they had wasted all the daylight in. I could smell the petrol scent of their skin waiting to ignite as my mother rushed down the hallway to her room and slammed the door. James chased after her but she'd locked the door before he could get into their room. He banged his fist on the door and kicked the wall, making the whole house shake.

"*God dammit Vicki, open the door, you stupid cunt,*" James shouted as he contin- ued to bang on the door.

I didn't rush out to see what was happening. I had long since learned better than to insert myself into their adult world on days like that, but I was summoned to the edge of my bedroom door by my mother's screaming, "*Go to hell you fucking pervert.*" I pressed myself flat against the wall and peered down the hallway.

James was red and sweaty and his fist hit the door so hard I was certain he would break it down any second (eventually he would). That word, *pervert*, pinged around inside my head, its letters barbed with the sharp edge of my mother's voice. Instinctively, I pulled my bedroom door closer to the frame so that it left only a crack through which I could see. *Pervert.* I'd thought that same word one of the first nights that James Dixon had crept into my darkened bedroom while my mother served plates of greasy french fries and hamburgers to truck drivers.

His body had been heavy on top of my small frame. He smelled of cigarettes and bile but also of pine and musk. Even before his hands had slipped below the waistband of my pajamas, while he did nothing else but lie on top of me, breathing heavily and stealing all the air from my lungs, I had thought the word, *pervert*. His thick fingers pushed inside of me as he grinded his body against me. I'd gasped, wanted to scream at him to stop, but no words escaped my mouth. My heart raced in my chest and temples and behind my eyes until eventually he stopped, a warm, wet spot spreading from inside his jeans and dampening the leg of my pajamas. He took my bottoms off without saying a word and from down the hall I heard the water begin running from the washing machine. *Pervert.*

"Is that what you like? Girls that ain't even old enough to leave their mama's house? I know that girl's mama, and she sure as shit ain't old enough to be at places like that getting groped by fat old fucks like you."

"We was just talking," James shouted back, his fists in reprise.

"I know what talking looks like and that ain't it you fucking redneck piece of shit."

"You on your rag or something, Vicki? You don't see right and you should know better by now than to talk to me like that with your filthy fucking mouth."

"I didn't sign up to spend my life with some cradle-robbin' cheat who can't keep his pecker in his pants."

"You threatening me?"

I remember his voice got low as he asked her this. It wasn't a real question. All the air in the house seemed to quiet with it, but my mom couldn't see the air change from her side of the door like I could.

"You bet your ass it's a threat, you dumb motherfucker."

"Open the door, Vicki." His voice was still low and I felt my skin prickle when he spoke.

"Fuck you, pervert."

A flash of red filled my eyes. I saw his body shift and with it my vision was in and out. From that moment, those consonants popping on my mother's tongue, the rest of the night blurred to static. His shoulder splintering the doorframe. My mother's scream jumping from performative to authentic and terrified. My face warm, wet with tears. Trying to keep myself quiet so he wouldn't remember I was in the house. My pants filling with warm liquid, followed by goosebumps from the chill of warmth gone cold. My mother's body an assortment of limbs, worms exposed to sunlight as he dragged her past my door by her hair. The sound of flesh and bone being bruised by walls and door handles and body. The smell of myself as my thighs chaffed themselves raw.

The next morning, while James was at work, my mother came into my room, her body moving as though she had aged a hundred years. She sat down on the edge of my bed, her back to me. I don't remember if we talked or cried or if anything deeper was exchanged between us. I remember only one line.

"Pack up your things. We are leaving in ten minutes."

The sweetest, most terrifying words I had ever heard. I didn't respond. I did what she said. I packed my Beanie Babies and my art pad. I packed some books that I had already read and a bathing suit in case where we were going had a pool. I didn't pack underwear. I remember this because in the car I got sick to my stomach and had an accident in my pants. When my mom told me to change I realized I couldn't and I had to sit in my own mess while we drove to the store to buy a pack.

After that, my mother didn't drink for a while. Like she needed to think straight for the first time in her life. The length of her time on the wagon wasn't something I knew to pay attention to yet. When my mother wasn't drinking, which was almost never, she entered a serene sort of quiet like she was all inside her head and she couldn't share anything that was going on up there with the rest of the world. It made me wonder if all her constant laughter and her loud voice were products of drinking. Maybe my real mom, the one that lived inside the small, dry space surrounded by drink, was quiet and reserved and had thoughts all her own that never left her care.

I wonder if that is how life is measured: by the periods of time in which we do or do not do something.

"Earth to, Sabine," I heard someone say and I realized the sad country song was coming to an end and Jesse was in the seat next to me, his head cocked in confusion as Spike licked my fingers which were wrapped around the sweating beer bottle.

"Sorry," I said, shaking my head like I was shaking the thoughts out of it, "My mother used to love that song."

"Geesh, I didn't mean to send you through the spiral. How long she been gone for?"

I laughed and Jesse looked at me like I'd admitted I'd murdered her myself.

"She's not dead," I said through my laughter, "She just doesn't listen to that song anymore."

"Well, you could of fooled me from the morbid look on your face. Hey, Nick," Jesse shouted down the bar, "another round for me and this little weirdo you let inside your bar."

"You know, they say it takes one to know one," Nick said as he poured another gin and tonic for Jesse and a shot of whiskey for me.

I could feel my insides had already grown soft with country music and whiskey and I could sense that another shot wasn't the best idea, but I also knew I'd been thinking about some shit I'd been avoiding for longer than I could remember and the best way I knew to get rid of thoughts you don't want is another shot that isn't the best idea.

SEVEN.

If we're talking Freytag shit, then I think what happened next is where the real story begins. The rest is background, exposition, whatever. I'd lost track of time drinking as one often does when they begin drinking in the heat of the afternoon in a foreign desert landscape. Jesse and Spike had left. I remember a kiss on the cheek, *"You should get yourself out of here before you get in too much trouble, chica."* The bar filled with people. The air around me felt damp and warm with bodies. My shot glass was empty. The two beer bottles beside it were empty. A mound of peeled labels sat in front of me. The bartender, a blur in the distance, wasn't looking at me. I had to shut one eye to see him as one figure instead of four.

What memory I have from the latter part of my time in The Whiptail is all fragments. The room spinning. My balance on the stool coming undone. Nearly eating shit as my feet somehow found the floor beneath my barstool. Stumbling away from the bar and down a hallway. Someone saying, *hey, hey, you ok?* Someone else saying, *woah, watch it.* Someone else saying *hey, what the fuck?* A pain radiating from my hip bone after bumping it against the corner of something. The stink of urine and artificial flora. My mouth warm and viscous with bile. Then, blackness.

More time must have passed, and I don't know how long I stayed like that, sitting on the bathroom floor, slumped over a toilet, drool and bile dried to my chin. I don't know why I am including this in the story. Maybe a smarter writer would skip ahead, but I never claimed to be a writer. I am just a person confessing, and so I guess this is just another event that feels necessary to get off my chest.

I came to, though only momentarily, when the door to the stall scraped my back from someone pushing it open. My eyes were narrow slits as I looked up toward the silhouette of a person backlit by flickering fluorescents. As my eyes adjusted to the light, the ghost of Janis Joplin filled my vision. Or, at least it felt like a ghost, but it was prettier than the real Janis. Her face less puggish, her teeth less tarnished. Her cheeks were fleshy, somewhere between youthful and jowly, her blue-green eyes something you could swim in, and her nose was short and pointed upwards so you could see the opening of the nostrils. She had the same easy way about her hips. Her hair was long and straight—dishwater blonde. I could see her lips moving, but if they made a sound, I couldn't hear it.

I wish I could recall more clearly the events of this night through the slush of my fucked-up-no-good mind, but all I had was the fever apparition of Janis—the inciting incident of my story mostly a blackened memory that never formed. That is, if we are agreeing to call the arrest the climax of my story, then this night must be the inciting incident, and for the purposes of orienting any sense of narrative into the otherwise disjointed series of events that are a life, I think it best to call the arrest the climax.

"What in god's name did Nick do to you?"

My head jerked back in surprise at the sudden clarity of her voice, but I couldn't open my mouth to respond.

My clothes clung to me like a long-outworn layer of skin that needed to be shed. My mouth was all sandpaper and ash. I squinted harder at the woman in front of me and thought maybe she wasn't Janis's ghost after all—just a woman with an uncanny resemblance to the deceased. Bell-bottoms. Long, untamed hair. The scent of incense and cigarettes. She kneeled close to me and brushed my hair from my eyes. Her hand brushing my hair back, caressing my neck, the kindest gesture I had felt in weeks. There was nothing ghostly about it, but in the haze of my drunkenness, there was something otherworldly about it.

"Who's Nick?" I slurred.

"That slack-jawed fuck behind the bar who is responsible for you hugging this toilet here."

"It's my fault," I said, and I retched into the toilet again, acidic backspray speckled across my cheek.

"Sugar pie, we are gonna have to get you vaccinated after the night is through cause of how close you're getting to the filth around here. Either that, or a good hose down."

She wrapped her arm around me and I was enveloped in her long hair and the drapey fabric of her Janis attire, her embrace like something I could dissolve into. She smelled of Palo Santo and vinegar up close.

"Up we go."

And then I guess she carried me out of the bathroom—my body in her arms like a limp toddler after a day at a theme park. And there it is, my first encounter with Howling Woman—the moment in my life that led to everything else, the one without which, I might never have even begun putting this story to paper.

EIGHT.

The problem is, nobody ever tells you that no matter how happy you are, you will never be happy enough. Maybe this is what my Victorian literature professor meant when she said that, unlike Victorian novels where the marriage is the end of the story, Chekhov said marriage was just the beginning. The point, I think, was that "happily ever after" was an easy way for a writer to tie up a story, but I never could find that Chekhov quote, and we never read any Chekhov in class. I might have understood the nature of marriage better if I had. I am not trying to rewrite history here as one often does when they discover the life they thought they wanted wasn't all it had been built up to be in their mind. I can understand the desire to do that—to refuse the events of a former life to validate the narrative of the present. But I am trying to be as honest as possible here, otherwise, what even is the point of a confessional? Rewriting the narrative to make my marriage some terrible thing would be a lie.

Maybe this confession is too little too late. Maybe my life would look a whole lot different if I'd started to dissect and talk about my marriage and feelings when I was still in California. Maybe I would have never left California or cheated on David in the first place if I'd been able to talk to him more. The things I couldn't share were mostly thoughts and feelings that seemed too embarrassing to name aloud.

That I worried my life was meaningless.

That I wasn't happy.

That I didn't know if I ever could be happy.

You can't tell your husband these kinds of things without him taking it personally. I thought, best to keep it to yourself or risk abandonment. I thought, better to have someone love part of you than to have no love at all.

Then there was my past, a thing that felt impossible to name in front of David.

That I'd grown up poor.

That my mother let strangers into her bedroom most nights of the week.

That we lived on knockoff Rice-A-Roni and Kool-Aid.

That a man used to come into my room and climb on top of me while I was still a child.

That my mother and I never talked about it.

That I never told anyone.

These weren't the kinds of things a man who'd gone to private school—first high school, then Stanford, then Berkeley—could understand. His father, a man who died before I'd met him, had been a lawyer. His mother employed a maid. With them, I ate meals that included vegetables I never even knew existed. Escarole. Kohlrabi. Fiddleheads. I remember the first time I met his mother. We'd gone to see a movie in the theater together. Afterward, David's mother invited us back to her place. She served us espressos in her living room and asked us what we thought of the *film*. Not just if we liked it or didn't like it, but what we made of the plot, how it was paced, whether we thought there was room for more character development, and so on. I didn't know there were people who talked like this outside of classrooms. It was so civilized. I wanted to be like David and his mother. The kind of person whose basic needs were met and therefore could strive for higher tiers of thought than how to survive. With David, I never could get rid of the feeling that I was on the verge of getting caught. This was true even before Avery.

At least after I met Avery I could focus on not getting caught cheating. That is so much less abstract than trying to hide an elusive sense of self. Either you get found out or you don't. With the past, the layers reveal themselves in small, insidious ways, slowly taking root in the mind until some darker image overtakes whatever was there before.

After the first time sleeping with Avery, I found myself thinking about him constantly. I summoned the image of his face onto the screen of my mind. A sort of meditation where I escaped the reality of my married life and the past I didn't want to remember by focusing my thoughts on a singular point of obsession. Breathe in. Silver stubble. Breathe out. Pock marks. Breathe in. Dimpled chin. Eggy breath. His face came to me in fragments. A spattering of freckles creeping from beneath the collar of his shirt. Salty beads of sweat at his temple.

The sex with Avery was the perfect type of distraction from reality. It was all-consuming. The type of sex that leaves you in a fugue state. Avery fucked me like he might actually die if he couldn't come inside of me, his hands digging into my ass as he pushed so deep into me I thought I might shatter. He was always pinning me against things and holding me down like he knew I didn't belong to him, like he thought if he loosened his grip I might get away. Sometimes, he would fuck me from behind, his arm wrapped around my throat, his cheek pressed rough against my own. Then, he would stop, mid-thrust, right before I was about to come. I would shake from the impending closeness of my orgasm.

"Do you want to come?" he'd ask.

"So bad."

"Then tell me you're my little whore?"

"I'm your little whore."

"You're a filthy slut, Sabine."

"I'm your filthy slut, Avery."

"Are you a whore who will do anything for my dick?"

"Anything."

"Then let me fuck your tight little ass."

"Please," I'd beg, and he'd jam himself into my ass and the ripe smell of semen and my innards would overwhelm me, and I'd explode into a glorious oblivion.

Sex with Avery reminded me I was disgusting. It felt good to be the thing I was.

But why am I writing these details? What does fucking Avery have to do with shooting a man? What does admitting to lying to my husband prove to anyone? Certainly nothing redeeming. Maybe I'm just trying to show you who I am—a desperate woman looking to escape herself. Is that so monstrous?

NINE.

After I came to in The Whiptail bathroom, I blacked out again. This happened sometimes. Hours, and occasionally whole evenings, lost to darkness. The problem was I never knew when exactly it would happen. Sometimes all it took was a couple drinks. Other times it took an ocean. The other problem, besides the obvious dangers one might associate with existing in a semiconscious state, is that during the blackouts I was often functioning. More often than not, I appeared to the outside world as a conscious person. I might have whole conversations with people, go from one bar to the next, make a new friend, or even prepare a meal in my kitchen.

Blacking out is never not a hazard, but I think it is especially dangerous when you're having an affair, especially if in your blacked out state you are prone to engaging in conversation, as, it turns out, I was. I worried, though obviously not hard enough to avoid drinking altogether, that I might slip up in front of David and mention Avery. I worried one morning I'd wake up and he'd be gone because we'd had an entire discussion about what a philandering bitch I was and no matter how hard I tried I would never be able to remember how it all went down because the part of my brain that transcribes action to memory was turned off during the event.

One moment I'm awake, the next I'm transported from wherever I was to a bed or couch or floor. There is no bridge from one place to the next. It is a type of dark magic.

This is how I woke up in Howling Woman's house, only I had no idea at the time that it was Howling Woman's house. My memory of the night before ended in the bathroom, so when I woke to the sound of footsteps on tile floor, sun penetrating my too-sensitive eyes, I had absolutely no idea where I was. I squinted through the pain of waking up and saw I was on a couch in an ungodly bright room. I could make out the blurry edge of a person and instinctively I reached for my crotch. My shorts were still on, fully buttoned. At least there was that. I felt my chest. Shirt still on. I rubbed my face with my palms and the smell of cigarettes and vomit filled my nostrils.

"Morning, Buttercup."

It took me a minute to place the tall woman smiling before me. She bent over and brushed the hair off my forehead the way a mom in a made-for-TV movie might do. As her face came into focus, I had a feeling of recognition.

"I bet you feel like a semitruck rolled right over you," the woman said. I don't know why, out of all the images and sounds I'd come into contact with during my blackout, her voice was the thing that had formed a memory. Again, I don't want to read too much into the story of my life, looking for symbols where there aren't any, but I think there might be something to the fact that I saw this stranger's face, recalled it belonged to Janis Joplin's ghost from The Whiptail bathroom, and instead of utter fear, experienced relief. My face was still in her palm, and she was smiling at me. I had this odd sense of comfort, or, maybe it wasn't exactly comfort, but it wasn't what I might expect from a situation of waking in a strange town in a stranger's living room, which is to say, I didn't feel terror.

"Hey," I said, the word scratching across the drought of my mouth, "where am I?"

"Casa de Howling Women," she said, releasing my face and extending a cup of coffee to me with her other hand. I sat up and my vision turned to stars.

"Easy there." She propped me up by the shoulder with her free hand. "Drink this. It will help."

I nodded and accepted the mug. I took a sip of the sludgy coffee. It was sugary and strong and it went down like molasses and Drano. I looked around the room, trying to stir up some type of recognition, but it was all new to me. I didn't have even one fragment of memory of having arrived.

"How did I get here?" I asked. In the past, especially with David, I never liked to let on that I didn't have any recollection of the night before. Sometimes I didn't even know that I couldn't remember what I'd been up to while drinking until people started referring to conversations we'd had or places we'd been. Usually, I would act real coy about it, answering their questions with another question or smiling and nodding in agreement. There wasn't any need to do it with this woman, though. At that point, I had absolutely no plans to have her in my life long-term. In fact, it was probably right around that moment, sitting on her couch, drinking her coffee, that I had the thought that I should get the fuck back to a bus station and head far, far away. I'd give the whole fresh start another try since this one hadn't gotten off on such a great note.

She smiled and sat down on the coffee table in front of me. "You weren't in any shape to be alone."

"God, I am such a fucking mess." I looked around the room where we sat, hoping something might jog my memory, but it was all totally unrecognizable. Large, exposed wooden beams supported the ceiling; the wall behind her was painted turquoise with a woven tapestry hanging in the center; and the floor was clay-colored tiles. Succulents of all varieties grew out of cut-up milk cartons and coffee mugs with missing handles or big chips in the side. They lined the windowsills and were cluttered on all the flat surfaces of the living room. Of all the places I could have ended up, it wasn't the worst-case scenario.

"Ain't nothing to beat yourself up over."

"I'm sorry, this is so embarrassing, but can you tell me your name again?"

"Howling Woman," she said. Her face didn't flinch or reveal judgment. She just said her name, calm as ever, and then leaned into the space between us. "And let me tell you something, you don't need to go on wasting your *sorries* on me. Lord knows there's enough women in the world apologizing for things that don't need apologizin' for."

Howling Woman, I thought. Was this woman messing with me? I looked at her, still smiling like it wasn't a totally strange thing to invite some drunk out-of-towner to sleep off a blackout on your couch. She looked to be somewhere in her fifties and her hair was shorter than I'd remembered from the night before. I could see streaks of gray in her mass of golden hair. She looked normal enough in her terry cloth robe and moccasin slippers. A harmless older woman with a generous spirit, who, apparently, went by a name that didn't seem to fit her at all. It was, as far as I could tell, the strangest thing about her. To my surprise, and a testament to the degree of my hangover and shame, I didn't get hung up on the name. I don't recall thinking right then and there, *oh wow, this crazy bitch. This woo-woo wannabe native with her fucking moccasins and bizzarro name.* I don't recall reaching into the recesses of my liberal California college degree and thinking, this cultural appropriator—the worst type of white woman—taking from cultures what you like and leaving the rest in order to create a sort of enlightened, spiritual-hippie persona. It was a type I found insufferable. Cringey. Uneducated. The exact type I would normally distance myself from in a heartbeat. In California, I had worked hard to put myself in spaces filled with people who knew the right way to be, with people who knew what political views to have and books to read and comments to make. David was one of these people. But at that moment, I don't remember wondering what the appropriate or politically correct thing to say would be. I felt an impulse to reach out to this woman who hadn't let me wander into the night alone. How many people did I know in Oakland that would be willing to take a stranger into their house? I couldn't think of one. It is so much easier to say the right things than to actually do them.

"I'm Sabine," I said, my voice trembling. She reached out and put her hand on my shoulder.

"You're okay," she said. I nodded, fighting back tears, but I didn't believe her. Nothing about my life felt okay.

"Women are entitled to a little crazy every once in a while."

I shook my head, too afraid that if I opened my mouth again I'd start crying.

"It's not anything worth beating yourself up over. Nick and I set you up on the couch in the stockroom until closing time and you didn't bother anyone."

"That was so nice of you. I'm not normally like that. It's just, I've had a lot going on in my life and I think it must have gotten me all mixed up or something. I don't even know what to say. Thank you for letting me stay here and for the coffee and…" I looked up at her, at her sweet smile, at the blanket on my lap that she must have covered me with in the night, and I felt an urge to bury myself in her like a little kid. It was so kind. "Thank you."

"One thank you is enough. I don't mind a bit."

"So is this typical for you then, letting drunk strangers sleep in your living room?"

She laughed and squeezed my knee again.

"Not exactly, but I've been known to lend a hand a time or two."

"Well seriously, thank you." I looked around the room again, realizing I didn't know if my backpack had made it with me.

"Behind you."

I reached behind the couch and felt the canvas of my bag.

"See, it's all okay."

"I should probably get out of your hair, though. I'm sure you've got things to do. This was so generous of you to…"

"Don't be silly. Why don't you stay for breakfast? You must be hungry after last night."

As if on cue, my stomach grumbled. I couldn't remember the last thing I'd eaten. The pizza at my mom's the night before I got to Yu? Maybe a granola bar on the bus ride? I couldn't remember eating one bite of food the day before. No wonder I'd blacked out. What an idiot!

"I shouldn't. I feel I have probably already overstayed my welcome."

"Go on and get yourself cleaned up. I'll have something ready for you in a couple minutes." She gestured across the room to the bathroom and then stood from the coffee table and walked toward the kitchen, which was really just an extension of the living room. She opened the fridge like nothing about the situation was even the slightest bit odd.

TEN.

In Howling Woman's bathroom mirror, I saw the version of myself I hoped no one else saw when they looked at me. Dry brown hair, pock-marked skin from having cystic acne as a teenager, ruddy cheeks and chin, oily forehead, narrow lips that formed deep parentheses at either end. Every time I ever looked in a mirror, all I could see were the ways my face was wrong. Acne and wrinkles, too-large pores across my nose, bushy eyebrows that were too light for my face, hair that didn't know whether to be a mass of tangled curls or a staticky shock of frizz. I couldn't believe that I had tricked a man into marrying me. Another one to regularly fuck me. It was hard to imagine that another man would ever desire me again. I was nearing thirty. Everything seemed like it was about to end. I'd wasted my window of youth. Before, even if I couldn't be called beautiful, at least I could be called young. The only people that call women in their thirties young are women over fifty. Now, I wasn't anything worthy of desiring. Not young. Not beautiful. Not employed. Not loved.

I turned the sink faucet on and splashed water on my face. It felt good to have clean water rinsing away some of my filth. I dug through my backpack and found my phone. It was dead, which seemed fine enough. It wasn't like there was anyone I had to talk to. My cigarettes and wallet were there. I dug around for my deodorant and gave a quick slick to each armpit. Then I pulled down my shorts and sat on the toilet to pee. It was a dehydrated pee, the kind where you can feel your kidneys working overtime to release the toxic waste from your body. My urine was dark yellow and had that sweet fecund smell of rotting stone fruit. How was I even alive? I must have sat there for a while, blanketed by the smell of my own pungency, because Howling Woman knocked at the door some time later to say that breakfast was ready.

Howling Woman didn't have a kitchen table. The kitchen and living room all bled into one sprawling room. At the center of what was the kitchen half of the room, was a kitchen island with two tiers—the lower side a countertop and stove, the raised side an extended flat surface which functioned as a dining counter. There were only two bar stools pushed in beneath it. It all gave the impression that she wasn't one for hosting much.

"This looks great," I said, setting myself up at the counter as Howling Woman plated eggs and toast for us.

"We got the girls out back to thank. Fresh from the nest."

"You have chickens?"

"Better pets than dogs." She put our plates down in front of the bar stools and poured hot water from a kettle over coffee grounds in a French press. On the counter, she'd set out a little pitcher of milk, butter in a butter dish, and jam in an unlabeled jar like she'd made it herself. It was all so domestic, so homey. It made me think of when my mother had started going to the farmers market during my last year of high school. It had come out of nowhere, her sudden interest in going, and sometimes I'd go with her if I happened to have the day off from the little coffee shop where I worked. We'd walk past vendors, not buying anything, and she would say stuff like, *one day when I have money, I'm gonna buy myself a farm and set up one of these stands*, or, *one day when I don't have to work so goddamned much, I'm gonna learn to make my own jam.* She was like that, always talking about some future that might exist after I graduated high school. Her dreams weren't big. Just little stuff like the farm, or growing a garden, or reading a book, or losing a couple pounds and trying yoga. I don't understand what was holding her back all those years. We were broke, sure, and she worked constantly, but on her days off she sat around in the dark living room, drinking her Diet Sprite and vodka, watching television. Surely, there was time to plant a tomato or open a book or make a jar of jam. For my entire childhood, we had subsisted on 10-for-10 boxes of artificially flavored rice and macaroni products. The only produce in our house had either come from a can or a freezer bag, and even then, it was stuff like *fruit cocktail* or *broccoli and "cheddar."*

I never really got why my mom went to the farmers market each weekend. Maybe it was all part of her fantasy making. For all her visits there, she only ever purchased one item—an eggplant she'd been coerced into buying. My mother had been tracing the curves of its oblong body when a vendor, a soft looking blond woman in a soil-stained apron, said, "It's the perfect time of year for ratatouille. Tomatoes stay good here longer than most places because of the heat."

"Oh yeah?" my mother said, removing her hand from the eggplant.

"Have you had it before?"

"Maybe," my mom said, looking over her shoulder at the path out of the vendor's tent.

"Did you see this squash over here?" The woman gestured to a crate of star shaped vegetables that didn't resemble any food that I had ever seen before. "They go great in the dish."

"Just this is fine." My mother practically tossed the eggplant she'd been caressing at the woman.

"Okie dokie." The woman reached into her apron and pulled out a small square of paper with an image of colorful cooked vegetables in a stoneware bowl on one side and text on the other, "Here is the recipe for that ratatouille." She smiled a big horsey grin and extended the small slip of paper out to my mother.

"Great." My mother accepted the piece of paper and shoved it in her pocket.

The eggplant sat on our kitchen counter for weeks untouched. It grew divots that looked like cellulite on the back of middle-aged thighs. I finally threw it away after I'd lifted it up to wipe the counter and felt my fingers slip into its fibrous mushy center. When I pulled my fingers out, they were sticky and slick, reeking of the overly sweet scent of a once living thing gone to rot.

Howling Woman's house, her scrambled eggs and toast breakfast she'd whipped up in the time it took me to rinse myself off, felt like something out of a Hallmark movie—all good-hearted strangers and new beginnings. It called to mind the life my mother imagined for herself—a life better than the one she'd been dealt.

"This is so generous of you," I said, watching Howling Woman press the plunger of the French press.

"It's nice to make breakfast for someone." She filled two mugs of coffee for us and walked them over to the side of the counter where I was sitting. "So, tell me, Sabine, how did you end up in Yu?"

"It actually feels too weird to even say out loud."

"Try me."

"The bus I was on broke down outside of town."

"It's a sign," she said, a chewed-up bit of bread falling out of her mouth. She slapped her hand across her leg, "I could sense it from the moment I saw you." She tilted her head toward me and whispered, "The vortex."

"Oh god. Not you too."

"You heard about it then?"

"Nick."

"It's the truth, powerful stuff that vortex we got. It's been here long before any of us arrived."

"I don't really believe in stuff like that."

"Well, it's a good thing it don't need you to believe in it in order to exist then."

"What even is a vortex?"

"You see those mountains on your way in?" She gestured out the window above the kitchen sink, but she didn't wait for me to answer, "We call her la Chupadera. That tall one in the middle, that's la Chupadera's peak, and god herself carved up the flesh of the earth to birth it. La Chupadera surrounds the entire town of Yu. She separates us from everything outside of the valley. She is a barrier between good and evil, but most importantly her vortex cleanses evil from the good."

"You think a mountain can do all that?"

"You tell me, Buttercup," she leaned in close to me, propping her arms up on the counter between us and rested her chin in her palms, "what is it you think brought you here to this middle of nowhere town?"

"I told you, the bus I was on broke down outside of town."

"Sure, but you didn't have to walk down the hill from the shop now, did you?"

I took a bite of my eggs and considered what she was saying. There was some truth to it—that I had felt a sort of magnetic pull from the town (were vortexes magnetic?)—but I could think of a hundred reasons, none of which were magical, that explained that feeling. I was prone to restlessness; I didn't want to wait in a hot garage for another bus to take me somewhere equally as random as where we'd stopped; I didn't have any place better to be; or, the simple, age-old reason for half the shit I did, which was I wanted a drink and my chances of finding one were better if I walked down the hill than if I'd stayed put.

"I don't know. I wanted a beer?" I said, grinning.

"Joke all you want. I know the truth. I can see it all over your face. It's the vortex."

"That sounds like the type of thing a person believes in when they are looking for meaning where there isn't any."

"Spoken like a true lost soul."

"Oh god. You can't be serious."

"It's the truth."

"What does that even mean?"

"People like you, Sabine."

"You mean fuckups?"

"Girl, don't go talking about yourself like that in my house."

"I guess I'm not sure if I believe in the whole *soul* thing is all."

"Soul *thing*?" she laughed, "It doesn't matter what you believe. La Chupadera doesn't care. The vortex sucks 'em right up and keeps 'em here until they're ready to leave."

"And when will that be?"

"As soon as it's done working through all the mess inside of them that's keeping them from enlightenment."

"Is this like some sort of new age *come-to-Jesus* type thing? Don't tell me you're an Alan Watts fan."

"Call it whatever you want to call it. It's there no matter what you name it. It's bigger than us and whatever we've got planned."

"So you're saying that if I wanted to leave right now, I couldn't?"

"That's not the point. The point is, you got something you're running from or something that's running you, and the vortex brought you here to deal with it."

"That sounds a little unbelievable, don't you think?"

"You'll see," she said, smiling at me with confidence.

"What about you then? The vortex bring you here too?"

"Something like that."

"What were you running from?"

She smiled and patted my knee.

"Go on and finish your breakfast before it gets cold. We don't want to hurt the girls' feelings by tossing their eggs out." She took a heaping bite of her own eggs on the last little bit of her remaining toast and stood from the stool, plate in hand, and began cleaning up the kitchen.

"What I really want to know," she said, her mouth full as she walked around to the sink, "is where you were headed."

"That's a good question."

She put her hand on her hip and looked at me from across the kitchen. "Well then?"

"Utah."

"What's in Utah?"

I took a bite of my eggs and chewed slowly, probably thinking about how best to answer her question. I'd bought the ticket because it was the cheapest and earliest departure out of my hometown. It wasn't a dream of mine to live in Utah, but I liked the idea of starting over in a place famous for its breathtaking landscapes. I read about it in a Terry Tempest Williams book during college and I couldn't ever get those descriptions of red earth out of my mind. It was an abstract thought, just a thing I'd read about. That it wasn't notorious for being an expensive place to live like the Bay Area was also appealing. I wasn't exactly working with a heavy cash flow. David's salary and family money had paid for a good chunk of my life. I'd maxed out my personal credit card getting the ticket to my mom's place and had pulled out a grand from our joint bank account the day before I left. I wasn't stupid enough to think I could go around using my debit card freely if I wanted my location to remain a secret from David. I've watched enough Lifetime movies to know better.

"I don't know. I always thought it would be cool to see Zion though."

"Hmm…" she looked me up and down for a minute and cocked her head to the side, "You don't strike me as much of the nature type."

"You just met me."

"Well, are you?"

"I'm not sure. I think I could be."

"So it's settled then, you are going to Utah." She looked over at me and raised her eyebrows, "To Zion," she said, but she didn't sound all that convincing. It was more like a question, like she was asking if I was challenging the vortex.

"I don't know anymore."

"You thinking you might stay in Yu instead of leaving then?"

"That is sort of the question I keep asking myself. You know…" I started, but the thought trailed off and I felt my voice tremble. It hit me, sitting in her kitchen being questioned about my very near future, how uncertain I was, how precarious my situation was—I had cheated on my husband, gotten pregnant, gotten an abortion, left my husband without any real explanation, had barely any money, had absolutely no clue what to do next. How was I supposed to be trusted to make the next right decision? In books and movies, characters always make starting over look so simple—you just leave one place and enter another—but how did it actually work? How did a thousand dollars pay for the in-between time it took to get to a new town and find a new place to live and get a job to keep paying for the new life?

"Hey Buttercup, you alright?" Howling Woman's voice had gone all soft and she was walking toward me, but she looked blurry. I realized my eyes were welled up with tears. I felt her take my hands in hers and it all became too much—my situation, how stupid I felt believing I could start over, how afraid I was that I'd irrevocably ruined the only good thing I had going for myself, that I had absolutely no idea what I should do next. I felt like I was old enough to know better, to know how to be an adult, to know how to live, and yet it felt absolutely evasive to me—impossible to know the right way to live. Tears streamed down my cheeks. She squeezed my hands tighter in her own.

"Hey now."

"I really fucked up bad," I said, "like really really fucking bad."

"I'm sure it ain't as bad as you think."

"No, it is. I am a horrible, stupid person. I was in a perfectly good marriage to a nice man, and I fucked it all up. My marriage. My life. My future. Now I'm here in this town and I don't even know what to do next and I wish I could start over again and be a good person and not such an idiot, but I don't even know how to find a place to stay or where to go or what to do. It's all a mess."

"It's alright, Buttercup, this ain't the worst that's ever happened to a person."

"I know," I said through sobs, "that makes it worse. So many people have it worse than me and here I am, totally ungrateful for the life I had. I went and ruined everything, and now I got no one to love me or care about me and I am going to die alone as a worthless, awful, terrible, no-good human."

I was really crying then, my words all one wet, stuttering mess, but she must have got the gist because the next thing I knew she was pulling me up from the stool and wrapping her arms around me. She smelled like patchouli and coffee, and she held me like I belonged to her, like I wasn't just some stranger she barely met.

"Hey now, it's all gonna be okay." She pressed me close to her and petted my head. I let her. I kept crying into her chest. I don't know if anyone ever held me like that, petting my hair, cooing that I was alright. I don't even think my mother had ever consoled me like that as a child, but Howling Woman stood there, letting me cry myself tired like it was the most normal thing in the world to do. This is the image I keep coming back to now that I know who she really is, now that I know what she did all those years before we met. It is hard to reconcile the woman holding me in the kitchen with the woman they say she is.

"Take a breath, Buttercup. Sometimes it's hard to see the light when we're in the dark, but I promise it's still there."

I nodded into her chest, my breathing finally slowing, and she leaned back, putting her arms on my shoulders so we were face-to-face.

"Better?"

I shrugged.

"I have an idea."

"Yeah?"

"Why don't you stay with me for a little while?"

I wiped my nose with the back of my hand, and looked at her through bleary eyes.

"I couldn't."

"Why not?"

"That's too much. You don't even know me. What if I am some horrible person? A murderer or something?"

"You're not a horrible person," she said, her response so quick it felt like the truth.

"I think I am," I said. I could feel a lump in my throat, like more tears were on their way.

"Hey now," Howling Woman squeezed my shoulders, "I know you're wrong. I get a sense about these types of things. You're good."

"You think?"

"I know."

"I'm sorry. I don't normally break down crying in front of strangers."

"Hey, no sorries. I got a futon out in the shed that's just collecting dust. Besides, it sounds nice to have someone around other than those clucking chickens. Why don't you stay here for a little while?"

"Are you sure?"

"I am," she said and pulled me into another hug.

Now that everything has happened, I keep thinking back on that moment, trying to remember if I got the details right. I'd been so concerned wondering if I should stay with her that I hadn't thought much about why she invited me. I still don't know the answer to this. Maybe it was just a feeling she had like the one I had that told me to stay. All I can remember with certainty is a feeling of yearning. Before I met Howling Woman, I never had any close female friends. Men consumed my emotional energy. I wanted to be adored, to be the center of someone's desire. Self-erasure through romance. But Howling Woman had something I wanted. Even then, standing in her kitchen, I could feel it. The kitchen window emitted a halo of light around her, the steam coming up from the coffee like an enchanted fog surrounding an ethereal spirit. She was Klimt's Athena in *Pallas Athene*—ambiguous, golden, self-assured, so powerful as to overwhelm the canvas itself.

There's so much I still need to write that I'm not going to waste time trying to answer why I stayed. Sometimes, when you've run out of options that sound good, you accept the thing right in front of you.

ELEVEN

I'm not sure if writing this all down is the right thing to do. I can hear the voice of my lawyer, his smoke-strained voice like something from the mouth of a rugged cowboy, not the frazzled, thin man he is, saying, *Just keep your mouth shut. It's always a gamble when the defendant speaks. I'm not sure you want to take your chances with stakes this high.* He doesn't want the jury to hear my justification for why I shot a man. He says it won't hold up against the facts. Such a wild thing to distill a story down to a single detail. That's no story at all. Simply a search for facts. I am not so sure a fact matters without context. Not sure anything can exist in isolation. What does it mean without the story behind it? People talk about objectivity like it is some aspirational virtue—the news is supposed to be objective, the court is supposed to be objective, history is supposed to be objective—but everything, even so-called facts, are just what someone saw—a matter of perspective. A fact can't exist in a meaningful way until language is ascribed to it, and isn't the point of collecting facts to create some kind of narrative—the truth, a belief, a story? If you're going to use a fact to form a narrative, then it's only fair to know the story leading up to the fact. So, yes, the *fact* is I shot a man, but that doesn't even begin to tell you what happened.

After that morning in Howling Woman's kitchen, I helped her clean up breakfast then followed her out to the shed in the backyard. The shed was next to a small chicken coop, and the girls, as she liked to call them, clucked around our feet.

"Here, give them a treat and introduce yourself." She reached into her pocket and scooped out some chicken feed then placed it in the palm of my hand. "Bend down and open up your palm. The girls will come right up to you, but don't make any sudden movements."

I bent down and the four chickens swarmed me, clucking and pecking until the food was gone. Once they realized I had nothing left to offer them, they turned and wandered away into the enclosed backyard. One stayed by my feet, looking up expectantly.

"That's Penny," Howling Woman said, pointing to the copper-colored chicken. "She likes to be held."

"I've never held a chicken before."

"It's not too hard if they like you and I think she likes you. Put your hands on either side of her wings and scoop her up gently. She'll let you know if she doesn't want you to touch her."

I leaned toward Penny slowly and followed Howling Woman's instructions. I was surprised she didn't try to get away from me. She was lighter than she looked, and she fit in my arms the way I imagine a baby might. She looked up at me and her head twitched back and forth as I petted her.

"That's right, Penny, we like Sabine, don't we?" Howling Woman said in a sweet voice.

"She's so soft."

"She's the princess around here, but watch out for that one," Howling Woman pointed to a large speckled black and gray chicken that was running around pecking at the dirt, "That's Ozzy. She's my little satanist."

Howling Woman slid open the door of the metal shed and kicked some boxes to the side. "Here, give me a hand with this." She reached for a corner of a wooden futon frame and pulled it toward her. I put Penny back down on the ground and she stayed close by as we pulled the futon and a folding room divider out of the shed. We carried it all into the house and rearranged the living room so that a corner of it was sectioned off as my room. Howling Woman pulled out a set of clean linens from the closet by the bathroom and we made the bed up, finishing it off with a pillow Howling Woman pulled off the couch where I'd slept the night before.

"It's not anything special, but it beats the stockroom."

"It's perfect," I said.

"Go on and get yourself settled in. I got some things to do out back."

I watched her walk toward the backdoor and once she was gone I crawled into my new bed and slept for nearly thirty-six hours straight. I don't remember ever sleeping like that before as an adult. It was as though I'd fallen under some spell that had made everything inside of me go slack and heavy.

It had been a restless kind of sleep, though—the sort where your body is slick with sweat, and you feel as though you are straddling the world of the living and the world of the dead simultaneously. I slept in a fevered state, my brain on a tread-mill of half dreams and anxieties. A montage of faces played on repeat—my mother, David, Avery, James Dixon, Nick from the bar, Howling Woman. I slept so long that the faces started to dissociate from the bodies and memories from which they belonged, and when I finally woke up, I had lost the sense of my past, the people in it. All that was left was an exhausting sense of faces like phantoms haunting me.

Like déjà vu, I awoke with Howling Woman hovering above me, a Groundhog Day type feeling of awakening, only more than a day had passed, and this time she didn't have any coffee in her hand.

"You planning on getting out of this bed one day, or you just gonna waste away in your own stink?"

Howling Woman was sitting on the bed beside me, her hand on my thigh like she was a mom waking up her sleeping child—the gesture gentler than the question.

"What time is it?"

"It's time to quit stinking up my house with your June Gloom attitude, that's what time it is."

"No, for real?" I asked, reaching around for my phone.

"It is five o'clock in the damn evening. You've gone and slept the whole day away."

"You're joking."

"You wish, now come on. Get up and rinse yourself off so you can help me with dinner."

It wasn't exactly the way I imagined being talked to by a roommate, but then again, we hadn't really talked about rent. I was more of her guest than anything, so I dragged myself out of bed to the shower. It sounded like it might help to wash off whatever literal or metaphorical filth was coating me.

I turned the water as hot as it would go. It burned my skin, and I shifted back and forth between wanting to be overtaken by the pain and wanting to avoid it. Eventually, I settled into the sting of scorching water running down my body. I acclimated to it until it was no longer painful, until it was pleasant. I felt as though everything and nothing had changed. I'd had an abortion, left my husband, Avery, and my mother. I'd returned to the desert but was somewhere entirely new to me. I'd changed nearly everything about my external circumstances, and yet, I was still in the same body I'd always been in, carrying everything that I'd experienced between birth and the present moment. I stayed in the shower until the hot water turned cold, and by the end of it, nothing eternal had been washed away. It was all still there, just dampened. Even so, I had a feeling that my whole life was about to change, something more internal. My skin sensitive and alert, feeling the slightest changes in the air, absorbing the atmosphere in my cells and readying my body for whatever was coming. I could sense that Howling Woman would be a part of it. I wasn't wrong, of course.

In the kitchen, there was a straw basket full of squash, tomatoes, and freshly trimmed basil. A record player emitted the sound of Heart's *Alone*, and Howling Woman was singing along as she diced an onion.

"That's better now, isn't it?"

"Yeah, I don't know why I feel so tired."

"Here, drink this." She gestured to a big plastic cup with bubbling pink liquid inside. It smelled tannic and sharp. I took a sip and felt bubbles burst in my mouth, tiny holes of my brain opening to the wine and the chill of ice. "A little hair of the dog that bit ya." She tossed the onions into the pan and reached for the tomatoes from the basket. "Dice these for us, will you?"

"I can't believe it's already dinnertime."

"Yeah, it comes quick when you're sleeping your life away." She turned on the burner beneath a big pot of water and threw a pinch of salt in.

"I don't remember the last time I slept like that. I'm sorry."

"Hey, what did I say about sorries?"

"I forgot."

Howling Woman nodded as she stirred the onions in the pan with a wooden spoon. She was wearing a pink and lime-green kimono, her long hair in a fat braid, no makeup on as she sang along to Heart.

"Life's a process," she said, not looking up from the pan, "but you can't let it win—if life fucks with you, you fuck it right back."

"That sounds like something a gym coach would say."

"Go on and finish those tomatoes up, will you?"

"Where do you want them?"

"With the onions." She stepped away from the pan making room for me to add them with the onions. "I'm serious—fuck it right back," she said again.

"I don't even know what that means."

"Sure you do. You didn't end up in Yu for no reason, and I'm guessing that you probably left something behind, and I might even go so far as to say that whatever you left behind is also something you're running from."

"I wouldn't exactly put it like that."

"Well, how would you put it then?"

"I don't know—a fresh start or a new start or something like that."

"And what is it that you're leaving behind then? You don't get a fresh-new something without abandoning something else."

"Jesus, I'm gonna need another one of these for this conversation." I chugged the rest of my drink and Howling Woman took the cup from me.

"It's the vortex that does it," she said, putting her hand up between us as if to stop me from objecting, "and before you go and make some twisted up face about our precious vortex, just hear me out a second. You might think it sounds like a crock of shit, but don't deny that there isn't something special you felt about this town—something magnetic—that drew you in. You might not believe in the vortex yet, but you can't tell me that you coming down here from that hilltop didn't feel the least bit out of your control."

I nodded, taking it all in—what she said, the two of us standing there together, no longer exactly strangers. The kitchen smelled good with the onions and tomatoes cooking. I realized I was hungry after sleeping through a normal person's day worth of meals. I stirred the tomatoes and onions. Howling Woman poured me another drink, tore pieces of basil into the pan with the tomatoes and onions, squeezed my shoulders. I felt my breath catch at her touch.

"What about you? What were you leaving behind?" I asked, taking my drink from her.

She took the wooden spoon from me and brought it to her mouth to taste. She nodded her head in approval and turned the heat down. "It's been so long since I got here that I've started to lose track of everything that happened in the past. Feels like another lifetime or person ago. What matters is, I'm right where I need to be. My life feels the way it's supposed to be." She smiled at me and reached for my hand. She wrapped her own around it and gave it a gentle squeeze. That's another thing about Howling Woman. She always knew when to reach out. That's not something I'm so good at. Maybe it's the kind of thing you learn from your mother, if you have that kind of mother, which I certainly didn't.

"I'm still married," I said, looking down at our intertwined hands.

"Is that so?"

"That's why I left California."

She nodded and let go of my hand, took a drink from her cup. "Your husband the kind of man that's going to show up on my doorstep demanding things from you that you don't want to give him?"

"David? No way." I laughed, trying to picture my husband showing up on Howling Woman's porch in one of his chunky sweaters, transition lenses, and New Balances. He didn't belong here. Even if he did find me, he wasn't the type to bang on doors. It was exactly the sort of reason I'd picked him to be my husband, though there was a part of me that felt a bit sad knowing there was no one in my life that could be compelled to extreme gestures in the name of passion.

"What kind of man is this husband of yours then?"

I looked into my drink, the small bubbles floating to the top and bursting at the surface.

"He's pragmatic. A professor. He's not the dramatic type."

"I could see how that could be a bore. Life's short."

"I think I'm going to have a smoke."

"I'll come with."

Outside, the sun hung low in the sky, all dusty roses and sherbet. In the middle of the desert, the horizon line is a dramatic thing. There aren't any tall buildings or trees to disrupt it. It gives the illusion that things are endless, full of unseen possibilities, and it's easy to imagine how a person could walk for miles through it without stopping, pushing themselves to keep going, even when they are thirsty and dried out to nothing. That illusion of something more just a little farther enough to stupefy them into dying beneath the sun. Even the mountain emerging from the flat earth had a split in it, like you could walk up it or go straight through to more ever-expanding possibility. It wasn't like the Bay Area where cities and suburbs jutted out of the landscape, where even in nature there was an endless flow of people walking their dogs and FaceTiming their friends. In the desert, you didn't need to go far to disappear, for the earth to swallow up everything else.

"So, Sabine, what do you do for work?" Howling Woman asked as we lit our cigarettes.

"Well, right now I guess I don't do much of anything. But I was in school."

"What'd you study?"

"I got a degree in English, but I haven't really done anything with it yet. I was working at a restaurant my whole way through school. I was still waitressing up until I left California."

"I always loved reading. Did you ever read anything by Anne Waldman? There's a poem of hers, I can't remember the title, but a line in it goes something like 'Turn yourself inside out and you might disappear.' I like that. Do you know the poem?"

"I don't."

"I like poetry. It's a lot like music in how it says so much with so little. But music's more physical. It connects people even if they don't know the lyrics. You don't have to worry about meaning or anything like that. It's something you feel."

"So, you're a musician then?"

"I guess you could say that. For the most part I sing covers at The Whiptail. It's a trip how all it takes to become someone different for a night is a wig and a little bit of makeup."

"Yeah, I thought an English degree would make me different in some way. More intellectual or whatever, but it turns out reading books doesn't pay a living the same way serving burgers does."

"I think there's something humbling about serving others. It's good to be of service. You can be a part of someone's story in that way."

"That's one perspective, I guess. Personally, I always feel a bit humiliated every time I have to put on an apron."

"That reminds me. I got you a job."

"What? Where?"

"The Whiptail. And you don't even have to wear an apron."

"Oh god, no. I can't imagine ever showing my face in there again."

"Don't be so dramatic. You're not the first person to ever throw up in The Whiptail bathroom. At least you aimed for the toilet."

"Nick wasn't upset about the other night?"

"That old fool? No, he's smitten. Happy to have you."

"I don't want it to be weird."

"Idle hands make the devil's work," she said, and as if preempting that I might think bringing talk of god or the devil into all this would make me more resistant, she looked at me with a big smile on her face and said, "I'm no Bible-thumper, but it will be good for you to work. Get your mind off things. Live in the moment. 'Start over' as you said."

"If this is about money, I can get a job. I will pay rent. You don't have to worry about that."

"I think you're turning this into more than it is. It's a great job, only a couple days a week, real easy stuff. Besides, there aren't many options out here unless you want to commute to Albuquerque."

"I must have made a real fucking fool of myself the other night. I'm too embarrassed to go back."

"You worry too much about what others think."

"Doesn't everyone?"

"You gotta open yourself to the gifts of the universe."

"I don't deserve gifts."

"Phooey. Everyone deserves gifts."

"What about women who cheat on their husbands and leave them without explanation?"

"Buttercup, this isn't the olden days. No one's gonna make you stitch a scarlet *A* on your tank top."

"It's more than that. I was cruel to someone who didn't deserve it."

"If you were a bad wife there was probably a reason. Just 'cause a man's good to you don't mean you owe him your life. There's a lot of ways men take advantage of women without even knowing it. I'm not saying your husband did this or anything. All I'm saying is you didn't do what you did for no reason."

I thought about saying something else to prove that David was good—that I was bad, that I was greedy and selfish and unwilling to put in the hard work of being a wife—a partner. The whole time I'd been seeing Avery behind David's back, I'd been convinced that it was all me who was terrible. Maybe those things were true, but maybe there was also something about David or our marriage that shared the blame. It was nice to consider it as an option at least.

I'd lied to David, kept things from him about myself, but maybe there was something nearly imperceptible about him I'd picked up on that made it impossible for me to open up. I remembered that once I'd thought about telling David the story of how James Dixon had come into my room all those times in my childhood. We'd been married just a couple of months. We were in bed together, him on top of me, looking into my eyes full of adoration. He was looking at me, but he wasn't seeing me, not the real me, and so I said the words I'd said so many times during sex with other men, *hit me, please, slap me, tell me I'm your whore.* It was automatic. They came out of my mouth so quickly. Just as quickly, he stopped thrusting into me, his body suspended above me, him still inside of me, shaking. He pulled out and rolled onto his back next to me, his face twisting up in confusion.

"*What?*" I asked.

His eyes were closed like he didn't want to look at me and he was shaking his head back and forth on the pillow.

"*I can't,*" he said, then inhaled deeply, exhaled, breathed in again, "*Why would you want that, Sabine?*"

"*I'm sorry. I know I'm disgusting.*"

"*No.*" He turned toward me and put his palm on my stomach, "*I love you too much to do something like that. I don't want to hurt you.*"

I started to cry, and he held me. The tears felt violent coming out of me. I remember thinking that if he loved me then he'd hit me. Then I thought, *what the fuck kind of awful human thinks this way?* I wanted to explain myself, but I didn't know how to put it into words—that it wasn't that weird to ask your partner to hit you, but also, I wanted to try and analyze why I was like that, like if I could explain my desire, it wouldn't be so offensive. I wanted him to see me as a woman with agency and choice, not a woman who had been abused. It's such a dirty word. They're all dirty words. Abuse. Molest. Assault. Rape. If I told him, I'd be conflating my entire identity, my sexual desires, to a set of actions done to me without my consent. It didn't seem fair that I could be judged by the things that were done to me rather than the woman I was trying to be. I'm skeptical of the notion that all my desires are entirely tied to what happened to me It seems too reductive to say that my desire for a certain kind of violence attached to sex is a result of trauma (another word I hate). It seems too obvious. Too simple. I don't think we are smart enough to truly get the complexity of desire. I don't think every twisted fantasy I've ever had is directly rooted to what happened to me, but I don't think it is totally removed from it either. Maybe I just like the way pain enhances pleasure—the way being slapped makes my skin prickle, heightening all my senses because I'm anticipating more. It heightens the orgasm in that way too—my body increasingly attuned to the sensations of foreign objects impacting it.

For a moment, in his arms, I thought about telling him the thing I'd never told anyone. I wanted to defend myself. Prove that I wasn't the terrible one in this situation. Let him know that I was still lovable, maybe in need of love even more than others as a result of my childhood. But I didn't believe it enough to say it. The words didn't come, and I fell asleep like that, cry-tired and ashamed, grateful in a way to be loved by someone who wouldn't love me in the gross way I wanted to be loved.

I took another sip of the sparkling wine concoction Howling Woman made me and tried to shake the thought from my mind.

"Thanks for getting me the job. And for everything else."

"I'm glad you're staying."

I looked over at Howling Woman, surprised to hear this from her. That someone I hardly knew could share such an earnest sentiment of gratitude for my presence. It felt good to be looked at by her, smiled at by her, like it meant something about me that she wanted me around.

"It's been a while since the vortex brought someone in."

"Oh jesus, not the vortex again."

"You might not like the sound of it, but I can tell you're supposed to be here. It's like a feeling in my soul telling me that you and I were supposed to meet."

The sun began to settle behind the mountain, the cool night air coaxing itself in like waves. I looked out at the landscape beyond Howling Woman's backyard. The sky was an expanse whose vastness seemed too big to fill. A halo of orange light bled into pink wash across the mountain range. That single high peak, la Chupadera, appearing to pierce the setting sun and make it bleed its orange rays into the pink haze. Soon, all the color would be swallowed up by darkness and a sliver of moon and constellations would be left to light the world around us. Is it so crazy to believe there was a magnet in that mountain? That something so striking could be so powerful?

TWELVE.

My first shift at The Whiptail was *Two-Step Tuesday*. I hadn't exactly packed my bag in anticipation of bartending, so I was wearing a tank top, jeans, and Tevas. It wasn't the worst outfit for bartending, but the sandals would have to be replaced as soon as possible.

"You excited for your first shift?" Howling Woman cut the engine to the truck in the gravel parking lot outside the bar. She was performing as Wynonna Judd and her big red wig flickered beneath the moonlight as we hopped out. It was a weird gig she had—performing as other women at The Whiptail. It was one of the things that drew me to her—the way her existence was unlike anyone else I knew. I'd spent my entire life trying to mold myself into a person that could blend into normal society. Polite society as the novels I read called it. Part of my desire to leave where I'd grown up was that it all felt too much like something that might be on a daytime television talk show—the kind where poor white trash sits in front of an audience that can't stop gasping at their lack of civility. I didn't ever want to be a spectacle. I thought of my mother like that, a *spectacle*. Her with her raucous relationships, fighting with men in bars, walking around in too tight T-shirts exuding sex with her enormous tits and collecting stares from every single passerby. The thought of people looking at me with their mouths agape, drooling with judgment, was more than I could bear. I wanted to become small enough, conventional enough, that I could go unnoticed. But it is tiring to whittle yourself to nothing. Looking at Howling Woman crossing the dirt lot of The Whiptail, her stage makeup and sequins an act against disappearing, I thought maybe I'd been doing it all wrong.

"I don't know if that would be my first word choice for it, but yeah, I guess I am looking forward to a bit of normalcy."

"Ain't nothing normal about The Whiptail and that's a blessing, Buttercup."

It was after eight p.m. and there were only a couple of cars parked in the gravel lot beside The Whiptail. Two women stood smoking outside as we walked up. One of them had shoulder-length red hair and wore a denim skirt and flip-flops. She had a cigarette in one hand, a bottle of Coors Light in the other, and she was leaned up against the painted nose of the lizard on the outside wall of the bar. The other woman was stout with spiky hair, and she had her hand pressed beneath the fabric of the red-head's tank top. We pulled open the heavy wooden doors of the bar and they both turned toward us as though suddenly realizing they existed in public.

"Giddyup, ladies," the woman with the spikey hair hollered at us.

The bar was surprisingly full for how few cars had been in the parking lot. The bar stools were mostly taken up by droopy-faced men staring into their empty glasses. Interrupting the row or men was a woman in a baby pink velour tracksuit sipping white wine through a straw. It was the same woman I'd seen my first night in town. The jukebox played some country song, raspy male vocals waxing on about loosing your one and only, the only salvation left the light of a neon moon. Couples pressed their bodies into one another on the dance floor by the stage. I couldn't help but acknowledge how meta the song was on a Tuesday night in a bar in the middle of nowhere. I hadn't lost my one and only though. I'd lost two men, or rather, I'd left two men. I didn't even know if I had a one and only. But I was alone, or at least without a partner, in a bar. Always a bar. Always that sacred neon moon coming to the rescue. There wasn't anything romantic about it. Yet there they were, couples on the dance floor clutching one another as the pained lyrics of the male vocalist bellowed out of the jukebox.

David hated Country music. Everyone with a college degree seemed to hate country music. But I could feel the song pulling me into the bar, into the daze of dancing with abandon and drinking until the world was as simple as cowboys drowning their sorrows, awaiting the return of the lovers that left them. In California, I never admitted I liked country music. It was like you were admitting to being a republican or sleeping with your cousin, but now that I was back in New Mexico I didn't have to pretend so hard to be someone else. It was perfectly acceptable to like country music, and really, is there anything truer than songs about whiskey and loneliness?

"Hey there, Champ. Welcome back," Nick said as Howling Woman and I approached the bar, "You look like a brand-new woman."

"I guess that's what a shower will do," I said.

"That, and a vanishing coat of bile." He winked a theatrical wink at me.

"Hey now, play nice, Nick." Howling Woman kissed him on his cheek.

"I don't mean nothing by it. Sabine and I go way back," he said, filling a pint glass halfway with pink wine and topping the rest of the glass off with seltzer from the gun, "And might I say, Ms. Judd, you are looking quite fiery tonight."

"Let's see if I'll catch." Howling Woman smiled and reached for the glass Nick had prepared for her. "Have fun you two," she said, disappearing into the crowd of people swaying in the smoky light of the dance floor.

"Always," Nick shouted after her before turning to face me, "So, it seems like you'll be sticking around after all then?"

"Looks that way."

He walked over to the taps and poured a pint of something light. "Well, it ain't California," he said in a voice loud enough for the men at the bar to hear, his own personal audience. He set the beer down in front of a guy with a big shiny bald spot, "And thank the good lord for that. Can I get an *amen*?" he shouted to the bar.

"Amen!" a chorus of men at different stages of drunk sang from their seats. Nick slapped the bar and laughed. He walked back over to where I stood waiting for direction.

"You work in a bar before?" he asked.

"It's basically the only thing I'm qualified to do," I said, trying to make it sound like a joke, but I could feel it catch in my throat on its way out, that chip on my shoulder to be different than my mother heavy as ever.

"That makes two of us. Tonight will be a pretty easy shift for you. It's Charity's last rodeo here." He pointed across the room to a petite woman with big blond hair holding a tray of empty bottles up above her shoulder. She was wearing a white tank top and a denim skirt, the official uniform of Yu I was quickly learning. She looked my age, maybe a little older, and she had a tattoo of a snake with an apple in its mouth wrapped around her slender bicep.

"She's moving to Albuquerque to study nursing in the fall."

"Good for her," I said, hoping it sounded genuine and not condescending. I wondered how many people from this town came and went. Howling Woman's vortex theory had given the impression that it was the kind of place that sucked you in and barricaded you from the outside world, but already she stood corrected.

"Sure is. Not every day people leave Yu," he said. Charity looked over at us and smiled. Nick motioned for her to come join us and she rolled her eyes up to the sky and tilted her head back and mouthed *thank you.*

"You must be Howling Woman's new roomie," she said as she began unloading the empty glasses onto a mat at the bar, "Sabine, right?"

"Word sure spreads fast around here."

"Get used to it, girl." She laughed and dumped the bottles into the recycling bin at the opening of the bar and then set the tray down on a shelf beneath the bar top.

"Congrats on nursing school," I said, realizing that I already knew something about this stranger as well.

"Ready to get the hell out this town."

"School starts in August?"

"I know I'm leaving early. Wanna get me a job before school starts."

"That sounds practical."

"Mostly, I want to get the hell out of here."

"Albuquerque is pretty nice," I said, even though the only thing I knew about Albuquerque was that it was the city people moved to when they wanted to get out of other small New Mexican towns but were too scared to leave the state.

"I wouldn't know. Never been, but I figure anything beats this place." She reached her hand out to me and set it on my shoulder, "Not to give you a bad impression of Yu or anything. It's different when it's the place you're from."

"You don't have to explain that to me. I get it."

"But you're gonna be living with Howling Woman and working here. What a trip."

"Well I don't know how long I'll be staying."

"No plans?" Charity shook her head and made a *pft* noise with her mouth, "You're something else. You know?"

"How so?" I asked, not at all sure what she meant.

"You know, moving to a place you don't even know and moving in with Howling Woman of all people." She shook her head.

"Yeah, she's really generous."

"You'll love her. Everybody loves her. A little weird, but lovable."

"Yeah, I know, it's a little weird, right?"

"I think it's great. You're great."

I don't know what it is about Yu, but people are different here. Maybe that's part of its appeal and also part of the way it sucked me in a little bit. The sheer kindness of strangers unlike any other place I've ever been—like the town and the people were all casting a spell on me. If I had to assign a genre to the story of my life upon arriving in Yu, it was more fantasy than reality.

For the next thirty minutes I trailed Charity as she shimmied through the crowd, picking up empty beer bottles and delivering fresh ones. She was like a local celebrity, customers knew her by name, some even cheered when she delivered a round of drinks. You never would have guessed by her big smile and loud laughter that she was ready to run from the place.

"Is it always this busy on a weeknight?" I asked as we waited at the bar for Nick to fill our drink order.

"No, just Two-Step Tuesday, otherwise it's your normal small-town bar."

"Nothing about this town seems normal."

"Guess I wouldn't know," she laughed, "Why don't you deliver this round, I gotta check in with Howling Woman real quick."

"Sure," I said. It was a round of beers for a small group of middle-aged hippie types in baggy linen pants, with long hair, and patchouli perfuming the air around them. They were dancing near the front of the stage and they barely noticed me as I set the beers down on a high-top where all their belongings were piled.

I looked around the room to see where Charity was and that's when I saw him for the first time.

So, now is probably as good a time as any to mention there was another thing that led to me and Howling Woman down state with a gun. I hate to admit it, but it was a man. I didn't want this to be my story—you know, girl runs away from problems in search of finding herself and meets a man, falls for man, secretly hopes this new man will be part of what makes her new life better. I had already tried living out that trope once, and look where it had gotten me. You'd think I would know better, but maybe life is just repeating the same cycles over and over until we die. I think this is where writing classes and books and movies get it wrong—always insisting that characters be somehow changed by the end of the story. It creates a false sense of reality. A belief in the human capacity for change.

The point is, and this is important, it was him who was staring at me first. He was more than staring. I think the proper term is *eye-fucking*. He was *eye-fucking* me from across the bar, though I don't want to be presumptuous and say that he was into me from the first time he saw me. Maybe that's part of the story I'm trying to tell here alongside everything else. A story where I'm seen as a beautiful woman that a man might desire. If that's the case, others might desire me, or desire good things for me. Maybe then I won't spend the prime of my life in prison. Beautiful women aren't meant to be behind bars. Beautiful women are meant to be free, adorning the landscape and distracting from the grotesque reality of life on earth.

The man, who I now know as Angel, was wearing black denim jeans, a Black Sabbath T-shirt, and a denim vest. He was leaning up against the wall near the stage, playing the handsome loner role and looking impenetrable. I locked eyes with him for a moment to see if he would beckon me over for something, but he didn't. I dropped my gaze, my heart growing fast in my chest from having been caught in a staring match, and I picked up an empty glass at a table nearby and made my way back to the bar. I instantly wished I'd put on some makeup for my shift, or had worn something more flattering than a baggy old tank top. Then I shook my head. No. Who cares. No more men. Even then, wishing I wasn't interested in gaining a man's attraction, I could feel the yearning to be wanted. It is a compulsion I have—a need to be validated by others. Especially men. As I set the tray down at the bar, I looked back to where the man was standing to check if he was still looking at me. He was, and he smiled when our eyes met. I don't recall what I did with my face, something stupid probably. It didn't matter. He wasn't my type, but he was handsome, seemingly enigmatic in a way I imagined made women want to orbit around him in hopes they might be the one invited to peek into the mystery of him. He had tawny skin, a long, jet-black ponytail, and pursed lips it was easy to imagine kissing.

"Don't let that pretty face fool you. He'll break your heart."

I jumped at the sound of Nick's voice beside me, my sexy stare-down interrupted. "Huh?" I said, pretending I had no idea what Nick was referring to even though my face was on fire and my pulse was probably visible. Caught, doing the very thing I said I wouldn't be doing. No men. No sex. Forget the sexy eyes and the kissable lips. I didn't even like ponytails.

"Angel, the man in black over there who appears to have caught your eye." Nick gestured with his bar towel across the room to where Angel was leaned up against the wall, no longer looking my way.

"Not really my type."

"He's everyone's type, the lucky bastard. You should see the bar on nights he works here."

"He works here?"

"Sure does."

"Well trust me, he's really not my type."

"Oh yeah? You into women?" he asked, his eyebrows raising.

"Would it be a problem if I was?"

"Hey, I'm not here to judge. To each their own."

"It's not that. I'm just off dating or whatever," I said, hoping that if I said it out loud to someone else it might hold me more accountable.

"Or *whatever*?" Nick asked, arching an eyebrow and smirking.

"Sex. I'm off sex," I said in a loud whisper.

"Ah yes, or *whatever*." He pulled two shot glasses from the shelf below him and set them on the bar between us. "Aren't you a little young to be doing a thing like that?"

"I'm going through a divorce," I said, though I hadn't thought of my leaving David in such technical terms yet. Divorce sounded so pragmatic, so official. Divorce required at least some form of communication. All I had done was leave.

"Yeah, I been through one of those before. It's rough stuff, but it's not so bad." He lifted his shot glass and motioned for me to do the same. "Cheers to the lonely-hearts club," he said.

I clinked my glass with his and threw my shot back. I could see Angel watching me as I wiped a dribble of whiskey from my chin. He wasn't even my type. But neither was Avery. Neither was David. It's possible my type is just men who want me.

THIRTEEN.

My next shift at The Whiptail started before noon the following day and I was sweaty and sun-tired by the time I got there. Nick, Howling Woman, and I had stayed after closing time the night before. She was all amped on her set and they kept telling me how excited they were that I was there working with them. Nick kept pouring us shots as we wiped the bar and took out the trash and I felt like I did an okay job not getting totally sloppy drunk in front of them even though I'd lost track of how many times Nick had poured us whiskey. The drive home was blurry, but I remember lighting a cigarette in the truck. I remember Howling Woman singing along to the radio. After we turned off the main drag of Yu, it was a long stretch of dirt road to Howling Woman's house. There weren't any streetlights, and the surrounding mountains were a midnight shadow beneath a thick tapestry of stars. I remember stumbling into my section of the living room, which means I hadn't totally blacked out, which also meant that presumably I hadn't embarrassed myself too bad. Besides, Nick and Howling Woman had been going drink for drink with me, so they probably weren't at their sharpest either. Still, I hated having to return to the scene of the crime the day after a night of drinking. You never know what kind of things might be revealed about yourself. But here I am, trying to do the thing I've always avoided—revisiting the past. Committing my memories to the page, though everything I write feels like a lie, like I'm different even just seconds after I come to the end of a sentence. And what will it matter anyway? My story. The truth. Lies. None of it will change the fact that I shot a man. What do I expect to get from explaining what led to it? Justice? Catharsis? Freedom? I can't settle on an answer here. My intention changes with every sentence, with every passing day that brings the trial closer to the present. It won't be long now until I won't have to wonder. Maybe that's the point of all this writing—an act to escape the waiting. At least by writing it all down I'm in control. I decide what goes in and what stays out. Soon enough, I won't have that luxury.

The door to the bar was still locked when I arrived, so I lit a cigarette and hid from the already too-hot sun beneath the awning of the building. The sign by the door was a hand-painted wooden board that listed the hours of operation as *Noonish – 12am(ish)*. I'd worked at plenty of bars before, but never one that didn't have set hours. I looked out into the empty dirt lot and beyond it to the rest of the town. Later, I'd learn that it wasn't technically a town. It was a Census Designated Place. A desert hideaway the government only ever thought about every ten years.

"Sabine?" I heard someone say, and I looked up to see a silhouetted figure walking around the corner of the bar toward me. I squinted and cupped my hand above my brow to see who it was. The voice came together in fragments. Tall body. Black Denim. Band tee. Long, black ponytail. Angel.

"I thought I was supposed to be meeting Nick here."

"I'm covering for him today." He was standing right in front of me then, keys in one hand, a paper bag in the other, and I could feel the heat coming off his body from the late morning sun. He smelled like myrrh and citrus. I felt my face tilt toward my pits. Filthy. An animal on its way to rot.

"Can I get by?" Angel jangled the keys, and I realized I was blocking the entrance. I took a drag of my cigarette and stepped aside.

"Nick said he'd be training me today."

"Looks like you're training with me instead." He opened the door and held it ajar for me. "Don't worry, it's not rocket science or anything. I think I can manage showing you how to tend bar at this old dive."

"Sure. Okay." I put my cigarette out and walked past him into the bar. He closed the door behind us, and I heard the lock turn.

"Nice thing about this place is you don't have to rush to set up and open at any exact time, but the locals might get a little unruly if the door's still locked by one o'clock."

"Good to know."

"It's Angel by the way." He flipped a switch by the door and the dim lights of the bar came to life.

"Sabine."

"Yeah, I got that. Those your only shoes?" He gestured to my Teva's.

"I haven't had a chance to get to the store yet."

"There's not really a place in town for something like that."

"I'll figure it out."

"Here," he held out the paper bag toward me, "I had a couple things at my place I thought you could use. I'm not sure if they'll fit, but they were collecting dust. Consider it a housewarming gift or some shit."

I eyed the bag in his hands.

"Trust me, you aren't going to want to work all day in those sandals."

"Sure." I took the bag from him.

"There are lockers in the stockroom if you want to change."

I walked toward the stockroom door and heard him behind the bar clanking bottles around.

"Hey Sabine…"

"Yeah?" I turned around to face him. He was holding up a bottle of well vodka and a Coors Light.

"Can you grab a couple bottles and a six-pack of Coors while you're back there?"

"Sure."

I felt jittery walking away from him, concerned he was watching me, and even then, I told myself I didn't care what he thought of me, but my body wasn't listening. My gut was a wave roiling up my throat, and every move I made felt riddled with fragility, like a limb might go and shake right off me. In the stockroom, I set the bag from Angel down on the couch and looked inside. I pulled out the top item which was a large Thin Lizzy T-shirt. Beneath that was a T-shirt that had obviously once belonged to a woman. It was pale yellow and, on the front, in glittery pink lettering, it read *Bossy*. There was a pair of denim shorts that were about my size and at the bottom of the bag was a pair of faded pink Chuck Taylors and a brand-new package of socks. I was mortified thinking that Angel's perception of me was of someone so poor off. We'd never even spoken and here he was perceiving me in some very specific way that wasn't at all how I saw myself. My face was hot with shame, but I couldn't deny that the sneakers were better than my sandals for working in the bar. I looked at the tag on the Chucks, nine, a half size too big, but it was better than my sandals. I sat down on the couch and traded my Tevas for a pair of fresh socks and the Chucks.

"They fit?" Angel asked when I came out of the stockroom.

"They're a little big."

"What about the other stuff?"

"Yeah, it's fine."

"Great. Let's get this place opened up. You want to do the honors of picking our soundtrack?"

"Sure."

Angel unlocked the door and went outside to hang up the flag while I scrolled through the jukebox until I found a track to start with.

The guitar started in, and it was nice to have the quiet of the bar cut through with a familiar song.

I love your lipstick, Baby Face
It makes me all shades of red

"Nice pick," Angel said, stepping back into the bar.

"I figured you'd approve with the shirt and all."

"Yeah, but most people would go for something from the *Jailbreak* album."

"Overrated," I said, "Except for 'Cowboy Song,' which is highly underrated."

"I didn't expect you to be a fan."

"Why'd you give me the shirt then?"

"It didn't fit me."

"Well, thanks, but just so you know, I'm not like homeless or something."

His face shot back in surprise, and he dug his hands into his pockets. "I didn't…"

"It's fine. The shoes are nice."

"Good," he said, and walked behind the bar and started unloading the beers I'd brought from the back into the fridge.

We didn't talk much the rest of the shift and it was surprisingly busy for a Wednesday afternoon in a small-town bar. He was all instructions and information, nothing like Nick who had been more *let's have a drink* than *this is how you do it*.

Working at The Whiptail, as weird as it was, wasn't much different than working anywhere else. Customers mostly wanted beers from the tap and the side work was the same as it was anywhere—fill the ice well, stock the snacks, wipe the bottles, chit-chat with strangers like you're all long-lost friends. It was one of the many things I loved about bars. They were dependable no matter what side you were on or what state you were in. A universal language.

Not surprisingly, the afternoon clientele was a lot of regulars. They acted like they owned the place, all of them welcoming me like I'd shown up on their front door step. Mostly the bar talk was the usual questions and obvious advice one gets asked at any new bar where the demographic is predominantly regulars: *You new in town? Where you coming from? Where you staying? Make sure you eat at such and such place.* The Whiptail locals also offered more specific sage wisdom like, *watch out for Angel, he may be nice to look at, but he'll break your heart*, which garnered a lot of eye rolls and *hey now, hey now*. It was the kind of exchange regulars lived for—bartenders willing to play along with an inside joke that made the regular feel clever, but which was obviously overplayed and required a level of dissociation on the part of the bartender to respond jovially to something they heard more times than they could count. More than one person responded to the story of my arriving in Yu with some version of *Ah, yes, the vortex*, but didn't say anything else about it. It was like some false collective truth they'd all learned in school, and I nodded my head, pretending I didn't think they all sounded fucking crazy, because who was I to question them and their home's mythology?

Around five o'clock, Nick rolled in all smiles, no sign of a hangover.

"Sabine, look at you, I swear you were made for this place," Nick said, his hands in the air as he walked around the other side of the bar. "Has Angel been treating you right?"

"Yeah, he's been a real professional."

"That so?"

"Someone's gotta be," Angel said, serious but smiling.

"Don't forget who signs your checks now, Bucko."

"You wouldn't let me if I tried."

"For real though," Nick wrapped his arm around Angel and squeezed his shoulder, "I appreciate you. Thanks for covering me."

"I live for it."

"Yeah yeah yeah, now you're being fresh. Go on and line 'em up and you can get outta here early."

Angel lined up three shot glasses on the bar top and looked at me, "Whiskey, right?"

I nodded, and thought of the night before. If we'd talked, I couldn't remember it. I worried I'd hit another kind of blackout state, but none of the regulars or Nick had given any indication that I'd gone full psycho. Maybe it was as simple as the fact that apparently Angel was an observant dude and he'd seen me and Nick taking shots. I scanned through the images of my memory but came up blank. As far as I could remember, he stayed leaning against the wall the whole night and eventually disappeared without me ever seeing him go.

Angel poured whiskey in two of the glasses and Nick sprayed a splash of Coke from the soda gun in the third glass. Angel raised the shot of Coke up in salute. "Cheers."

"Cheers," Nick and I said in unison, clinking our whiskeys against Angel's Coke. I threw my shot back, watching Angel do the same with his soda. What the hell? A bartender that didn't drink. Who the fuck was this guy?

FOURTEEN.

This isn't a love story. Let me say that right now in case there is any confusion as to where this is going. This isn't Cheryl Strayed's *Wild*. I'm not a woman who left a man she was unfaithful to only to find a happy ending with another man after a long journey through the wilderness with nothing but the solitude of memory. This will not be a story that ends with a glimpse at a future life beyond my own depravity where I have a husband and two wonderful children and I take them to a bench near the wild place where I found myself, the four of us licking ice cream cones, my past a portal to the future. Even now, even if the trial goes my way, I know this to be fact.

The thing about Angel is, he immediately took up space in my mind. We didn't work another shift together for those early days in Yu, but I kept anticipating his appearance at shift change. As time ticked toward five o'clock, I could feel the prospect of his presence in my body—my eyes darting toward the wooden doors every time someone came in, my pulse strong behind my eyes, my hands running through my hair, trying to tame it to something a man like Angel might want to run his own fingers through. I didn't know him yet, but like most men, the idea of him, of me with him, inspired an image of someone new I might become.

I keep circling back to those early days in Yu, trying to remember what it felt like to be in a totally new place for the first time in over a decade—not just in a new place, but in a new life. I feel like I should have felt weirder, more out of place, more obsessed with the past, than I was. Experiencing disillusionment, leaving your husband, having no clear plans for the future, all seem like the types of things that should weigh heavy on a person, and maybe they did, but mostly what

I remember about settling into Yu was how simple it was. In just a matter of weeks I'd fallen into a sort of routine—working at The Whiptail, chatting with regulars about the weather and music like I'd done at a dozen other bars and restaurants before, smoking cigarettes on the back porch of the house with Howling Woman after day shifts, watching the chickens chase each other around and peck the ground, helping Howling Woman tend to the little garden she kept in the backyard, making simple pasta dinners together while we drank wine from coffee mugs and listened to bluegrass from her record player. It felt like I'd lived in Yu forever even though it hadn't even been a whole month. Maybe it's because for the first time in as long as I could remember I wasn't trying to fight fate. I was finally accepting that I wasn't anything special—just a small-town girl serving drinks to people who didn't have any dreams bigger than what could fit inside of a dim-lit bar. They welcomed me in like they'd been reserving me a seat my whole life.

"So, you're from California?" Sissy, a regular, asked one afternoon as I dusted the Jack Daniel's bottle for the fifth or sixth time that afternoon. I'd seen her a handful of shifts, but usually she came in around shift change and flirted with Angel instead of paying me any attention, but she was there earlier than normal, and it was just the two of us at the bar. Nick was in the stockroom taking inventory which took him longer to accomplish than any other manager I'd ever had. A laudable feat considering the limited selection of alcohol from which there was to take stock of and order.

"A couple hours south of here actually," I said, putting the bottle of Jack down.

"Yeah, but you've been living in California before this." Sissy raised her finely plucked eyebrows and gave me a *don't even try to bullshit me* face. She wore terry cloth joggers and had long brown hair that grew thin and frayed at the ends.

"It's true," I said, and pulled the Sauvignon Blanc from the ice and gestured toward her glass.

"What the hell? Why not? As long as you don't charge me for the top off."

I'd seen Nick constantly topping off beers and shots of whiskey without ever charging anyone for more than the first glass. That was another difference I noticed about The Whiptail. Nothing was free like that in California.

"So, what in the good lord's name would prompt a pretty little thing like you to leave California and come to this place?"

"Have you ever been to California?" I asked.

"I have a cousin that used to live out there. Fresno or Fremont. Something like that."

"I've never been to either."

"You know," she said, cocking her head and looking me over, "you look like you're from California."

"Ha," I said without actually laughing. I didn't know what she saw in me that gave her this impression. Despite living in California for over a decade, I never felt like I belonged. There was a certain type of cool that native Californians gave off which I couldn't acquire. Growing up, I'd worn orthopedic looking sneakers from Payless and high-water jeans because my mother couldn't afford to buy me pants as fast as I grew. It wasn't all that different from the way California college students and bartenders dressed, but they had tattoos and piercings and disaffected attitudes that made cheap clothes look fashionable. I never had the right amount of money or culture to make dorky and poor look stylish. For me, it was a matter of income, not aesthetics. I couldn't help but think of my husband, the way even in his too short pants and ratty New Balances, he gave off an air of cool. His thick glasses and the way he always pressed them up close to his eyes. All these parts screamed *dork*, and yet, I'd been so drawn to him, to what he represented. Berkeley born. Intellectual class. Too smart to worry about things like *coolness*, and so, he exuded a certain type of cool.

"I say something funny?" She took a big swig of wine and some of it dribbled down the side of her mouth leaving a river of flesh bare beneath her thick foundation.

"No, no. I just never heard that before."

"Oh yeah?"

"I never really felt like a Californian the whole time I was there is all."

"Did I ever tell you I was *Miss Teen Yu* in my glory days?"

"Doesn't surprise me," I said, though I'd heard her say this to another bar patron more than once in my very short time working at The Whiptail.

"I woulda been *Miss Teen New Mexico* too if it weren't for that anorexic bitch Jillian De Martino." She looked into her glass, her face twisting as if she was trying to do the math of how much wine she had drunk. "You plan on sticking around awhile?"

"You know, everyone keeps asking me that."

"We're a nosy bunch."

"You can say that again."

"Angel says you're staying with Howling Woman. That true?"

"Angel told you that?" My cheeks grew hot hearing that my own name had been in his mouth, talking about me to a regular.

"Sure did. He says she got you this job too."

"Sounds like you got yourself a spy," I said.

"Nope, no spy. Don't nobody need spies around here, darlin'. Everyone always has something to say and not anyone does anything without somebody seein'."

"Well that's not creepy at all."

"Hey now."

"I mean it. I always wanted a neighborhood watch. Who needs surveillance drones when you live in a small town?"

"Now why don't you watch your tongue and spill already?" Her face had grown slack, but her eyes narrowed in on me, crooked, intent.

"Spill what?"

"Well," she said, lowering her voice, "Nick says you didn't hardly know Howling Woman until you got to town."

I nodded, waiting for her to go on.

"Oh come on. Do I have to drag it out of you, child?"

"I guess so."

"You guys seeing each other or something?"

"You aren't serious."

"What?"

"You ever hear of boundaries, Sissy?"

"Ah, so it's like that. I knew it."

"No, it's not *like that*. It's not like anything."

"My gut tells me it is."

"Your gut is full of Sav Blanc."

"Hey missy, no one likes a judgy bartender. All I'm sayin is that it's just a little odd, you staying with Howling Woman all out of the blue. Don't you think?"

"It is *odd*, I guess, but not in the way you think."

"Come on and top a gal off," Sissy said, lifting her wine glass. I looked toward the stockroom hoping that Nick would finally return and interrupt this whole exchange, but the door remained fixed in its place.

"She's just helping me out. I thought it was a little weird at first too, but the more I think about it, if I was in her position and could help another person out, I would. Maybe it only seems weird because as a society we're so concerned with our own independence that we confuse self-sufficiency with self-centeredness. Honestly, I aspire to be more like Howling Woman."

"Okay, don't go getting smart with me. I'm just calling it like I see it, and the way I see it is that Howling Woman is a strange woman and you seem normal enough, so there's really only one reason I can think of that would make sense why the two of you went and shacked up together so quick."

"I don't love where this is going."

"Oh don't be a drag, hear me out. The theory is," she made a dramatic gesture out of looking over her shoulder to see if anyone was listening even though it was still just the two of us inside, "either you're her long-lost daughter or you're her lover."

"Are you joking?"

"You got to wonder with a woman like that."

"What do you mean *a woman like that*?"

"The kind that don't ever have a man around. I've known that woman for nearly twenty years, and as far as I've seen she's only ever been with one man and that was a total fluke. Ask anyone." She tilted her head and raised her eyes as if the statement spoke volumes beyond the words said aloud.

"Well, not that it's any of your business, but I'm not her daughter and I'm not her lover." I tried to make my voice light, as if we were nothing more than a bartender and patron having a playful conversation, but I didn't like where we were headed. It felt like we had crossed the line into the personal too soon and I didn't know how to walk us back to the other side.

"You didn't hear this from me, okay?"

"Hear what?"

"Her and Angel used to be an item if you know what I mean."

I stepped back and looked at Sissy, trying to see if she was bullshiting me. For the last couple of weeks I'd been trying to put the pieces of Angel and Howling Woman together in my head. I imagined each of them as a type of outsider, inscrutable with their idiosyncrasies which I figured they only revealed to a select few. Angel with his shots of Coca-Cola and his all-black outfits, his thoughtful gesture of bringing me a bag of clothes, but how he also hadn't been eager to strike up a friendship. Howling Woman with her gregarious self on the stage that shifted into a calm, domestic loner once she got in her pickup truck and headed home. In my eyes, they each seemed above the material in some way. Certainly not like me, in a constant pursuit of the desires of flesh. I hardly knew them, yet I had such a clear idea of them. This new information didn't fit.

"Scout's honor. Strangest thing any of us ever saw. Two people that don't ever seem to have any time for romance suddenly together. Just between you and me, I think it might have had something to do with his mom."

"What do you mean?"

"They got together right after his mom passed," Sissy whispered, "cirrhosis. I wouldn't normally trust a bartender that don't drink, but Angel practically grew up inside The Whiptail."

"Jesus."

"Darndest thing was Howling Woman and him seemed like they might honest to goodness be into each other, which was, you know, weird, but whatever, who is anyone to judge, and then one day, practically out of the blue, she dumped him. Now you tell me, what kind of woman lands a man as fine as Angel and dumps him?"

"How long ago was this?"

"Two summers ago. What a shocker. I could have warned him she'd break his heart. Nearly eighteen years and I never saw her with a man, and then just like that she's getting down with Angel and then poof," she snapped her fingers, "she's kicked handsome 'ol Angel to the curb. Celibate again as far as I can tell. And then, here you come, moving on in with her so quick."

"I think you've watched too much daytime television."

"I'm just saying, that woman's got secrets." Sissy finished her wine with one large gulp then put a handful of bills on the bar. "It's been a real treat getting to talk to you. You're a hoot, but I got to get the hell out of this bar before I become one of them animals on the wall."

At shift change, Angel showed up in his usual uniform: black denim, black converse, band tee. I hadn't thought too much about his age until then, but I assumed he was close to thirty like me. After that afternoon with Sissy, I tried to see him with a new set of eyes. His skin was taut, but when he smiled there were fine lines around the corners of his eyes. Near his temple I saw a thin streak of gray hair. Other than that, he still looked young, but not so young that it would be entirely scandalous for a woman Howling Woman's age to sleep with him.

"How'd it go today?" he asked us, his usual greeting.

"Sabine and Sissy became best friends," Nick said with a shit-eating grin.

"Sissy doesn't have friends," Angel said, "She has victims."

"Well then, what are you?" I asked.

"What do you mean?"

"Apparently all her intel came from you." I said, sounding more spiteful than I'd intended and not exactly sure why it was manifesting at Angel's presence.

"What intel?"

"Oh, not much, just that I'm living a derelict lezzy life with Howling Woman."

Nick laughed and slapped his hand on the bar, "Oh, she's on one, man. Been like this ever since Sissy left."

"The whole town knows you're living with Howling Woman, and I didn't say anything about you being a lesbian." Angel laughed, but a nervous edge surrounded it. "Damn, this town."

"Pour us a shot, won't you, Angel? I gotta get out of here," Nick said, still laughing.

Angel pulled three shot glasses off the shelf and he and Nick ran through the muscle memory of shift change, Angel pouring a shot of Jack for me and one for Nick, Nick splashing Coke into a glass for Angel. I thought of what Sissy said about his mom dying of cirrhosis while we clinked glasses and felt even more self-conscious than usual shooting my whiskey in front of him, but I also wanted the shot. Even more, I wanted to not care what he thought of me. I was starting to form a new narrative of him in my head, and it changed the way I imagined how he saw me. It felt wrong knowing more about him than he shared with me. It was my own biggest fear—that people could know more about me than I wanted them to, that they could form a story of who I was that I didn't consent to. That's what I'm realizing now as I write all this down—how little control we have over the stories that are told about us, how even the stories we tell about ourselves can be interpreted in a way we don't agree with. That's what it's like with the shooting. People are going to make up their minds about me, the type of person I am, with only a specific set of details. Too much is going to be left out, and even if they get to hear everything, the whole story, they might still see it differently than I do.

Nick pulled his pack of cigarettes from his back pocket and offered one to me. "You coming?"

"No, I'm good," I said.

"Alright." He made his way out the front door. He always said he had to get out of the bar as soon as Angel arrived for shift change, but what he really meant was that he had to get on the other side of the bar. I was pretty sure that he spent most his waking hours at The Whiptail, which was something he could get away with without looking too bad seeing as he owned the place.

"You sticking around today?" Angel asked as he began draining the old water from the three-compartment sink.

"I shouldn't."

"Says who?"

"Me."

"Well that's a shame," he said in an even tone, and I couldn't tell what he meant by it. If it was just a thing he pulled from the bartender script he'd created or if it was genuine, if he honestly did think it was a shame I was leaving. I felt that same flush and prickling from earlier when Sissy had told me he'd been talking about me, but I tried to breathe through it, grateful again that we kept the bar so dark.

"Seems like you're part of the family now," he said, and smiled at me.

"How so?"

"Getting an earful from Sissy makes you one of us."

"That's all it takes?"

"It's a start."

"It's not the worst family I've ever been a part of," I said and instantly thought of his mom, his dead mom, and regretted it. He didn't seem to notice.

"So, how are things going with Howling Woman?" He looked down at the sink as he asked this, and I wondered if this was his way of keeping tabs on his ex, but they saw each other enough at work that I didn't think he needed me in order to know what was going on in her life. It was the first time we'd really talked after a shift. Up until that point, I usually left after the first shot, avoiding a repeat of my first night in town. I wanted to get to the house so I could drink with Howling Woman, and then alone in the privacy of my bed, so it was new for me to navigate talking with him. I didn't have a sense of what he was after.

"They're good,"

"Yeah, she's good people."

"I think so."

"Can I ask you a question?"

"Sure," I said.

"Why'd you leave California?"

"California's not so great."

"Is it true about the bus?"

"Yeah," I said and laughed, "What about you?" I asked. "Are you from here?"

"Born and raised."

He ran his fingers through the ends of his ponytail. I tried to imagine him next to Howling Woman, kissing her, embracing her, but I didn't like the picture in my head. I didn't want to watch her strong jaw and steady eyes soften and go all doughy in front of a man. I didn't want to imagine him, gentle and smitten, looking at Howling Woman as though she was the queen of his heart. I liked where they were in my brain: separate.

"You ever think about leaving?"

"Sure," he said, "but we're not all as bold as you."

I felt myself flush and was reminded of Charity, how she'd seemed impressed at my moving to the desert on a whim. I thought *if only these people really knew*, but I didn't want to correct him. I could see how he would be drawn to Howling Woman, to her boldness, and I wondered what had happened between the two of them that had ended their relationship—if there had even been a relationship.

"I got to get out here."

"You hear about Jesse's party Friday night?"

"Hard not to."

"You going?"

"I don't know. Probably not."

"That's a shame."

"Howling Woman keeps telling me I have to go with her."

"Maybe you should."

"We'll see. It's not like I really know Jesse super well."

"You're family now, remember?"

I laughed and stepped off my barstool.

"See you tomorrow." He smiled at me as I turned toward the door and fought the feeling of heat rushing through my body.

FIFTEEN.

Hearing that Howling Woman had been in a relationship with Angel aroused a surprising sensation in me. I thought, *I could fuck* him. And then a thought, a picture. Us in the stockroom, door locked, my hands gripping the Gorilla Rack shelves, his fist pulling my hair, his cock pounding into me from behind. It had been in my mind vaguely before that, like it was with all men really—more like an undertone of possibility rather than a clear thought or desire. When it announced itself as a wholly formed idea, an action I ought to carry out, I felt my head shake. *NO!* I thought to myself. *YOU WILL NOT HAVE SEX WITH YOUR ROOMMATE'S EX, YOU PSYCHO BITCH.* I had to think it like that, in all caps, to myself, because this was something I'd done before—slept with the exes of women I wanted to be friends with (and sometimes even their boyfriends) as if it would prove my worth—like if I could get another woman's ex/partner/love interest/etc. to have sex with me, then it was like I was as good/beautiful/etc. as the other woman by proxy. It was probably part of the reason I didn't really have any close female friends and why my mother was one of the first people I thought to house me after leaving David.

On my way home from work that day, the sun was a fiery touch on my bare arms. I tried to shake Angel from my mind. I said, out loud, as I walked away from the bar, *You do not want to have sex with Angel. You do not want to have sex with anyone.* I think I must have started to believe in the little spell I was casting because by the time I got back to Howling Woman's I wasn't thinking so much about Angel as I was thinking about how Howling Woman had become a woman that no longer dated men. It hadn't been something I'd thought about until Sissy pointed it out, and when I became cognizant of it, I started thinking about how there weren't any women I'd ever met in my entire life that weren't in the middle of some process of dating—whether it was binging sex, actively looking for a sexual partner, or in a full-on relationship with a partner—every woman, probably every person I knew, was irrevocably tied to sex or romance or needing validation from someone they were intimate with, yet I'd created an image of Howling Woman in which she was liberated from this part of life.

Briefly, I wondered if I could be a woman without men. I thought about Sissy implying that we were lesbians and I tried to give way to the possibility of it, that there might be something more between us than two women sharing a house. It was true that I felt a pull toward Howling Woman that was more physical than logical, but was it desire? Attraction? Did I not recognize the sensation when it was affixed to a woman? I tried to envision the angles of our faces fitting together, her long hair curtaining us off from the world, my lips reaching to meet hers, our bodies coming together with so much sameness. There was something comforting about the thought of our bodies connected in that way, but it felt gentle and delicate, like affection between companions, not people ravenous to consume one another.

The house smelled of dill and vinegar and something sweet when I walked in. Gillian Welch and her accompanying banjo were softly wailing from the record player. Howling Woman was in the kitchen, singing along. She was wearing long, turquoise rubber gloves that went up to her elbows and a taupe-colored apron with line drawings of herbs printed on it. She was standing over a huge steaming metal pot with a thermometer in her hand. I shook my head at this woman who could be both a flamboyant vocalist by night and a country homemaker by day. I wondered how one woman could contain such multitudes. If I did too.

"Give me a hand with this, will you?" she hollered as she walked over to the counter where a bunch of mason jars were lined up and filled with sliced cucumbers, squash, garlic, and onions.

"Sure," I said. I unlaced the Chucks that Angel had given me. I'd thought about getting a different pair of shoes, but I'd only gotten one paycheck so far and tips weren't all that impressive at The Whiptail. I was living on a budget, so what if the Chucks weren't something I'd ever have bought myself. I needed money for cigarettes and wine. Shoes would have to wait.

"Go on and ladle this brine into the jars while I boil a fresh pot of water."

I walked across the room and picked the ladle up off the counter. The smell of vinegar was sharp in my nostrils.

"How was work?"

"Same old."

"Sounds like you're settling in okay then."

"Too well actually."

"I knew you would."

"It's kind of strange to be honest."

"How so?"

"I don't know exactly. It's just, I didn't think it would be so easy."

"Well you've done it before."

"I mean the whole starting over thing."

"You know, Buttercup, there isn't such a thing as starting over."

"You know what I mean. You left your life too, didn't you?"

"I didn't *leave* my life. I moved."

"I know that, but what about the people from your past? Do you like keep in touch with anyone from before you moved here?"

"There is no one to keep in touch with."

"Well what brought you here anyway? Be real with me."

"Same thing that brought you here."

"God, please don't say the vortex."

"Sabine, I swear you're gonna know what it's all about in a matter of time. It don't matter if you believe it or not. Some things don't need belief in order to exist."

"So the vortex brought you here too, but what else?" I waited for her to reply and felt annoyed at this idea of some spiraling energy in la Chupadera. A magnet that supposedly collected lost souls. It didn't seem fathomable, not any more so than a naked woman in an orchard talking to a serpent and taking a bite of an apple that was somehow linked to the origin of human consciousness.

"The truth is, I wouldn't be here without that vortex. I'll take you up to see it soon. On a full moon is best. You'll feel it and know."

"Didn't you say that the vortex is supposed to help like free people of all their toxic bullshit and then allow them to move on?"

"Something like that."

"Well then, what are you still doing here? How much toxic baggage did you bring in?"

"Real cute."

"All I'm saying is, if you believe in the vortex and all..."

"It ain't about belief."

"You know what I mean."

"It sounds like you might be feeling the pull of the vortex is what I think you mean."

"Do you want a drink?"

"I'll have one," she said, screwing lids on the jars. I pulled our mugs off the drying rack and opened the fridge as she loaded the jars onto a circular metal tray. I poured wine into the mugs. Topped them with seltzer like she liked and brought one close to my face, feeling the air fiz around my mouth. I watched her cross the kitchen holding the tray by its long handle before she lowered it into one of the pots on the stove. She pulled off her rubber gloves and reached for her wine. She brushed a stray strand of her goldish hair off her glistening forehead and tucked it behind her ear. She had a nice face, babyish in some ways with her big round cheeks and doe-eyes, but it also formed a severe square at her jaw that was a sort of a masculine scaffolding for the rest of her feminine facial features. I tried to see her the way Angel might. At first glance, she had a face that wasn't exactly pretty. It was possibly even confused as ugly with its competing shapes superimposed upon one another, but it was the kind of face that made you look twice, as if you needed to put your finger on what exactly was incongruous about it, but as you looked, you discovered that she was beautiful, like beautiful in the kind of way that doesn't fade. It was easy to imagine a man, or a woman, falling in love with her. The kind of woman who is more than one thing—a person who will forever hold someone else's interest. I wondered what Angel saw when he looked at me, if he thought I was a bunch of incongruous parts made beautiful like Howling Woman.

"Why you looking at me like that?"

"I'm just thinking."

"Don't hurt yourself now."

"It's hard to believe you didn't leave someone behind too. You're beautiful, and talented, and nice. You can tell me, you know."

"How many shots did Nick pour before you left work?"

"I'm serious. Please?"

She took another small sip of her wine and scratched her forehead, "There ain't much to tell."

"Come on. I've told you about David."

It was true. I'd told her some about David in the weeks that we'd been living together. Not much, but enough that she knew I'd been an insecure and unfaithful wife. I told her about how it was hard being married to someone with such a clear vision of the future when you feel so uncertain about yours. Maybe some other things too, but it wasn't a topic I wanted to talk about too often, so it was greedy of me to ask her to divulge more of her past.

"Sure, there were people I left. A man, too, if you really want to know, but it wasn't just one man. It was a whole life of bad men."

"Is that why you're not seeing anyone now?"

"You sure are a nosy lot this evening."

"I'm curious is all."

"Make yourself useful and pull those jars out," she said, pointing to the pot of boiling water they were in. "If you must know, I'm not seeing anyone anymore for the simple reason that I like being alone."

"Yeah, well Sissy has some thoughts on your singledom."

"Oh, I bet that wino does."

"She thinks we're a lesbian couple." I cocked my head and smiled, watching the information settle on Howling Woman's face.

She laughed. "Wouldn't that be something? I swear that woman is the definition of idle hands makin' for the devil's work. What else did she have to say?"

"Not much."

"My ass *not much*. What are you after?"

"Well, she also said that you and Angel used to date."

"Aren't you just little Miss Encyclopedia Britannica now."

"So, it's true?"

"Why you want to know?"

"Just curious."

"Mmmhmm. Pass me my wine. Let's go out for a smoke."

The sun was starting to set behind the mountains, turning the whole sky a deep orange, practically sepia. It wouldn't be long before it was replaced by a purple backdrop of stars. I sat down on the porch steps and waited for Howling Woman to join me, but she lit a cigarette and busied herself with feeding the chickens.

"I mention the name Bison West before to you?" she asked from across the yard.

"I don't think so."

"He's a guy I once knew right before coming to Yu."

"Like *the* guy?"

"Buttercup, there isn't one guy—they all been bad. He just happened to be one of the last in a series before I got myself here." She walked back over to the porch, picking up a watering can and filling it with the hose. "He was a real type of evil, I can tell you that much."

"What'd he do?"

"Same thing they all do—he thought women belonged to him and that he could do whatever he wanted with them." Her back was to me, watering the herbs that lined the porch railing, so I couldn't see her face as she said this, but her voice came out softer, more distant, than normal, and for a moment I felt a pang of guilt for having pushed the issue of men and dating like it hadn't occurred to me that there might be things she didn't ever want to tell another person. I could relate to that and should have known better, but she kept talking, so I went on smoking my cigarette and listening.

"I met him when I was traveling with another man, actually. I was only a little bit younger than you are now, and, you know, I was all into the whole free love scene or whatever people were calling it by then."

"So you were a hippie?"

"Sure, hippie, but that was a little before my time, free spirit, slut, whatever you want to call it."

"I'm not really surprised, you know, with a name like *Howling Woman* and all."

"What's that supposed to mean?"

"Oh come on, like you don't know."

"Well, it's funny you should mention my name actually, because it was what happened with Bison that led to the birth of *Howling Woman*, and before you go and say something cute, don't act like it's some hippie-dippy woo-woo shit to be changing your name—whoever thought it was totally normal to accept the name you were given by someone you might not even end up liking and who doesn't know you at all—now that is some crazy shit."

"I guess I never thought of it like that."

"Something new to chew on."

"What was your name before?"

"Don't matter. That's not the point of this story."

"I didn't mean to pry. You don't have to talk about it if you don't want to."

She set the watering can down on the iron plant stand and took a long drag of her cigarette. "The thing is, Bison was the type of guy that all the women in the circles I was traveling with would drop their drawers for without so much as blinking, but I thought he was a creep. I'm not saying I was better than those other women, but if you've known bad men, then you can spot one from a mile away."

"Isn't it crazy how there are some men you know aren't right? I always think of that phrase *women's intuition* as a little ridiculous, but it's the truth. Sometimes you just get a feeling."

She bent down beside me and picked up her mug of wine. "Can I let you in on a little secret?"

"Please."

"There isn't any better feeling in this world than getting even with a bad man."

Her voice was so close to my ear that it sent a ripple of breath down my spine and I felt my skin prickle with goosebumps. There was a seriousness that surrounded what she said, and thinking back on it, I should have thought more about what I'd just said, about intuition, about the weird feeling it gave me when she talked about getting even with bad men. She downed her wine in one gulp and stood back up, "Let's go make some dinner."

SIXTEEN.

Jesse lived in a small, one-bedroom adobe style home down the street from The Whiptail. It was already ten o'clock when we got there, and it looked like the whole town had shown up. People stood smoking and talking loudly over each other in the front yard, and no one even seemed to notice me and Howling Woman walking up the pathway to the front door. Inside the house, people glistened with the sweat of too many bodies packed into a confined space. Half the party was singing along to Fergie's *Glamorous*. When Jesse caught sight of me and Howling Woman he started whooping.

"OAKLAND!" he sing-songed, and gestured for me to come and hug him. He wrapped his arms around me and shouted over the music, "Everyone, this is my new friend from Oakland. She just moved to town."

The room whooped and Jesse shouted even louder, "Someone get these beautiful women a fucking drink."

"I didn't expect so many people to be here," I said.

"What?" he asked, half looking at me, half looking around the room.

"This party is great."

"I know. I am so fucked up already!"

"I gotta catch up," I said, but he wasn't listening. He kissed Howling Woman on the cheek and then whooped at someone else who walked in the front door.

Howling Woman took me by the hand and led me toward the kitchen. On the way, people said hi to her, but I couldn't hear what she said to any of them, and we didn't stop long enough for her to introduce me. I liked that about her, that she was the type of person to know it was important to get a drink before real socializing—that she didn't drop my hand even though others solicited her attention. It made me feel special in a way I didn't know I needed—that I was the person out of all the people there that she was with. Isn't that all anyone really wants? To be seen and wanted more than everyone else by at least one other person? It felt even more special that it was Howling Woman—a sort of magnet for others—who wanted me. When we got to the kitchen, Sissy was at the counter next to a bunch of liquor bottles. She called Howling Woman's name and Howling Woman led me to her.

"You two need a drink?" she asked, looking at me with a sly smile.

"Yeah, what are you having?" Howling Woman asked.

"Vodka soda."

Howling Woman looked back at me, "Sound good?"

"Let's do a round of shots first."

"Well look at you, life of the party," Sissy said, swaying a bit beside the counter.

"What can I say?" I grabbed two red cups from the stack and opened the whiskey bottle in front of Sissy, "May I?"

"Have at it."

"You want one?"

"I'll pass on this round." She reached for the counter, steadying herself.

"I'll have one for you." I poured two big shots for me and Howling Woman and then another one for myself while Howling Woman mixed us a couple vodka sodas.

"Look at you two. So in sync," Sissy said, that stupid smile on her face again.

"You know how it is with roommates," I said, giving her a look that I hoped said *cut the crap.*

"Right, *roommates*," she said, letting go of the counter and making air quotes as she said it. She stumbled and Howling Woman reached out to steady her.

"Jesus, I'm spent," Sissy said, and started walking toward the kitchen hallway that led to the back of the house without saying another word to us.

"Should we follow her?" I asked Howling Woman.

"She's an adult."

I nodded in agreement but thought about how Howling Woman and I had first met, me drunk on the bathroom floor of The Whiptail, her lifting me up and eventually taking me home. I'm an adult too. What made me different from Sissy in Howling Woman's eyes?

"I want to introduce you to a couple people," Howling Woman said, handing me my drink. I took a swig and followed her back out into the living room. I looked around to see if Angel was there. I scanned the room of heads, my heart speeding up every time I saw someone with black hair, but I couldn't find him. Maybe he'd already come and gone. I didn't know how late people stayed out at parties any-more, especially not people who apparently didn't drink. Maybe there was a strict cut-off time for sober people where it became too obnoxious to be around drink-ing people, but he worked at a bar, so I doubted that.

"Have you met Sabine yet?" Howling Woman asked a group of regulars from The Whiptail I'd seen but hadn't been formally introduced to yet. They all said their names, but it was loud, and I was distracted, so I'd have to ask them to repeat them to me again during my next shift. I took a long slug of my vodka soda and tried to appear like I was interested in whatever they were saying to Howling Wom-an, but I wasn't, not really, and I remembered then why it had been so long since I'd been to a party. The whole reason for socializing like this was to find someone to go home with, and the person I wanted to go home with, if I were to go home with someone, wasn't there. I hated parties. I wanted to leave. I could come up with an excuse to get out of there soon enough, I thought, but then the scent of myrrh and citrus filled the air. I felt someone step close behind me and when I turned around there was Angel.

"You finally made it."

"Yeah, I took a nap after my shift, so we got a late start," I said.

He unscrewed the cap to his Coke and took a swig. "What do you think?"

"Of the party?"

He shrugged like he realized that it was a lame question, but I humored him anyway.

"I forgot I didn't like parties until I got here."

"Yeah, me too."

Was this some kind of opening? In my past life, the one from just a couple of weeks prior, this would be the kind of line that read like an invitation, and I'd have jumped at it, said, *why don't we get out of here then,* but I was not the old me anymore. I left her in California, at least part of her, and so I didn't say that. Instead, I took another long sip of my drink until it was mostly gone, and I could feel the sharp edges of existing in public soften a little.

"This a lot different from the types of parties you go to in California?"

"I don't remember. It's been so long since I've been to a party. But yeah, I think so."

"There's not much else to do out here."

"Isn't that a little weird for you?"

"What do you mean?"

"I don't know, living in a place where the two main pastimes involve drink-ing?"

"Who says you gotta drink?" He lifted his Coke bottle up as if to prove a point.

"I guess."

"What were you doing out there anyway?"

"In California?"

"Yeah."

"Usual stuff. School. Work."

He leaned back on his heels, a gesture of his I'd noticed in the short time we'd known each other. Rocking from heel to toe, thinking before opening his mouth to speak. "That's cool, what were you in school for?"

"I got my degree in English, but I didn't really do anything with it."

"So, you're a writer?"

"I'm a bartender, remember?"

"I took a couple art classes at the community college in Albuquerque a while back, music mostly, but I never finished them."

"Oh yeah?"

"Long commute, life. I don't think real musicians go to school for that kind of thing anyway. It felt a bit try-hard. Phony."

He rocked onto the balls of his feet again then back down. I didn't know what else to say, because that word *life* lingered in his summary and all I could think about was his mother, how she was part of the *life* that kept him from commuting to study music. Another question felt like it could veer into the too personal, and I didn't want to be stuck in a situation where one second we're greeting each other, talking casually about college, and the next we're talking about his dead mom. I was trying to think of something else to say, but I was aware of the way bodies were blurring into a single fuzzy haze after the drinks, aware that he was totally sober and I wasn't.

Howling Woman turned away from the group of regulars she'd been talking to and her mouth turned up in a smile.

"Well it's nice to see you've made it out for once," she said, reaching her arms out to hug him, and he smiled at her and opened his arms up in return. They hugged, and the way their limbs wrapped around each other looked so seamless, so natural, and I felt jealous of their ease with one another, and that I hadn't gotten the same kind of greeting from Angel, but we'd never hugged before. We'd never even touched.

"You know Jesse would never let me live it down if I missed one of his parties."

"Lord knows that's the truth, though he might not remember much of this one." Howling Woman winked at Angel and the way their eyes caught made me wonder how serious it had been between them—if it had fully ended or if they were one of those broken up couples that never truly breaks up until something else more serious comes around.

"I'm gonna go out for a smoke," I said, "You want one?"

"I'm okay for now, Buttercup," Howling Woman said, breaking eye contact with Angel. "If you need moral support I can join you though." She winked at me, but I felt annoyed with her suddenly, like seeing her wink at Angel and then seconds later at me made it less special, made me less special.

I didn't know where the jealousy was coming from. It was physiological. A sharpening in my chest. A grinding of my teeth. An urgency to leave. It was the first moment since moving to Yu where I felt the reality of my aloneness. They were standing there smiling and everyone was a stranger. Even them. No one knew me. Not really. Up until then, that's what I thought I'd wanted, but now I wonder if we all long to be known. Everyone says you can't ever truly know someone, it's the crux of any good thriller or mystery (that a person is unknowable, that they can be a doting spouse or parent, a standup member of the community, but behind their persona of goodness exists a more nefarious double, a truer self comprised of violent urges and secrets), but aren't we all trying in some way to show ourselves to someone else, little by little, until they prove trustworthy enough to see the whole?

"No, I'm okay," I said, then looked at Angel to see if he'd give some sign that he wanted to join me, but he didn't say anything. "Alright then," I said, but neither of them responded. I walked toward the backdoor through the kitchen, dumping my ice into the sink so I could refill my cup with whiskey.

"Easy does it," a guy with a waxed mustache said as I filled my SOLO Cup halfway to the top with whiskey.

"I'm a thirsty, growing girl," I said, adding another splash for good measure before heading out the backdoor.

Outside, I walked to the side of the house away from the groups of people standing on the patio and lit a cigarette. I could see Howling Woman and Angel through the side window, and I alternated taking sips of my whiskey and drags of my cigarette as I watched them. The room was full of people, so they were forced to stand close to one another as they talked. Occasionally Angel laughed. Once, Howling Woman squeezed his shoulder the same way she'd squeezed mine on that first day I'd spent in her house. The whole time they didn't take their eyes off each other, and I wondered why either of them had feigned caring about whether I showed up or not. They looked like they'd be just as happy, happier even, if they were in a room alone together.

I took the last drag of my cigarette and chugged the rest of my whiskey. I thought about going back inside, but I didn't know how to reenter the space between Angel and Howling Woman. I'd never been good in groups. I preferred my conversations one-on-one. It was so much work to keep track of the emotional energy of more than one person. Soon, the whiskey I'd chugged would make it impossible. I could already feel it sloshing around in my brain, making it so thoughts were disconnected by the river of it. I needed to leave. I needed to protect myself from ruining whatever it was I might have with the two people inside who I felt I cared about regardless of the short time I'd known them. Each of them had taken up residence in my heart, I could feel them inflating larger, buoyed by the whiskey, as I watched them longingly through the window. How to emit the sudden adoration blooming inside of me without embarrassing myself? It was something that happened sometimes, whiskey turning my thoughts into a sentimental slop. It wouldn't come out right. Even thinking about it confused me, their faces and what they symbolized distorting before me. Tears trickled down my face and the taste of salt filled my mouth. I dropped my cup and my cigarette on the ground and walked around to the front of the house and headed down the gravel driveway.

The tears were really coming as I turned out of the neighborhood and stumbled toward the dark, dirt road that led to Howling Woman's. Under the night sky I couldn't recall whether to make a left or a right. More tears came as the overwhelm of confusion turned the desert into one undistinguishable expanse. Maybe it was a sign that I should go back, wait for Howling Woman to drive us home, or at the very least ask her for directions. I lit another cigarette and pulled out my phone. I clicked on the map icon, my thumb hovering over where the search bar would appear as I waited for it to load. When it did, I went to type in Howling Woman's address but realized I didn't even know it. I closed the maps and opened my messages. I didn't know her phone number either. How was it possible to believe I was so close to a person whose phone number I didn't even know? I tapped the search bar, typed in Avery's name, a habit of crisis as automatic as breathing. I felt the pang of rejection as his last message to me loaded on the screen.

I understand.

I typed a message out and hit send.

I miss you so bad.

I put my phone in my back pocket and turned right. I started walking, hoping that some deep intuition would cut through the alcohol and get me to where I needed to be. I made it a couple hundred yards then stopped to open my messaging app again. He hadn't replied. No little dots dancing. I typed another message.

I wish you were here with me right now.

And it was true, I wished I wasn't going home to an empty bed. I wished there was someone who could hold me and fuck me and drown out the emptiness that I was feeling. But he was just a person on the other end of my phone whose life I couldn't see. I'd broken it off. He'd barely reacted. Of course he wasn't going to text me back now. I put my phone away and continued down the dirt road.

I felt a panic in my chest the whole walk to Howling Woman's, certain that some creature or person would jump out from behind a cactus and attack me. The moon was a sliver, and the desert was filled with shadows that could be anything. It felt like the start of a story people tell when a reckless woman is found dead on the side of the road. I picked up my pace, my head feeling clearer from the fear. My steps were certain and straight as if I hadn't had a drop to drink. *This is how I'll die*, I thought, and then told myself I was being dramatic. *You're okay, you're okay, you're okay*, I said to myself, trying to drown out the voice telling me I was in danger. I cried and walked and cried and walked. My heart lunged at the sight of each house with a porch light on. They were all so spread out. One of them had to be Howling Woman's. After what felt like an eternity, I stopped in front of a small stretch of dirt driveway that led to a faded yellow trailer aglow in its jaundice by a single porch light. I couldn't remember if I'd ever seen it before. Maybe I should turn around and go the other way, but I'd already gone so far and what if it was only a little farther now? I'd be out all night wandering if I didn't commit to a single direction. For a moment, I toyed with the idea of walking up to the front door of the trailer and knocking. It was a small enough town, maybe they could tell me where Howling Woman lived, point me in the right direction. Or maybe they'd pull me in and I'd never be seen again. I kept walking until I saw another porch light glowing in the distance. I jogged toward it and was overcome with the relief of recognition. My mouth broke into a smile. I started to really run, my body suddenly able to do something it never did, but I had to get out of the darkness, I had to get into the safe confines of the house that had promised me a new start. I needed to fall asleep so that I could wake up and start over again, until everything preceding sleep was nothing but a nightmare I'd eventually forget. I pressed my body up against the door of Howling Woman's casita and could hear the thud of my heart against the wood. I'd made it.

As soon as I was inside, I pulled my phone out to see if Avery had texted me back. He hadn't. I put my phone down on the counter and grabbed a mug from the cupboard. I opened the fridge and filled the mug with wine from the box and took the first long sip with the door still open. It tasted sour after the whiskey and my cheeks twitched into a pucker, but it was good to have something to put inside my body, something to cut through the salt of my tears. I heard my phone vibrate on the counter and wine splashed out of the mug and onto the floor as I turned around to grab it.

I wish I was with you too.

At the sight of those words on my screen I felt my mood shift. Thank god. I wasn't in-fucking-visible. Another text came in, an image box, and I walked to my bed with my phone and my wine in hand while I waited for it to load on the screen. Then another text. The words appeared before the image finished loading.

I miss your mouth so bad. Can you come over?

The picture loaded and it was Avery's erect cock, reddish and veiny in his hand. Maybe at another time this would have excited me, but it wasn't sex I was after. It was a different kind of intimacy I needed, and more tears streamed down my face at his inability to sense the loneliness permeating my being. A dick pic. After everything. Who was I in his mind that this is what he thought I needed? He didn't know me. No one did. And whose fault was that?

No one ever sent dick pics in the books I read. Not even in romance novels. I try to imagine Jane Austen writing about lovers communicating via text, what Mr. Darcy would be like in contemporary conditions, if he would have ever sent Elizabeth a dick pic. Maybe. Probably.

I exited the messages between me and Avery and selected the thread between me and David. I opened it and his last message to me appeared.

I love you, darling! Want me to pick up Indian food on my way home from school?

I hadn't responded and of course no new messages had populated because I'd blocked his number. I swiped my thumb across the screen, our life in text scrolling before my eyes. There were so many *I love yous* and mundane lists shared between us about groceries and things to do before a weekend away or the start of the semester. It was all so gentle. Sweet. Civilized. I clicked on his contact information and saw the word *Blocked.* My thumb hesitated above it. I had a real sensation that I'd made a huge mistake. If two people can never really know each other, then maybe we could make what we had work—knowing only the versions of ourselves we'd decided upon sharing. I thought about the way he always held me all the way through the night, never letting me go to adjust to the needs of his own body, the way he brought me coffee in bed, and washed my hair in the shower on mornings he didn't have to rush out the door. I couldn't imagine another man ever doing that for me again. In the drunken fugue of my loneliness, I thought about taking it all back, but too much had happened, and even in that state I knew better than to believe it would work on the second try. I dropped my phone on the side of my bed and chugged the rest of my wine. I wanted another glass, but I was too tired and sad to leave the bed. I crawled under the blankets and willed myself to sleep.

SEVENTEEN.

It was bound to happen of course—David getting through to me—and I blame it on my text to Avery. It was like sending him that message opened up some kind of invisible portal that let my past flow right on into my present. I had been pushing the thought to the back of my brain ever since I'd been away. In my first meeting with Dr. Camille, she'd said, "Substances just anesthetize you to your problems, but the problems are still there even if you can't see them." Then she asked me if I agreed, like there was any possible way that I could feel differently than her, the *expert*, as though my future didn't depend on at least ostensibly converting my beliefs to hers. I'd been in an obstinate mood, and I'd told her I didn't know, but the truth is I think most of being alive is an attempt to anesthetize yourself to all the suffering that is being alive. It isn't strictly a drug and alcohol thing. It's a being alive thing. A survival instinct not to suffer.

Blocking David's number from my phone before leaving him was an example of this. The problem was, we were still married. Legally, it didn't matter how far I ran or how long I was gone. How is it that words on a page can be so binding? You would think that miles of mountain and desert were stronger—more erosive— than they actually were. I knew I was existing in a liminal space, that eventually the pieces would begin connecting and leading my old life back to my present one. Then, there it was, a phone call from my mother as I applied mascara before heading into The Whiptail. It was the first call from her since I'd left. I answered it without thinking.

"BABY. . ." she projected into the phone, her voice loud and high-pitched. I could tell instantly that something was off. *Fuck*, I muttered to myself, putting the tube of mascara down on the bathroom counter and closing my eyes as I listened to her cluck her tongue into the phone, waiting for me to say something.

"Is everything alright? I'm kinda in a rush," I said, hoping to end the conversation before it could even begin.

"Hold on a minute, Bean, I will be quick. I swear," she said with a forced giggle, the kind she used when in public, and I could tell someone was with her. Everything about her voice—the high pitch, the giggle—was performative.

"What's going on?"

"Well, Bean, I am calling to see where you are. I haven't heard from you since you left, and we are just a little worried about you is all."

"*We?*" I said, my teeth beginning to grind in my skull.

"Oh, yes. Well, you will never guess who showed up on my front porch this morning looking for you."

"I bet I can." My jaw locked as I spoke, imagining my husband sitting in the stool at the kitchen counter watching my mother speak into the phone the same as I'd done when he'd called her while I'd been there. David had never been to my mother's house before, and it sent a wave of shame through me picturing him there against the backdrop of my mother's organizational systems which consisted solely of little piles everywhere: little piles of dirty laundry, of mail, of magazines, of folded laundry, of shopping bags. In all the years that she had lived in that house, nothing ever had a home. Mine and David's apartment was clean and organized, the traces of our lives mostly invisible: the mail in a hanging wooden box near the front door with hooks for our keys, our laundry either in a hamper in the closet or folded and tucked into drawers. Thinking of him in my mother's house was like thinking of him lifting the skin off my bones and seeing the part of me that wasn't meant to be seen. I wanted him to leave. For my mother to get rid of him. I would call him eventually, maybe. I ended it. It was futile—him chasing me like this. I felt a rush of anger pump through my veins like he had done something terrible by going to her house without my permission—for not leaving me alone when I told him I no longer loved him. I hated knowing that he was smelling the vodka on my mother's skin and the water rot of the walls. It was a part of me I had kept hidden from him and now it was exposed. I wanted to scream into the phone at my mother loud enough for David to hear, *GET THE FUCK OUT*, but my teeth were still gritted down.

"It was such a shock really," she said with another giggle, "but your sweet David is here with me."

"Oh really?" I said, my voice flat in my mouth.

"You know, Bean, he is worried about you."

I didn't say anything, and I could feel the open ears and held breath on her side of the line. I could feel her leaning in to hear me, awaiting news she wasn't sure she wanted to hear.

"You know, this all has *me* a little worried too, Bean. I don't know what to make of it. Will you just tell me where you are now? Stop being silly. David says he needs to see you." She inhaled sharply and I heard his voice disrupt the air in the background but couldn't make out the words. This is the real problem with marriage—that it is a permission slip for someone to access the most private parts of your life. I hadn't given him permission to go to my mother's house. I hadn't told him where I was going and there had been a reason for it. These things belonged to me.

"You know, he says you haven't been answering any of his calls or texts," she went on.

"I can't talk right now. I am on my way into work."

"You got a job?"

Again, I heard David's voice in the background, *ask if she's gone back to California*. I felt my grip around the phone tighten.

"Yeah, I did."

"Are you back in California?" she asked.

"I have to go."

"Sabine, don't you fucking be like this god dammit," she shouted.

"Fuck, I am not being like anything. I really have to get off the phone."

"Don't you play this game with me. I don't know what the hell happened between you and David, but you don't just leave a man with no explanation."

"Oh this is rich." The phone crackled and the whispering on her end of the line came to a halt.

"Sabine?" A low voice, the voice I'd woken up to and gone to bed with every night for the last three years. "Sabine, I don't know what to say to you, but we can't leave things like this. I know there is someone else. I saw the phone bills." His voice trembled, and I could almost see him pushing the frames of his thick glasses up toward his eyeballs as he spoke. "Where are you Sabine? Are you with him?"

"I'm not," was all I could say.

"Can we please talk? In person…" he paused.

I couldn't find the words to respond.

"I can meet you wherever you are. Just tell me where you are." His voice was gentle and pleading, like he thought we stood a chance, and I didn't know how it was possible for us to have two such differing views on the future of our marriage.

"I'm sorry," I said, "I have to go. I am late for work." I hung up before he could respond but I didn't move. I stood in front of the mirror where I had been getting ready and looked into the drain, avoiding meeting my eyes in the mirror's reflection. It had been stupid of me to think that having left him would be my last interaction with him. He was my husband. There was paperwork and belongings and rent and all the things that made a life together. You couldn't just disappear forever from that sort of thing. What surprised me most though, wasn't that he'd found out about the affair in such a short amount of time, but that he'd sounded like he might be able to forgive me. I had been so afraid to tell David about the affair all this time, and he had gone and figured it out anyway. I wondered what else that meant he knew about.

My phone began to buzz on the bathroom counter, the name *mom* appearing bold and back-lit across the screen. I reached out and silenced it, then changed the settings to *Do Not Disturb*.

Outside, the sun felt close to the earth, a weighted blanket amplifying the gravity of my body. The air was a static wall of warmth hitting my chest and lungs, a sort of punch to the organs that cleared out anything other than bodily consciousness. This was one of the things I loved most about Yu, something I hadn't appreciated as a child growing up in the desert, the way weather can whittle away at your thoughts until you are nothing more than an organism overcome by atmosphere. It was nearing one hundred degrees, and it wasn't even noon yet. I was in a tank top and cutoff jeans. The uniform. It was hard to wear much else in the heat. I liked the oppressive feeling of the sun, the way even the ground emanated with heat, so that you could feel a fire coming at you from all sides. I liked the way sweat attracted a film of sand to the body, subtle enough that you didn't know your body was coated in it until dark liquid ran into the drain of the shower. The desert has a way of reminding you that you're just a body, that you attract filth, that cleanliness is temporary.

It was a fifteen-minute walk to The Whiptail from Howling Woman's house. Most of it was down the long dirt road leading to the main drag of town. I wanted a cigarette, but I hated walking and smoking. I preferred to smoke standing still, focusing on each inhalation of smoke like it was a thing that could set my mind right and not a thing that was killing me slowly. So I walked with my fingers wrapped around a lighter in anticipation of when I would arrive outside The Whiptail and could lean up against the wall to smoke with pure concentration. Walking in the heat, thinking about smoking, feeling beads of sweat forming in the divots of my spine and between my breasts, I was becoming a person who hadn't received a phone call from my mother and estranged husband. It felt like I was shedding the skin of them through my pores. Nearly new by the time I hit the main road.

I could see The Whiptail at the end of the only paved road in Yu. Stepping onto the main road was like entering a time portal to the Wild Wild West of the Hollywood screen, only more modern and less lively. Most of the squat adobe buildings that lined the road were sun-faded and cracked. The majority had wooden boards in the windows. The only businesses in operation were the coffee shop, a gas station with a single oil-stained pump, a tiny pizza shack called Mama's, an apothecary, and a La Fiesta Mercado, which was in fact, not a fiesta at all, but a run-down grocery store that smelled of warm cabbage and rotting citrus—a sort of old school organic market that was only really alive on Saturdays when tents popped up along the sidewalk for a small farmers market where locals sold produce and various arts and crafts. It all looked so vacant, fake almost, like I was living in a make-believe town. I dissociated a little bit, and I couldn't tell what felt more real—the call from my husband or that I lived in this town now. All I knew was that I wanted a drink. Does this make me an alcoholic? An addict? I don't think so, but I did want to anesthetize my problems as Dr. Camille might say, because they all felt a little too heavy and I wasn't equipped enough to sort through them. Isn't it human nature to want to take a break from reality every once in a while? I don't think we've evolved enough to handle the amount of emotional experience enabled by living in modern society. It's too much. A person shouldn't be able to interrupt your escape from reality with a single phone call.

"You look a little rough, Kiddo," Nick said when I walked in.

"I'm all good."

"You sure?" he asked, and for a moment I thought about telling him about the call from my mother and David, but it felt like a lot to get into so early in the day. It required too much context, and I didn't know what would happen if I opened that gate.

"I think it's the heat."

"It'll get you if you aren't used to it." He reached for two shot glasses and filled them each with a heavy pour of Jack, our usual commencement routine. We clinked our glasses together and then threw them back. Instantly, a cold sweat came over my skin and I felt my insides ease with warmth. I wanted another one immediately, and then another one after that. I wanted to keep drinking until I was asleep, until a new day came and washed away the one I was in.

Nick walked around the bar and selected a song on the Jukebox. A fast, heavy guitar filled the speakers and soon enough Roky Erickson's grizzly voice took over the room.

My shift went by torturously slow. There wasn't the usual stream of regulars coming in, so there was little to distract me from my thoughts. Nick spent most of the day in the stockroom, coming out to the bar occasionally to grab a beer from the fridge and take it back with him. I wanted another drink, but I didn't trust myself to pour my shots without Nick's presence, so instead, I opened a bag of bar nuts and ate them. Then I opened a bag of Funyuns and let the salt and chemicals smother my feelings. I ate two beef jerky sticks in quick succession. My appetite felt insatiable. I wanted a shot, a cigarette, every bag of processed food in existence behind the bar. None of it seemed like enough to fill the void. I kept snacking until I was bloated and uncomfortable in my body.

When Angel showed up at shift change, I was so relieved that I could finally have another drink.

"How's it been today?" he asked, not even looking at me. He was busying himself with getting a bar towel and moving around glasses, avoiding making eye contact. With the call from my mother, I'd forgotten about the party the night before and I got the sense that Angel was irritated with me.

"Slow," Nick said as he reached for three shot glasses from the shelf. "And I don't know what y'all did to this one here last night, but she's been a real zombie today."

I was already on the other side of the bar waiting for my end of work shot.

"Hey, don't look at me. She disappeared on us last night," Angel said, pouring the whiskeys into the shot glasses for me and Nick.

"That right?" Nick nudged the shot of Coke toward Angel and one of the whiskeys toward me.

"I wasn't feeling that great."

"Apparently in California if you're not feeling that great it's okay to ditch your friends without any explanation."

"Well you're in a mood today aren't you?" Nick said. "The both of you are. Must be something in the air."

"I'm fine," I said, "just a bit distracted is all."

"Distracted, huh? What's on your mind?" Nick tapped his index finger on my temple and smiled.

"My ex, actually."

"The husband?"

"Yup, that one."

Angel looked up at me for the first time since arriving at work. His face was scrunched up like he was trying to make sense of what Nick and I were talking about.

"Let's take these already. Some of us have to get to work," Angel said.

"Yeah, yeah. We all know you only come in here to brood." Nick winked.

"It's harder than it looks."

"I didn't say it looked easy."

We clinked our shot glasses and I threw my whiskey back. Angel gestured to the bottle of Jack and I nodded in agreement.

"So, you were married? I guess town gossip doesn't spread as fast as I thought," Angel said.

"Still am, and it turns out he's looking for me."

"Woah, woah, woah. Back up a minute," Nick said, slapping his hand against the bar top, "I thought you said you were getting a divorce."

"It's a little more complicated than that."

"What, you just up and leave him one day with a post-it note or something?"

I looked down at the drink in front of me and wrapped my fingers around the glass.

"No shit. Is this guy dangerous or something?"

"No, no, no," I said, wanting to stop that thought before it grew in their minds. "He's an art history professor."

"What does that mean?"

"He's nice. Gentle. He's a really sweet man."

"So why did you up and leave the poor fool if he's a 'really sweet man'?" Nick asked.

"Haven't you heard that's what they do in California? Leave people without saying goodbye." Angel's voice was sharp as he said this, and I regretted opening my mouth. I'd known it was a bad idea from the start. It's why I hadn't said anything at the start of my shift, and of course, I'd been smart not to. There wasn't any way these two men would understand a woman abandoning a sweet man.

"I am still trying to put this all together," Nick said, scratching his head.

"I'm over it," Angel said, "Nick, where'd you put the strainer?"

"Hold on a minute. Tell us where this husband of yours is now?"

"Angel, will you pour us another round?"

"Sure, if you'll tell me where you two left the strainer."

"It's under the sink," I said, clacking my fingers on the shot glass in anticipation. "He is actually at my mother's house right now."

"Who? Your husband?"

"Yup."

Two regulars, Josúe and Cat, pushed through the big doors of the bar and hollered hellos at us. They loved the jukebox almost as much as they loved light beer and public displays of affection.

Nick put a cigarette in his mouth and narrowed his eyes at me, "This isn't over yet," he said in a dramatic tone before walking toward the door and slapping Josúe's back hello.

"Got the whole crew here," Cat said, crimping her tight blonde curls in her palm.

"I was just about to leave actually," I said, not sure I was willing to continue discussing my marriage in public. I took the shot Angel had poured and pushed the empty glass away from me.

"Oh, come on, Sabine, stay for a quick one," she said, sitting down next to me. I hardly served Cat as she usually came in at the end of my shift, but she always talked to me like we'd known each other longer than a couple of weeks. I'd met plenty of customers like her at other restaurants where I'd worked. The kind that love the establishment so much they pretend to be a part of it.

"You two staying for the show tonight?" Angel asked, setting two Budweiser's down in front of them.

"Nah, man. I'm working a site out in Albuquerque. Gotta be up fuckin' early." Josúe took a swig of his beer.

"Bummer. I'm gonna play a short set before Howling Woman goes on," he said, and I sat up straighter on the bar stool at the sound of Howling Woman's name on his lips.

"Oh no, I love when you play," Cat said, making a big pouty face. I thought of the guitar that was always tucked in the stockroom and tried to picture Angel on stage under a spotlight singing some angsty acoustic set.

"Well, I'm out of here," I said, scooting my stool back.

"Ahh," Cat said, but she was already turned toward Josúe, clinking her long-neck bottle with his.

"Hey, hold on a minute." Angel was holding the bottle of Jack Daniel's in front of me, and I felt a twitch in my face at the sight. I twisted back in my seat and nodded. He poured a nice full shot to the brim of the glass. He leaned close into me and passed me the shot, "Not sure what all the mention of your husband was about, but you look like you need this." He said it softly so Cat and Josúe couldn't hear him, and I felt a jolt of gratitude shoot through me that he hadn't invited these two regulars to join in on the discussion of my husband. His voice sounded good in a whisper, and I thought about the way it would sound muffled beside me on a pillow.

"Thanks." I took the shot in one big swallow and hoped it would be the one to drown the memory of the morning.

"What about you? Going to make it out tonight?"

"It's been a long day."

"That's too bad," he said, and I wanted him to lean back into me and whisper something so I could feel his breath on my ear again, feel the closeness of a man who cared about me. It was exactly what I didn't need. I'd been so good. I wasn't going to let one call from my mother fuck everything up for me. "I didn't know you played."

"I told you I studied music."

"I guess I didn't make the connection."

"So, be honest, what happened last night?"

"I don't know. I think I was feeling awkward being at a party with so many people I don't know."

"You could have said something."

"You're right. I should have." I looked down at my empty glass, sad there was nothing left to drink, sadder that what'd I drank so far wasn't doing much. "You think I could get one more for the road?"

He nodded, but I noticed his lips formed into a tight pucker and he wouldn't look at me as he filled my shot glass for the fourth time in a matter of minutes.

"You sure you're okay?"

"No," I said, reaching for the glass, but he didn't unwrap his fingers from it.

"If you need a friend, I've got some vacancies left."

"Thanks," I rolled my eyes, "but I was just in a bad mood. It's all fine."

He let go of the shot and I pulled it close to me, taking a whiff before shooting it back. "I should probably go."

"If you change your mind about tonight, I go on at eight."

"I'll keep that in mind."

I left the bar with no intention of returning to see Angel play. I felt too ashamed to come and stand around watching him on stage, hoping to catch his eye, avoiding making small talk with regulars that recognized me from the other side of the bar. I had my own plan for the night, and it involved a private drinking to oblivion in the solitude of my own bed.

EIGHTEEN.

For the next couple of days after the phone call, I thought that David would pick up momentum, that he'd be able to tell by some tone in my voice exactly where I was. That he could pick up on my exact geographic location and, any minute, would waltz through the swinging doors of The Whiptail or pound on the front door of Howling Woman's place. I'd worried that the guilt I'd felt over that phone call, over having dismissed my mother so quickly, would catch up with me and I'd drink too much one night and unblock David's number from my phone and call him myself. Instead, I turned my phone off completely. I didn't have anyone I needed to talk to. At least, if I did, it would be on my own time. A day passed. Then another. No David. No Avery. Just the petrol haze of desert sky and heat. It was officially summer and the days were long and hot and easy to get lost in.

Intentionally or unintentionally, Howling Woman and I didn't cross paths for the three whole days after the party. I mostly worked days at the bar, and she performed in the evening. It was easy enough not to see each other, though I didn't know exactly why I felt nervous to be in the same room together. Jealousy maybe? That she'd say something about my disappearance from Jesse's?

Then, four days after the party, I came home to find Howling Woman cooking in the kitchen. The house smelled like garlic and onions and fresh herbs. There were candles lit on the bookshelf that sat across from the couch, opposite from where my little makeshift bedroom was. Lucinda Williams's voice drifted out of the record player speakers and Howling Woman sang along as she moved around in the kitchen.

"You hungry?" she asked, looking up from the cutting board when I walked in.

"Yeah, sure."

"Make yourself useful then and pour us some wine and set the counter."

I slipped off my Chucks and put them on the rack by the door then got us the wine.

"You been a real ghost these last couple of days. Haven't seen you since you went and poofed into thin air on us at Jesse's."

"Yeah, I've been meaning to apologize about that."

"Everything alright?" She raised an eyebrow and locked her eyes on me.

"I guess."

"That don't sound too convincing."

I took a sip of my wine and sat down at the counter across from where she was cooking.

"Here, why don't you finish chopping this veg for the salad?" She slid the cutting board toward me, and I took over on the cucumber.

"It wasn't cool you know, you leaving like that?"

"I know."

"You're an adult and entitled to do as you please, but if we're going to live together and go out together, I expect at least the courtesy of you not scaring me with that kind of bullshit." She was staring right at me, and her face was serious in a way I hadn't yet seen it. It hadn't occurred to me that someone would worry about me if I left, especially not a woman I'd only known a few weeks.

"Yeah, I'm sorry."

"Angel and I looked around for you for a good thirty minutes before someone finally told us they saw you walk off down the street. What was the matter with you?"

"I don't know. I think I got overwhelmed."

"Well next time, speak up. Don't go leaving without saying goodbye. It ain't right."

"Yeah, okay."

"And wipe that puppy-dog look off your face. You don't need to go getting your tail between your legs."

I nodded and busied myself with dinner prep. I took her words to heart. I wanted her approval. My whole life I always felt like I was being judged. In turn, I think I became even more judgmental—of my mother, of my upbringing, of where I'm from and the types of people that stayed there, of myself—as if casting judgment before anyone else has a chance to means no one can judge me as hard as I judge myself, but trying to live preempting judgment is a type of prison. The only real freedom is not caring what others think. Howling Woman doesn't care what other people think, and even now, her behind bars, she isn't concerned with how others might see her. She says she was right to do what she did. Says I was too. Says it's between her and the universe. Says she doesn't need anyone else weighing in. Maybe that's the point of all this writing. Confession as unshackling. Maybe unburdening myself from judgment will mean freedom no matter what happens when I go in front of a jury. Their judgment won't mean nearly as much if I can separate it from how I see myself. See it for what it is—a group of people with limited information assigning a title to me. That's the problem with judgment itself, the scope from which we view anything is always so narrow.

I kept quiet and waited for the tension between us to ease, for the impetus of domestic labor to erase any resentment. I slid the cucumber into the salad bowl, took sips of my wine, reached for a tomato, pressed the knife into its flesh, the skin expanding out around its edges, ballooning until it split open. With each cut I imagined myself deflating a little, becoming something less anxious and ready to burst.

After dinner, we poured another round of wine and went out back to smoke and watch the sunset. The air was still thick with heat, and it felt like a warm embrace—like even in all the desolation that was desert, there was something comforting about it.

"You know, my mom called the other day," I said, lighting a cigarette.

"You guys close?"

"Definitely not."

"Mother-daughter relationships are overrated. I haven't talked to my mom in nearly forty years."

"Wow, that's such a long time."

"I don't even know if she's alive."

"Do you worry about her?"

"I try not to think too much about it. Honestly, she feels like a stranger to me at this point."

"My mom was calling because my husband showed up at her place looking for me."

"So, it is like that then?"

"Don't worry, he isn't going to come banging on your door."

"Better not, I don't got patience for that kind of shit." She lit the citronella candles on either side of the porch railing, then sat down beside me.

"Why don't you talk to your mom anymore?"

"We just have a different way of seeing the world. That's all." She took a drag of her cigarette and leaned her back up against the porch railing so that she was facing me. "You sure I don't need to worry about this ex of yours coming and banging down my door?"

"Yeah, even if he did show up, he'd probably only knock quietly and leave if we didn't answer."

"Is that the truth?"

"David's not really a *banging on doors* type of guy."

"Hmm…" She furrowed her brow like she was trying to make sense of this.

"What?"

"It don't quite add up."

"What doesn't?"

"The way I hear you at night in the living room and your ex being a *real nice guy.*"

"I don't know what you're talking about."

"You don't got to lie to me, you know? Those nightmares you been having, those sounds don't strike me as the types of sounds that come from being married to a real nice guy."

"I didn't realize. . ." I started to say, but I wasn't sure what exactly to respond to. The nightmares hadn't stopped after I'd left my mother's house, but I hadn't realized they'd been anything the outside world could hear.

"I used to have them too," she said.

"It's not David, if that's what you're thinking. I'm not really sure what they're about."

"I won't pry. If you don't want to talk about it, you're entitled not to."

"What about your nightmares?"

She sighed and took another drag of her cigarette.

"You don't have to answer either. I'm just curious since you mentioned it."

"It's been the same dream as long as I can remember. I don't have it so much anymore, but it was recurring for a lot of years after I moved away from home. I always meant to read some Carl Jung and see what he had to say about it all. Did you ever have to read him in college?"

"A little, but I don't remember anything from it. Something about archetypes and symbols."

"I heard he was a cokehead."

"I think that was Freud."

"Right, weren't the two of them in love or something?"

"Maybe. I was never all that into the whole psychoanalysis stuff."

"Me either. It all feels like a real crock of shit. I don't believe in therapy either. Just people with too much education trying to feel in control of their own uncontrollable human selves and turning their own anxiety outward, convincing other people they need to partake in some specific set of healthy behaviors. They're another sedative for the masses. Who decides what's healthy and what isn't? The way I see it, therapy is rooted in men wanting to control women."

I nodded, not sure if I fully followed what she was saying, but it seemed to make sense enough. I wonder what she'd have to say about me meeting with a substance abuse counselor, Dr. Camille, about having to piss in a cup and stay sober all in the name of proving to the court that I am not totally depraved, that I too can be a woman coerced into submission in order to behave in a way some collective whole deems appropriate.

"What was the recurring dream about?"

"My sister mostly."

"I didn't know you have a sister."

"Had."

"I'm sorry," I said, and for the second time she didn't correct me for using the word.

"I'm the one that's sorry."

"I thought you didn't believe in *sorries*."

"There's an exception to every rule. Ain't that right?"

"What happened to her?"

"A man," she said, "Isn't it always a man?"

"You don't have to tell me if you don't want to."

"I haven't talked about him in a real long time." She took another drag of her cigarette which was to the filter by then. "It was our stepfather. I was only a teenager when she died."

I realized I was holding my breath, not sure where this story was going, but the space between us morphed into something new—more serious.

"My stepfather, Dick," she laughed, "Hell it's almost like a joke—too on the nose or something with a stupid name like that." She shook her head, "Dick, that stupid prick, he was the reason she died, the reason I never talked to my own mother again. I think she knew it too, but she wasn't the kind of woman that could live without a man, so she just held his hand and cried as she mourned the death of her baby girl."

At the time, I didn't get why Howling Woman was telling me this, how we crossed the threshold into serious conversation. I thought maybe she was trying to connect with me in the way so many women tried to connect, bonding through trauma. That probably had something to do with why I could never be friends with women—the way they're always making sense of their identity through the lens of past *trauma*, one-upping each other with the things that have been done to them. I hate that word trauma. I'd always been trying to forget the past altogether. I didn't think it was such an impressive thing to be able to say something bad had happened to you. Now, I know there are more reasons to tell a story than to bond. Some things have to be said aloud. They demand it, no matter how long you try to keep them quiet. Howling Woman knows this too.

"What was her name?" I asked.

"Phoebe. Her name was Phoebe."

We sat for a moment sipping the last of our wine concoctions, Phoebe's name a ghost consuming more air than the two of us combined.

"She killed herself."

"Jesus."

"She slit her wrists in the bathtub. She was only fifteen years old."

I opened my mouth to say something, but Howling Woman went on as though we both knew there wasn't anything I could say that mattered.

"She was pregnant when she died. My mother didn't think I knew, but I heard her praying one night for Phoebe and her unborn baby. I was confused at first. Thought maybe I'd misheard, but she prayed every night for the both of them. The thought came to me so naturally. Dick. I knew he was the father."

"Jesus," I said again, and it sounded trivial and wrong, but I didn't know the right response.

"Phoebe didn't have a boyfriend. She never even left the house except to go to school. She'd changed after my mother married Dick. One night, I climbed into her bed like I'd done when we were younger. I'd been smoking weed and snuck in through her window. When I reached for the covers, she started flailing in her sleep, making soft screams, and then she slapped me across the face." Howling Woman bit her bottom lip and kept her eyes on the distance. I wanted to tell her she didn't have to tell me all this, that she could stop, but I didn't know how. I wanted to hear the rest.

"I didn't put it all together right away. Not until after it was too late. Even before I found out she'd been pregnant, I'd felt like Dick had something to do with it. Call it intuition, but the day she died, he'd been the one to take care of it, and I don't know how to describe the energy coming off him as he carried her body out of the tub, but it was diabolic. Dark and twisted. He couldn't stop touching her the whole time we waited for the police to come. It was sick. For the longest time I couldn't get the picture of him with her dead body out of my mind, the way his eyes kept scanning her little body. Disgusting. Eventually, I figured it out, that she'd put the knife through her wrists, but he'd been the one to put it in her hands. That's why my mother and I don't talk anymore. That's our difference of opinions."

The sky was mostly dark by that point and the translucent moon was settling over la Chupadera. It was full and fat and fit perfectly between its peak and its twin as though it was being cradled. I thought of the possibility that there was a vortex inside it. How its magnet might be pulling darkness in and wondered what sort of power would be needed to rid a soul of all this history. Could there ever be enough?

"I'm sorry that happened to you. And to your sister."

"Me too, but Dick got what was coming to him. I made sure of that."

"What do you mean?"

She pinched out the cherry of her cigarette and watched it float into the night. "I made sure he wouldn't ever be able to look at another young girl again." She turned to face me and her eyes glowed orange in the moonlight like they were on fire. "The day I left town, I rode my bike down to the sleazy car dealership where he worked. The office was just a trailer, and he was the only one there. I had this bucket and when he turned to look at me I sloshed it all over his face. I never heard a person scream so loud until that moment."

"What was in the bucket?"

"Acid."

"Are you fucking serious?"

"Serious as a burst pipe in winter."

"That is insane." I tried to picture it, Howling Woman as a young girl, a backpack on, ready to run away from home, stopping first to assault a man. How had she thought to get the acid? Where had she even gotten it from? I couldn't imagine myself doing something like that. It seemed awful and yet totally appropriate. What would it feel like to do something like that, to blind a man, to feel self-righteous about it, to get back at him for hurting you or someone you loved instead of lying down to die?

"No." She grabbed my wrists tight in her hand and I turned toward her, struck by the intensity of her touch. "You got it mixed up," she said, her voice low, her eyes catching mine, trying to burn something into me as she spoke, "What's insane is fucking a little girl and making her kill herself and thinking nothing can touch you. Thinking you don't ever have to atone for the shit you done because you're a big powerful man and don't nobody care about what happens to women unless they're beautiful or rich. Men think they can get away with all sorts of evil if they do it to women who won't ever point a finger at them."

I nodded and waited for her to go on, but she let go of my wrists and turned back toward the mountain in the distance. I felt my body loosen with relief that it was over. But my stomach churned with sick, thinking about what had happened to Phoebe, about the violence men inflicted on women, about the ways they got away with it. Howling Woman was right. It wasn't fair that women had to carry every memory of violence in their body, but the men who harmed them could just move on with their lives, completely unfazed by how they permanently altered another being. It was too much for a woman to carry alone.

I thought about how Howling Woman said the vortex brought her here like it had done me. I was sure that she would have to spend the rest of her life in Yu to erase that darkness. I had the feeling that there was more too. More than a sister and stepfather. I knew, because I had told her about David and Avery, and that had barely skimmed the surface of all that I was carrying. I knew because she hadn't finished the story about Bison, and if he was the type of guy that I thought he was, a guy even remotely close to her stepfather, then it wasn't likely that she'd just let him go on the way he'd been going on.

Even then, making that association to Bison, the story she hadn't ever finished telling me, I didn't think of Howling Woman as potentially dangerous, and I should probably clarify that I still don't—no matter what people say, I don't think she's a criminal. Not for throwing acid on her stepfather, and not for anything else she did either.

It doesn't matter that I got to where I'm at now because she insisted that we pay the man from my past a visit. It might have been her that brought the gun, but it was me who shot it. More importantly, the part no one seems to care enough about, is that when a woman's on trial for shooting a man, it doesn't matter that the man was the one who caused harm first. If you don't have evidence, if you can't show it, then what happened to you to cause your unraveling is just a story. It's fiction. You're expected to say you're sorry, that you understand right from wrong, and it won't ever happen again. It's an apology they want. A woman shouldn't be so self-righteous as to take justice into her own hands unapologetically. One needs to atone to gain forgiveness. The truth is, I'm glad I shot him. He deserved it. He deserves worse as far as I'm concerned.

NINETEEN.

For most my life I'd tried to cut the events of my childhood out of my story. Namely, the bits about James Dixon. It's not like people believe women when they say a man has hurt them. It's not like I even had the language back then to say what had happened to me even if I had thought there would be a person who'd believe me. Then, enough time had passed that even when I did have a better understanding of how to say what he did, I knew it would be met with an interrogation.

Why'd you wait so long to come forward?

It was a long time ago, are you sure you're remembering right?

Is there any way you might be misinterpreting what happened?

Have you ever told this story to anyone else before?

Is there anyone who might be able to corroborate this story?

Are you sure?

Are you sure?

Are you sure?

I wasn't wrong. Look at me now, finally ready to tell the truth and my lawyer's over here telling me to keep my mouth shut. The only person I ever told was the only person I could ever imagine taking my word for what it was. The truth. That was Howling Woman. People can believe what they want about her now that her past has reared its ugliness, but there isn't a better kind of person than a woman who believes, without doubt, another woman when they confess the evils of man.

I hadn't spoken his name in nearly twenty years. It had always been inside of me, but time had a strange effect on it, rooting it in deeper rather than erasing it altogether. The name dancing on my tongue like it wanted to spread my lips apart and be heard. I couldn't make sense of it—how for years during my adolescence I was able to ignore it, push it to the recesses of my mind, and then the farther away I got from it, the more space it took up. It had been there my whole marriage, a thing that wanted to be set free, a thing that should be able to be named in front of the person you have chosen to spend your entire life with, and yet, it caught in my throat. I didn't know what kind of person I would be if I named him. Named it. I didn't know how my history would look on someone else's face after I spoke it aloud. I didn't know if it was possible to love a person after you learned that type of thing, like afterwards, all that you'd be able to see was their grossness.

Then Howling Woman, with her story about Phoebe, us going silent on the porch, another too big glass of wine, my brain heavy—her story, my story, the wine. Maybe this is the real inciting incident—the one that led to everything else. It's possible that it was bound to come out, and everything else was just coincidence. Secrets are like that. Always there even when you think you've forgotten them. They'll wait for any excuse to come out.

I had gone to bed right after dinner, exhausted from bearing witness to Howling Woman's confession. Exhausted from what it reminded me of. In bed, I wondered if I was going to spend the rest of my life shackled to this thing I could not name.

How would I even begin to explain it to another person in the first place? That had always been the question that smacked me across the face. As a child, language evaded me. I could sense that my mother didn't want to know, or worse, that she did know but couldn't bear the thought of hearing the words from my mouth. She had her own pain to carry. Shouldn't that be enough? Then, time passed and the nights in my room beneath James Dixon were hushed by time and distance. Still, even as I sat on the stoop beside Howling Woman, the events of my past vortexing inside of me as she spoke of Phoebe, I didn't know how to share my story. Not yet, though, of course, soon enough, I would.

My story: An older man, my mother's husband, had pressed his heavy body onto mine. He'd sucked the air from my lungs with each of his gasping breaths as his hand pounded hard against my pelvis. His clenched fist had grown harder and faster against my delicate bones until his whole body paused. He slipped his hand below the waist of my Rugrats pajama bottoms and his sticky fingers found their way into the small space inside of me.

It wasn't rape exactly. Was it? Was it really even all that bad? The nights spent beneath him like that? It was mostly heavy petting. Some humping. Sometimes a finger or two inside of me. Lots of sticky semen dampening my pajamas. I'd seen enough television and read enough headlines to know that, *no, it wasn't so bad*. Not compared to what others endured. Was there even a word to define this? Whatever it was that had happened to me wasn't as bad as the stories I read about other women—the ones whose names were left out of articles for weeks on end, the harm done to them described in vague euphemisms. I knew from watching every episode of *Law & Order: SVU* that the act is always more terrible than the euphemism—maybe it is simply that language fails us, or that language is too powerful. I never asked James to stop. How do you tell the story and include that part? How can I be a victim if I didn't beg for him to stop, to get off, to get out from inside of me? Wasn't that always one of the questions victims got asked?

Did you ask him to stop?

Did you scream for help?

Did you say no?

They never ask, *Did your body turn to a hard surface hoping biology was enough to shut a person out? Did your throat fill with stones weighing you down, blocking any sound from escaping your little mouth? Did you feel like the screaming inside of you, begging to be heard, would shatter you to pieces even before the man did?*

No one ever asks the right questions. No one ever asks. If you want to be heard it's up to you to open your fucking mouth.

That night in bed, after Howling Woman had told me about her sister, I couldn't close my eyes without the room spinning. My mouth felt full of bile and all the words I hadn't said. All the years I hadn't said them for. What would it be like to say them out loud? His name. The act. What would these words sound like in front of another person?

I tried again to close my eyes. Microscopic stars filled my vision and the bed was a merry-go-round beneath me. I pressed my hands to my eyes to dim the stars, but it made more appear and I thought I might be sick all over myself with wine spritzers and all the things I'd been carrying for too long. They were making me sick. They were begging to escape my body.

Maybe this is me interfering with the events, trying to make sense of how one thing led to another. Looking for a connection between my drunken, overwhelmed state to what came next. Maybe I'm wrong about everything being interconnected. Maybe it's the opposite—nothing is ever connected until we go and say it is in an attempt to weave together isolated incidents. This is what storytelling is: creating causality.

The point is, I couldn't sleep. Whether it was because I was too drunk or too disturbed doesn't matter depending on who you are and how you like a story told to you. What happened next was, I opened my eyes to the darkened room and swung my legs over the mattress. My skin felt warm to touch as I pulled my shorts over my legs and stood. I flipped the lamp on and found the balled-up tank top I'd been wearing earlier. I pulled it on over my head and examined myself in the small mirror on my dresser. My hair was wild from sweating and the short hairs around my face curled in perfect ringlets. My eyes bulged wildly from my face, dark bags beneath them. The heat and booze and mania of my mind rattled through me and I touched my flushed cheeks as if they belonged to someone else. The feel of my fingertips grazing my bones made my skin tingle and I knew it was touch, the touch of someone else, that I needed to clear my head.

On my way to the front door I slowed in front of Howling Woman's bedroom. I swayed in my attempt at stillness, and for a second, I felt the pull of her beyond the closed door. I imagined that I could crawl into bed beside her, wrap my body around hers. That whatever strength she had would transfer to me through our bodies touching under the covers. Maybe if I'd have just done that, crawled into her bed instead, then things would be different. But that's not what I did. I had shut down after her story about her sister, and I'd felt a wall forming around me, stopping me from crossing its threshold to the space that held her and her story and all the things that could connect us. But if I leaned into my need for her in that moment, what other vulnerable, unlovable parts of me might be revealed? My brain hurt from trying to make sense of what to do next, of how to feel about Howling Woman's sister, the urge to tell her about James Dixon, the urge to press my body into hers until I was absorbed by her, the fear that in doing so she would never look at me the same, that her face would reveal the grotesqueness of my past and I couldn't see myself on her face in that way. I needed a firm hand on my thigh, warm breath on my neck, a cool drink to wash it all down with.

TWENTY.

The Whiptail was dead. I hadn't been there that late into the night since I'd first arrived in Yu, and there was something both reassuring and eerie about walking into a nearly empty bar after midnight. There was a new country song playing on the jukebox that Cat always queued up about Tennessee whiskey and love, so before I'd even seen her sitting at the bar with her legs tangled up in Josúe's, I knew she was there.

"Sabine, my queen!" Cat squealed when she saw me. "Look at you, cutie butt."

"Does Angel know the lights are off?" I asked. "If it hadn't been for the music, I'd have thought the place was closed." I sat down a couple stools over from Cat and Josúe. They were the only two left in the bar.

"Yeah, Angel's sick of Cat's singing so he's closing the place early to get rid of us."

I looked around the bar, which was easy to see since Angel had turned the inside lights up. I didn't see him anywhere though. I felt stupid in the bright lights of the bar, not at all the dim, smoky picture I'd had in mind while I'd been throwing my clothes on and getting out the door. I hadn't given myself enough time to think it through, what would happen once I got to the bar, but I knew from the wobbly feeling in my gut that this wasn't exactly what I'd been looking for.

"We never see you out this late, girly. Whatcha doing here?"

"Couldn't sleep."

She eyed me. I couldn't tell if she was reading into my motivation for being in the bar alone this close to closing time. I wanted a drink. Something to do with my hands. Something to soften the jagged edges of my brain.

"I wish you woulda been here earlier. We ordered a pizza from Mama's and Sissy baked a cake."

"What was the occasion?"

"Nick's anniversary."

"I thought Nick was divorced?"

"He is. It's the anniversary of his divorce."

"That actually sounds like a really fucking depressing celebration."

"Nah, it was fucking hilarious," Josúe said, taking the last swig of his beer. "Ray, you know, the delivery guy from Mama's?"

"Yeah, I know him," I said, even though I didn't actually know him. I'd seen him dropping off pizzas occasionally for customers. He was a lanky, mid-thirties guy who always wore a neon baseball cap with a screen-printed UFO on the front.

"He's like all good with computers and shit," Josúe said, already laughing at whatever he was trying to tell me.

"Oh my god, you wouldn't freaking believe it." Cat slapped her own thigh in disbelief and laughed.

"Ray blew up a picture of Bertie and Stan all big and glued 'em to this big 'ol bride and groom piñata. Professional grade cut-outs. The best part was they were life size. So there was like this Bertie and Stan at the anniversary party," Josúe said.

"Who are Bertie and Stan?"

"Oh my gosh, you don't know?" Cat asked and leaned across the bar like she was about to tell me a secret. "Bertie is Nick's ex-wife and Stan used to be their roommate until, you know."

"Shit," I said. A flash of Avery's face came to my mind. I cringed thinking about how one of my old regulars might have discussed us to someone. How my sex life might be late-night gossip between strangers. Had anyone from the Tavern known about us? I wondered if Avery talked about me to anyone or if he'd compartmentalized me in the small space of his mind reserved for things he'd keep tucked away until he could eventually forget them altogether. I couldn't blame him. I was doing the same, but it seemed like he was better at it. He hadn't called or texted since the night he offered up a dick pic.

The door of the stockroom creaked open and Angel emerged carrying a box of liquor bottles and snack size chip bags. His face scrunched up a little and his eyes lasered into me. I coulda feel the air between our bodies grow hot and staticky like his body was a thunder cloud and mine was the earth from which the lightning bolted. The electricity made the hairs on my arms rise as Angel walked toward the bar. He didn't say anything as he set the box down, but his face tilted to the side, his eyes still on mine like he was trying to place me, and I forgot about feeling stupid.

"Ray, a fucking loco that guy, he filled the piñata with pop 'ems so when we all went to beat the thing it sounded like a machine gun." Josúe laughed to himself and Cat nodded in agreement like this was a truly hilarious event.

Angel set down a shot glass on the bar in front of me and poured it full of whiskey without so much as a hello. He raised his thick black eyebrow with a *yup, this shit's been going on all night and I'm done* kind of expression.

"It gets worse," Angel said, pulling a bottle of Budweiser from the fridge and twisting the top off for me.

"Worse?" Cat screeched with a huge giggle, "You know it was funny. Don't be a buzzkill just because you had to mop up the mess."

Angel shook his head and looked at me with a *just wait for it* grin.

"After all was said and done," Josúe said, "Nick pulled his dick out and peed on the piñata. Right on Bertie's smashed in face. Pinche gringo."

"Can you fucking believe it?" Cat screamed with laughter. "You should have been here. One for the record books. In all my years I have never seen Nick like that."

"Wow," I said, taking a sip of my beer and looking away from Angel, "That does sound like the most depressing celebration I have ever heard of." It was hard to imagine Nick, a man I'd known for only a month or so, but who was always calm and equipped with exactly the type of one-liners that put people at ease, peeing on a blown-up picture of his ex-wife in front of dozens of customers.

"That barely scratches the surface of depressing celebrations around here," Angel said, "Stick around long enough and you might make it to the annual party for Billy's missing left arm."

"Who's Billy?"

"Oh lighten up, will you?" Cat said, turning toward Josúe, "What do you say? Got it in you for another round?"

Josúe straightened up on his stool and yawned, "I don't know, baby. I got work in the morning."

Cat leaned in and kissed his cheek, "My sweet, responsible baby." Cat pulled a sweaty looking wad of bills from the back pocket of her cutoffs and threw it on the bar. "You keep the change, Angel. Lord knows you deserve it."

They both stood from their stools and Cat stretched her long, tan arms above her head. Josúe watched her stretching in front of him like she was the most beautiful thing he'd ever seen, and I felt my gut twist in the agony of not having someone to look at me the way he did Cat. I thought they were loud, and a little ridiculous, but it's hard not to love two people who are so wild about each other. I felt envious of the way their bodies fit so perfectly together, the ease with which they coexisted, the way they were always laughing and smiling like the world just looks different when you're in love.

Angel followed them to the door, laughing at something Josúe said to him, and then locked the deadbolt behind them. The sound of the lock thumping into place gave me a jolt of frenetic energy and I felt my pupils dilate. Angel walked behind the bar and I could smell him as he passed. Myrrh. Tobacco. Citrus. He set the bottle of Jack Daniel's down beside my empty shot glass.

"So, what are you doing here so late?"

"Couldn't sleep."

"Odd place to come when you're trying to sleep."

"I didn't say I was trying. I just said I couldn't."

"Something wrong?"

"I didn't want to be alone."

He folded his arms across his chest and stared at me. I tried to avoid his eyes, worried I'd see his face full of pity and it would make me feel pathetic. But when I looked up he smiled at me like maybe he was glad I'd come running to him when I was feeling lonely.

"Here, I'll change the music for you. Something to make you feel better."

He walked around the bar to the jukebox and queued up a song. An acoustic guitar played out over the bar speakers and Phil Lynott's soft voice, more of a speaking whisper than a song, accompanied it.

"This song actually makes me feel a little weepy."

"You played it on your first day here." He sat down in the empty bar stool next to me, his body angled toward mine. "I see what you mean, though. All the best songs are sad."

"What kind of music do you play anyway?"

"Why don't you come here at a normal hour when I've got a set and you can hear for yourself?"

"I will."

"So, you are going to stick around for a while then?"

"I don't really know where else to go."

"Not back to your husband?"

I cocked my head, eyeing Angel to see what he might be insinuating, but his face didn't give anything away.

"No, that's not really an option. I messed it up good."

"You?"

"Geez, don't make me feel worse than I already feel."

"I wasn't trying to…"

"No, it's okay. I just don't think we were meant to be."

He raised an eyebrow like he wasn't buying it.

"And I cheated on him."

"So, you're on the run from your husband and this other guy then?"

"No one's chasing me."

"That's hard to believe." He steadied his eyes onto mine. He had dark eyes and his face was all angles and knives. I stared back and could feel every inch of my insides igniting with heat. Tight knots of pressure formed below my belly and begged to be massaged. I felt the urge to rub my palms over his flesh and feel his bones pierce me—releasing the tension building up inside of me that could only be relaxed by touch. His lips parted and I could almost feel his heavy breath on me from where he sat.

"Where are you going after this?" I asked, the tingling beneath my skin made it impossible to feel shame for wanting something so bad and acting. All I could think of were the parts of my flesh that hadn't been touched in weeks. Each part—my stomach, my breasts, the edge of my spine and the hollow it led to—ached beneath my clothes as though they were expanding out big enough for a hand to find them.

"Home," he said, standing back up and going around to the other side of the bar. I watched him pull the money from the drawer and start counting.

"Would it be weird if I asked to come with you?"

He finished counting before he looked up to respond.

"Yes, it would be weird."

I looked down at the empty shot glass in front of me, bit my lip, trying not to cry. I wanted this to be easy, for our bodies to somehow magically transition into a state of symbiosis, but I couldn't remember how two people came together in that way. It always seems so easy in movies, passion overtaking logic until nudity and sex ensue. In real life, there is so much in between desire and action.

"But I'd like you to, if you want."

I nodded. "That sounds nice."

"Let me finish up here. We can leave in five."

"Okay. Do you think I could have another while I wait for you?" I felt embarrassed to ask, like he might change his mind if he thought I was too drunk, but he poured me the shot and slid it to me, told me to wash it when I was done and help him with the trashes.

TWENTY·ONE.

On the drive to Angel's house, I lit a cigarette and leaned back against the passenger seat, closing my eyes as I inhaled the smoke. The radio played a song I'd never heard. It was staticky and romantic, something about eternal love gone wrong and what sounded like a euphemism for heroin. All the best songs are sad. All the best songs are about tormented love and addiction and yearning. Angel rested his right arm on the center console while he drove, and I reached out to hold his hand. He didn't say anything, but he folded his fingers through mine and held it back. Maybe it wouldn't be so hard. Maybe he wanted the same thing I did.

When we got to his house, he was quiet, stoic, putting his wallet and keys in a bowl by the door, unlacing his shoes and slipping them off. He put a record on and lit a couple of candles. It took me by surprise that he seemed to be setting the mood. His house was a one-bedroom casita down the road from the bar. Like Howling Woman's house, the kitchen and living room were all one large room separated by an island counter. He didn't ask me if I wanted anything to drink, and of course he wouldn't have had what I wanted even if he did ask. I couldn't tell if us holding hands in the car would lead to anything else. I asked to use the bathroom, nervous to be so close to him in the routine of his coming home from work. He pointed down the only hall of the house and I locked myself in.

I waited in the bathroom for a couple of minutes, leaned up against the sink, my back turned toward the mirror, not wanting to look at my reflection. My heart was pounding, and I was thinking it shouldn't have felt so strange to go home with a man, to act on desire. I was almost thirty. Married. Had carried out an affair. This, sleeping with a man, was something I knew how to do, and yet I felt like a little girl hiding in the bathroom, unsure of how to proceed.

"You okay in there?" he asked, knocking gently on the bathroom door, and I realized I'd have to come out eventually. When I opened the door, he was leaned up against the frame. Our bodies were nearly touching.

"I can take you home if you want."

I reached for him and slipped my hands underneath his black shirt. His skin was hot to the touch. He placed his hands over mine, the fabric of his shirt separated the flesh of our hands.

"Is this okay?" I asked.

"I'm not sure. Is it?"

I closed my eyes and tilted my mouth up to meet his, anxious that he would return the gesture with words instead of bringing his mouth to mine. I heard him sigh, and I thought that was it, but then he wrapped his arms around me, and I felt his lips on mine.

The sex had been better than I thought it would be. The thing I'd needed and had been pushing aside for too long. Maybe sex can be an addiction. I think about the way I had sometimes thought about calling it off with Avery when the guilt became too much—how one time I actually did and then less than twenty-four hours later I was texting him *I miss you*, and then I was meeting him at a park in the middle of the afternoon and pulling my pants down to let him fuck me from behind, and then the affair resumed before I could even settle into the anguish of ending it— the sex so regular I was sure there wasn't any way that David couldn't have caught on. I wanted so badly to end it, but every time I tried I was torn open by my own desperate need for touch and there was never enough. Not from David. Not from Avery. How was it possible to have so much and still feel a lacking that radiated endlessly through me?

Angel had taken his time with me, moved intentionally across my body in a way that overshadowed everything else that had been on my mind hours before. He'd lit a candle by his bed—the flame the only light in the room— its soft flickering easing the hard edges of Angel until his form took on the safest shape of flesh and warmth. He'd pulled my shorts down and followed their trail with his lips. Hot air escaped his lips and greeted my bare skin. It sent a shiver through my spine.

"You're so wet," he said, his fingers brushing my clit.

"I want this so bad," I said. He put his mouth on me again, his tongue taking over for his fingers. It felt like it had been forever since someone wanted me like that, to take their time with me, and it was almost too much to bear. I ran my fingers through his hair and pulled his face free from between my legs. "Please, Angel, I need you inside of me." My voice was shaking, and I could feel myself on the edge of losing it, like I was too close to coming, too close to crying, and I needed him closer, his body consuming me. It was a relief that he could sense my need to be crushed by his weight. He placed his open palm down on my chest and pressed me into the bed as he kissed my bare stomach in one long line up between my tits until his face was close to mine and our bodies were flush against one another.

"It feels so good being close to you." He cupped my face so I had to look at him, and he watched my eyes as he put himself slowly inside of me. I tried to pull him in faster, desperate to consume him as fast as possible, but he grabbed my hands and held them down above my head.

"Wait."

I trembled beneath him and felt the swell of him building up slowly over time. It made the pressure excruciating, overwhelming, and my orgasm was building up beneath it like it would split me open. Was it possible for something to burst the pressure building up inside of you until there was nothing left? When it felt like he was as deep as he could be, I didn't think I could wait any longer for him to make me come, he gave a single hard thrust and I let out a cry of relief, the tension finally releasing its hold on me and he wrapped his arms around me, pulling me closer until our cheeks were sweaty and wet beside one another. As I came, he shuddered and I gripped him tighter until we both went limp in each other's arms. I fell deeper into the mattress, a heavy spell casting itself over me, paralyzing me in a gentle euphoria. For a moment, just before I slipped into sleep, a glimpse of Howling Woman's face began to form, but Angel's slow, steady breathing on the pillow next to me were waves washing away my thoughts, and quickly, I fell into the sleep I'd been dying for all night.

Eventually, the sun filled the sky and lit Angel's room. His room was four white walls adorned with framed lithograph prints of domestic looking scenes in nature—one I could see best was a woman in an apron with constellations inked into the fabric, she was kneeling in a lush backyard and planting a flower. Milk crates full of records lined most of the room and he had a big record player near the window and two guitars secured to the wall. In each corner of the room were huge hanging plants with curtains of leaves that hung over their planters. It was an odd mash-up of adolescent boy and earthy, artful adult—the mattress with no frame, the milk crates as furniture, the macramé plant hangers, and the orderly placement of all his things.

It was hard to imagine Howling Woman ever lying in this bed beside him with all the idiosyncrasies of his youth and adultness exposed in one place. An image of the night before flashed inside my head, Angel's fingers in the hollows of my torso, his slow, deliberate hands tracing my body as though he was marking all the vulnerable parts of me. I couldn't imagine Howling Woman being the one getting marked by a man, but I didn't want to think about what she was like during sex. What she liked. What she didn't like. How those things had existed in this bed with Angel. How they might have informed the way he'd touched me.

Angel was breathing heavy beside me, and his warmth and weight felt like restraints around my lungs. I shouldn't be here, I thought. I shouldn't have done this. Why did I always do this? I closed my eyes and took a deep breath in. I could smell his musk and the citrus-rot scent of his skin. I didn't want to think about what came next. About the awkward fumbling to reacclimate to life in daylight.

"Will you take me back to my place?" I whispered. Angel rolled over toward me. He didn't open his eyes, but his fingers found my bare stomach and circled my belly button.

"I'm surprised you didn't disappear on me."

"It's a long walk," I said, turning onto my stomach so his hand couldn't touch my navel.

"Can we do coffee first?"

"I don't know. I need to. . ."

"It'll only take a second."

"Sure."

He rolled away from me and planted his feet on the ground. His knees came up to his face because of how close the mattress was to the ground and he yawned as he stretched his arms above his head. He didn't seem awkward or concerned about what would change between us and I worried for a minute that he had used me, too. Only, what would that mean? If I was something to be used, did it have to do with Howling Woman? My stomach tightened and my brain whirred. I was too hungover to think about what purpose I could serve in the story of his life. I needed to figure out how I would explain this, but the thought made me sick. Howling Woman had just revealed the most vulnerable side of herself to me, and what had my response been? To go and sleep with a man she had supposedly been with? All because I couldn't deal with my own shit. I closed my eyes, blocking the light, squeezing my eyelids as though I could physically crush the memory of what I'd done.

"I didn't know how you like it, so I just put a little milk in," Angel said, when he came back. I hated how calm he looked in the doorway of his room with two mugs of coffee and toast propped on their rims.

"I'm not that hungry. I just want to go."

He sat down on the bed beside me and handed me a piece of toast with clumps of cold butter on it. "You should at least have a bite. Trust me," he said.

I took the toast and had a bite. The crumbs clung to all the dry parts of my mouth, and I thought I might choke as I swallowed. I took a sip of coffee to guide it down.

"You okay?"

"Feel like shit."

He leaned over and kissed my cheek, "Well, you definitely don't look like shit."

"That's hard to believe."

"Maybe you shouldn't drink so much."

"Who asked you?"

"You're the one who said you feel like shit."

"It's not that."

He put his hand on my thigh and brushed his fingers against my still bare skin. "What is it then?"

"Just stop."

"Stop what?"

"Being so nice to me."

"I'm confused." He retracted his hand from my thigh. I instantly regretted telling him to stop. My brain wanted two conflicting things and I didn't know how to be.

"Why are you being so nice to me?"

"Is it bad to be nice to someone you like?"

"Jesus, how can you like me, you don't really even know me? What is it with the people in this fucking town?"

"Why are you being like this?"

"I'm not a good person, Angel. I'm not someone you can date and be happy with like everything is all wonderful."

"I'm not a fucking idiot, you know. I didn't ask you to be my girlfriend, but I like you. I don't see the harm in wanting to get to know each other."

"And what about Howling Woman?" I asked, my heart racing as her name left my lips.

He closed his eyes and ran his fingers through his long hair, his hands stopping at his neck and bracing it. "What about her?"

"Well she's my roommate and supposedly your ex-girlfriend."

"That was a long time ago."

"A couple of years isn't a long time."

"Who made you the queen of timekeeping?"

"It doesn't matter. It still makes me a fucking shit." I could hear the harshness in my voice, and even though part of me wanted to freeze the moment in time, be completely invisible to the world outside his bedroom, I knew it wasn't possible. I knew who I was on a fundamental level. He would know too. I needed to speed it up to the part where he would hate me. It was inevitable. I just didn't want to wait for it to play its course.

"We're all adults here, and honestly, you don't even really know what you're talking about."

"So, you two didn't date then?"

"I was going through a hard time. She was kind to me, but it wasn't. . ." he trailed off and shook his head, "No, you know what. I don't need to explain myself to you. You're the one who is married. I should be asking you the questions."

"Jesus Christ." I went to stand up, not feeling like I could be that close to him a second longer, like being next to him made the night before too real, my mistake too palpable. My toast fell to the floor as I stood. The room was spinning and unstable. I felt his hand wrap around my forearm, a hot slosh of coffee on my skin.

"Hold on a second," he said.

"I don't know what's wrong with me." I sat back on the bed, exhausted from the spike in adrenaline and standing too fast with such an awful hangover. He took my hand in his and it felt nice to have it held, but also like I wished I didn't need it so bad.

"Sabine, I told you, I'm a good guy. We didn't do anything wrong here. It doesn't seem like you and your husband are together and me and Howling Woman, that was never going to be anything. She isn't going to be mad."

"Howling Woman is my only friend here. What does that say about me? Fooling around with her ex seconds after she lets me in? I don't know why I am like this." My voice broke and I could feel tears welling up behind my eyes.

"Hey, it's all okay. It's really not that bad."

"Can you just take me home?"

"Seriously, you don't need to beat yourself up over this."

"Please."

"Yeah, okay." He picked my toast up from the ground and walked out of the bedroom. I felt like retching, like smashing my head into the wall, like anything to have a source of pain outside my own mind, but I needed to get out of there, so I found my clothes and met him at his truck where he was waiting in his small driveway, sunglasses on, music too loud to talk.

TWENTY·TWO.

We didn't talk on the drive back to Howling Woman's. When he pulled into the driveway in front of the house, he didn't turn the music down or put the truck in park. He stared ahead, waiting for me to get out. I walked to the front door without looking back. I heard Angel's truck picking up gravel as he pulled out of the driveway and the void in my gut spiraled out farther, catching in my throat.

I opened the front door as quietly as I could so that I wouldn't wake Howling Woman. I didn't want her to see me sneaking in like that. I didn't want to have to explain myself and watch her face distort in front of me, taking in this real version of me, the one that would sleep with her ex. It wasn't just that I wanted her to approve of me. I wanted to be her friend. I'd never had that before. I'd been given a taste of a future where I had a woman to talk to, the kind of woman who would call me in the clutch, who I could cry into my wine with, and never feel like we needed a man as much as we needed each other. I didn't know how to be that person.

As a child, my favorite movie was *Beaches*. I watched it over and over again, imagining myself interchangeably as Bette Midler or Barbara Hershey. I liked to fantasize about a spunky red-headed girl appearing out from under the boardwalk to change my life. I loved the way they met one summer, and felt a connection instantly, without real explanation other than that they both felt the outsiderness of adolescent girlhood and offered each other a symbol of some alternate life, writing to each other as pen pals from their very different worlds, forming a lifelong friendship. But that movie always made me cry at the end. Barbara Hershey dies, and before that, Bette Midler is a struggling musician who is wildly jealous of Hershey. She marries a man that will always be in love with Hershey as if to become lovable by proxy. Hershey admits to being jealous of Midler's career. Throughout the film, the two women take turns cutting the other one down while yearning to connect. At one point, a blowup fight ensues. It appears their friendship is over. The whole movie, presumably about female friendship, but ultimately about the debilitating envy among women, was my ideal model of female friendship. Still, there was something beautiful about the ending, the two women brought together by a fatal illness, free of men, holding hands on the beach as Hershey awaits death. I wanted the messy passion of that kind of friendship, but I didn't know how to have it.

I made my way to the cupboard and opened it as quietly as I could. I pulled down a plastic pint cup and then filled it to the brim with wine from the box in the fridge. I took a gulp. The cold liquid stung my teeth, and the tannic, sweet wine reassured me that soon I'd feel a lot less hollow.

I tip-toed back across the living room and prayed that my steps were quiet enough that Howling Woman wouldn't wake to catch me sneaking a full glass of wine to my room first thing in the morning.

By the time I made it to my room, my head felt lighter, and the sharp edge of loneliness dulled into a manageable throb. The day loomed heavy in front of me as I sat on my bed. It was only the beginning and already I was anxious for night to come so I could fall into a deep sleep until it was tomorrow. The day was already tainted from having woken up at Angel's. Part of me wished I hadn't left, that I could have submitted to his kindness and stayed, staring at him through the soft light of his bedroom window, feeling him reach for my bare skin beneath the sheets. The logical side of me, the one that was trying to formulate some kind of female friendship which was wholly foreign to me, understood that what I had done was wrong. I needed to sleep, to have a physical reset via the hands of time. I took another gulp from my plastic cup, my head heavy in that way that makes the world before you blur.

When I awoke, it was dark, and I had that feeling of deep tiredness that comes from having slept too much. My skin had a film of sweat and the sheets clung and tangled around my limbs. I stretched my arms above my head and walked to the kitchen with my plastic cup. I filled it halfway with tepid water and chugged it down in one gulp. I felt dehydrated, my arms and legs leaden with sleep and booze, my mouth a desert. I could see the moon full and bright in the sky through the small kitchen window above the sink. The clock on the stove read eight p.m., which meant the sun had been down for nearly an hour and I had slept for more than twelve hours. I sighed, relieved that it was now an appropriate time to drink again. I reached for the fridge handle, but my hand stopped before I could pull it open. Maybe I should try and go one night without drinking, I thought. I couldn't remember the last time I had tried to.

Now, it's been over thirty days since I've quit drinking. It's not by choice. There are lawyers, and Dr. Camille, and piss samples, and meetings involved. There are forms of paper that have to be signed, and I am smoking around the clock, staring out into the desert sky, drinking water and wishing it was wine. I am walking miles in the morning and at sunset, my legs restless and my body unable to sit still with the chaos of my unknown future tornadoing inside my mind. I am writing these pages to escape the present moment, looking up every few minutes at the fridge and wishing there was something in it I could have that would make existence easier.

That is what I was doing then, too, looking for a way, the quickest way, to ease the discomfort of life. Despite feeling somewhat better in those early weeks in Yu, my body existed in a perpetual state of unease. A constant heavy pain settled in my joints, my stomach in knots from the alcohol and anxiety that arose in the moments I waited for it to meet my lips. My esophagus regularly felt coated in an acrid bile, still, I reached for a drink.

No, there was no point in drinking tonight, I remembered thinking as I hovered near the fridge. I was probably going to get back in bed soon anyway, but then I thought of how hard it would be to sleep without a drink after already having slept all day. My body would toss and turn in restless discomfort. My heart would likely beat in my throat, and I'd sweat until the entire bed was soaked. Shit. How had I let it get to this point? How long had I been this bad? I had so many half-formed memories of nights waking up beside David, his arms wrapped around me, the panic at having been thrust into consciousness in the middle of the night, my body slipping out from under him, trying to be quiet as I walked to our kitchen and opened the drawer of the oven, pulling out the bottle of whiskey I kept tucked behind the cookie sheets, taking a large sip with the drawer still open, the cap in my hand, waiting for it to soothe me back to a state of being tired enough to sleep. Sometimes I did this all throughout the night, waking up unsure of whether I'd slept at all, unsure as to whether I was even slightly sober.

I clutched the handle of the fridge door and pulled it open. The box of wine glowed in the halo of fridge light. Fucking church bells might as well have gone off as I opened the door for how beautiful the image was to me. I shook my head, quieting the church bells, and slammed the door of the fridge shut.

A shower. That's what I needed. A distraction. A moment to wipe away the grime that always seemed to cling to me. I set my cup down on the counter and turned away from the fridge. I took a deep breath hoping to exhale the urge to turn back around and pour myself a glass of wine.

In the bathroom, Howling Woman had left a note on one of her cactus post-its. *If you get your bag of bones out of that bed, come down to The Whiptail. I'm Lita tonight.* I pulled the note off the mirror and ran my fingers over the ridges of her loopy writing. I felt close to her, touching the words that she'd left for me, and I wondered if she didn't know about the night before, if I was still good in her eyes. I could go to The Whiptail, get out of the house, be around people, feel less isolated. The previous night, going looking for Angel, had been the first night I'd gone that wasn't for a shift. I'd eased into being a daytime drinker, which meant my time at the bar mostly took place after my shifts ended. A round or two and then I would head to the house and finish my drinking with Howling Woman on the back porch. If I left for The Whiptail, it would defeat the purpose of not drinking the wine. Or I could be one of those people that goes to bars and only drinks club soda. What was the reason for not drinking the wine again? Trying to clear my head? Trying to create distance between me and the reaper? Something like that, but the initial decision was feeling weak with Howling Woman's note in my hand. I took a step toward the bathroom door and stopped at the threshold. No. I didn't need wine to take a shower. I turned toward the shower and turned the hot water on. I stripped my clothes off and stepped one foot into the shower. Fuck it. A shower was always better with a glass of wine. Besides, I was heading to a bar soon anyway. Why wait to start what was inevitable? I stepped out of the shower and water droplets fell from my ankle to the tile floor as I walked across the house to the fridge and filled my plastic cup. Halfway this time.

Consider this an anecdote for what comes next—proof of what I've been saying this whole time. You can't change where you come from or where you're going. Maybe you can take a detour, make yourself believe you might evade the past merging with the future, but I was born and raised in a house full of booze and violence. No matter the measures I'd taken to ensure that my history didn't become my future, the fact was, I wouldn't ever escape. Maybe that's what I'll tell my lawyer the next time he suggests it's best we keep quiet—there isn't any point. You can't escape destiny.

TWENTY·THREE.

The Whiptail was packed by the time I arrived, but most everyone was standing around the stage waiting for the show to begin, so I found a barstool next to an older guy I'd seen before but never talked to. He had leathery skin and swollen hands and didn't acknowledge my existence when I sat down beside him.

"I'm sweating my balls off back here by myself," Nick said when he saw me sitting at the bar. He set two shot glasses down in front of me and filled them to the brim with well whiskey.

"You need me to help out?" I asked, wanting him to say *no*, but also feeling like it might be a welcome barrier for coexisting with others.

"No, no. It'll die down when Howling Woman comes on. We just had a fucking bridal party walk in before you got here, and those broads are a fucking handful." He lifted his glass to mine and we both threw back our shots in one go. I thought it was strange that The Whiptail, in this tiny town I'd never heard of before, was sometimes a destination spot for people who lived on unincorporated land surrounding it or in the next town over, which was even smaller. Maybe it was the live music and Nick's glowing personality that got the out-of-towners coming in.

Nick cleared the empty shot glasses and opened a Budweiser for me before walking to the other side of the bar where six women with penis necklaces immediately started asking for *Sex on the Beaches* and *Blow Jobs*. Nick reached into the well and pulled out three bottles and put them on the bar in front of him.

"I got Jack, José, and Captain Morgan. These three gentlemen will let you blow 'em on any beach you like, ladies."

The women all made gestures of shock and booed at Nick, but they ended up ordering a round of tequila shots with extra lime nonetheless.

I peeled at the label of my bottle and scanned the room. I could feel my heart fluttering in my chest at the prospect of meeting Angel's gaze in this room full of strangers. Maybe he'd been right. It was only sex. I'd proven I could go without it for nearly a month, and wasn't that all I'd been trying to do in the first place? Did I actually need to be celibate forever? I took a swig of my beer and tried to swallow down these thoughts. It was not a good idea. What about Howling Woman? What about being the type of woman that didn't need a man's touch to feel whole? And then an image. Angel across the bar, how he might nod his head toward the stockroom door for me to follow him in. How I'd put a napkin over the opening of my beer and slip into the stockroom behind Angel. My stomach felt like fire as I thought of him running his hands up my dress and pressing them onto my belly before inching them below the band of my underwear, his breath hot in my ear as I gasped once his thick fingers found their way inside of me.

A steely guitar interrupted my fantasy of Angel in the stockroom. I looked over at the stage. It was shadowed in blackness. A fog machine filled the dance floor so that it looked as though we'd all been commandeered by an eighties music video. A single spotlight came to life and cut through the haze, landing on Howling Woman in black tights and a low-cut studded leather top. Her silvery blonde hair was teased up big and fell like an electrocuted mane around her breasts. She was beautiful. Or rather, some other mystical word that couldn't be defined by beauty.

People in front of the stage began cheering, and one of the women wearing a penis necklace whistled. Howling Woman was strumming heavy notes into an electric guitar. On stage, she was almost unrecognizable to the woman I lived with. Her eyes were rimmed black, her body adorned with leather and spandex, her face pained with every word she sang into the microphone she clutched in her hand. As the rhythm of the song picked up, the bar felt as though it was throbbing, and people cheered, drunk and in love with the woman in leather on stage.

By the time she was on her fifth song, I'd finished my beer and Nick was pouring us another round of shots.

"Funny that this is always the best show."

"Yeah, I don't even know who Lita Ford is."

"I think that's the point. People think we have a real live celebrity in here when Lita comes out."

"She's like a queen up there."

"Yeah, queen of The Whiptail."

"To the queen." We clinked our glasses together before shooting our whiskey.

The song ended and the stage got dark again. I thought it was too early for the set to be over, and I scanned the room to see if Angel had shown up while I'd been engrossed in Howling Woman's performance. My eyes slowed on a tall man in a denim vest, but he was a pudgy white guy with a tattooed octopus wrapped around his bicep. The crowd around the stage began to hoot, and I saw Howling Woman had returned to her place beneath the spotlight. She was in a new outfit—torn up Levi's, the same leather top, and a bomber jacket. The fog machine worked overtime and Howling Woman's features looked ethereal beneath the soft light. When she sang into the microphone it sounded as though she was whispering to a lover.

Another spotlight appeared across the stage and revealed a man in all black. He had a microphone in his hand and his face was obscured by his teased black hair and the fog. His voice came over the speakers, as if crying out in pain, and Howling Woman's guitar was an electric buzz. I realized that the man on stage was supposed to be Ozzy Osbourne. The man lifted his face to the audience. I knew this man. Or, rather, I recognized this man. It was Angel. His usual long ponytail had been released and crimped out like Ozzy's. He had thick black eyeliner rimming his eyes, and he looked desperate and hungry as he neared Lita on stage.

The crowd went crazy—screaming and cheering. Some people lit lighters and waved them overhead. I felt the whiskey do a flip in my gut and reached for my shot glass. There was nothing in it, so I lifted it toward Nick to gesture that I needed another. Angel reached his hands out to Lita in prayer, but she turned her back on him and continued swaying. He pressed his back into hers and cried into the microphone. Watching the two of them up there together, their bodies finding one another in such an organic way, made me feel sick. Nick took the shot glass from my hand and set it back down on the bar before filling it to the brim.

"Our boy can sing, can't he?"

I didn't say anything. I just reached for my shot.

"They look good up there together, huh?" He shook his head and laughed to himself, "That fucking guy broods behind this bar all damn night, playing introvert, but then he gets up there and it's like he's a different person. My fuckin' guy."

I slammed my shot and turned back to the stage. Angel wailed into his microphone and Howling Woman whispered a sultry chorus into hers and the guitar screamed into the darkness of the bar.

I was enchanted by the two of them on stage. I felt a yearning unlike anything I'd felt before, like I needed Angel—or was it Howling Woman—a desire maybe to be Angel, to be on stage with Howling Woman, to have once been loved or at least desired by her. Or maybe it was the other way around. My thoughts felt all liquid with whiskey, and I couldn't sort one out from the other. My stomach sloshed as though I would puke, the sight of their backs touching, grinding against one another, made me feel as though Howling Woman had been unfaithful to me. As though they both had. As though either of them owed me something. I wasn't sure which of the two was responsible for what was happening in my body.

It was Howling Woman. Intimate and natural beside Angel. A relationship I had barely known about. A part of her, like so many parts, I didn't know. My chest was burning as the music went on and my hands began to shake. Why had she invited me here? Did she know I'd been with Angel? Was this some sort of sick power play? The truth is, no matter what sort of guttural pull I felt toward her, or toward Angel, I didn't truly know either of them. Not like they knew each other, not like half the people in The Whiptail probably knew them. And yet, here I am, writing about them, my life forever changed once they entered it. Maybe time isn't everything when it comes to relationships. Maybe closeness and connection are defined by something less measurable. Maybe, and really, I mean MAYBE, there is something to be said about that fucking vortex—its magnet pulling things out of people and bringing them all to one place, connecting them through something unseen. That's more powerful than time—nature holding you down, ripping you open, and releasing what you try to keep hidden.

I left my barstool before the song finished and went out front to have a cigarette. The night air was colder than I'd expected, and I rubbed my shoulders with my hands to warm myself up. I could hear the song had ended and that Howling Woman was thanking the audience. The show was over. My stomach did another flip at the prospect of seeing Angel. Of seeing Howling Woman. I lit my cigarette and the rush of smoke and nicotine mixing with all that I'd drank made me lightheaded. My vision was blurry, and I could feel bile lining my throat. I shifted beneath the neon lights of The Whiptail and felt unsteady on my own feet. I was drunk. Or, I wasn't sober. I could probably still form a complete sentence if I had to. A couple of people filtered out of the bar, but none of them acknowledged me as they walked to the benches on the side of the building and lit their own cigarettes or drunkenly stumbled to the parking lot to drive themselves home in their pickup trucks.

"Nick said I'd find you out here."

"I was about to leave," I said, turning to face Howling Woman. I had to squint to focus on her and my words felt wet in my mouth.

"Yeah, he said you might be." She laughed like I should know what this meant but my brain was too liquid to take hold of any meaning.

"Yup," I said, for lack of any other words, and pinched the cherry of my cigarette out and watched it float into the darkness of the parking lot.

"Come on, Buttercup," she said, her voice low and softer than usual, "Lord knows I don't need to hang around here watching people get any more sloppy drunk than they already are."

I took a step away from her and squinted my eyes again to see her properly. She nodded her head toward the parking lot and breezed past me like it was a done deal. Like it was obvious I was riding home with her and not walking in the dark. Why wouldn't it be? She didn't know about Angel. About the night before. About how I felt seeing them up on the stage together.

TWENTY·FOUR.

Gillian Welch's whiskied voice sang over a twangy banjo and Howling Woman hummed along. I stared out the window as we turned off the main drag of Yu and onto the long dirt road that eventually led to the house. The sky was so dark, the stars barely visible through the blanket of clouds. It felt good knowing that for once the weather matched my mood. I hoped that thunder would soon fill the air, overwhelming the sound of all the things I wanted to say but couldn't form into words.

"I didn't know you and Angel performed together," I said.

"He makes a good Ozzy."

I couldn't tell if she could register the jealous edge in my voice as I spoke. My words were innocuous enough and I thought the looming rage I felt growing inside of me made my words come out steadier and more sober than I'd anticipated. In the dark of the pickup truck, I stared across at her. I was scanning her face for something I might have missed before—lust maybe, a sign that gave something away about her relationship with Angel. I didn't know this woman at all. Not really.

"What?" She turned her gaze away from the road and looked at me.

"Nothing." I bit down on my thumbnail and pulled a sliver away. I could feel her eyes alternating between the road and me. "It's just, I didn't know that you and Angel were so close."

She laughed and shook her head.

"We're not *close*."

I felt my body stiffen at the casual tone of her voice.

"What? You got a thing for Angel suddenly?" she asked, her eyes lingering on me before shifting back to the road in front of us.

"No," I said, "I don't have a *thing* for Angel. Geeze."

"Well good. Lord knows he's been through enough."

"What's that supposed to mean?"

"It don't mean nothing."

"Are you saying you don't think I am good enough for Angel?"

"What the hell has crawled up your ass and turned you rotten?"

"You are so unbearable sometimes. You know that?" I'd never thought this before, but the words came out of my mouth as though the thought had been there all along and I couldn't stop myself. "All your evasive bullshit like you can just walk around the world with your fake name and your hippie-go-lucky personality and everyone will just fucking love you and not think it's weird how you act like you are happy as can be even though you live all alone in the middle of fucking nowhere."

"Sabine, you should probably stop now."

"And the advice. All the fucking advice. I don't need your words of wisdom."

"Oh yeah? Because you're so wise? And aren't you the pot calling the kettle black actin' like it's such a transgression to keep secrets to yourself. What about you? What about this whole life you gone and left?"

"I've told you about my past."

"Horse shit."

We were in the driveway then and she cut the engine, but neither of us moved to get out of the truck.

"Sabine, all I am trying to say is Angel is a good guy, and you seem like you're in a place where you should be focusing on yourself, not looking to some man to come in and fix you."

"Like you tried to fix Angel?"

"You don't know what you're talking about, girl."

"No? You didn't swoop in after his mom died and try to fill that void for him?"

"You're trying to boil something down that can't be reduced to syrup. Why don't you just let it go?"

"But it's true, you had sex with him?" The question came out like an accusation, and I didn't know why I couldn't drop it.

"Since when do you care who I have sex with, Sabine?"

I threw my head back against the window, trying to stop the thoughts that were coming too fast and leaving my mouth before I could make sense of them. A tear rolled down my cheek from the impact.

"Buttercup, what is going on with you? Why you trying to pick a fight with me like I'm your new worst enemy?"

I squeezed my eyes shut and took a breath as if preparing for the impact of fist to gut.

"I have to tell you something," I said, my voice trembling, more tears threatening to escape.

"In the morning." She reached across the front seat of the truck and squeezed my thigh like that could comfort me, like it was her purpose in life to comfort me. I pushed her hand away.

"I had sex with Angel last night," I said, my teeth chattering as I spoke. I don't know what had come over me at that moment, but I felt compelled to be honest with Howling Woman. Or to get a rise out of her. To go and do something that would force me to change everything all over again. To push a person to see what they'd inevitably see in me with enough time—that I was no good. If I am trying to find the inciting incident to this whole thing—my life, the arrest, how I got where I am now—then maybe this is the true beginning. Maybe everything else is exposition. Or maybe this is the climax—the turning point. I can't tell the difference really. Aren't they both essentially foreign forces redirecting a person's path? One minute I was a person whose whole life was the sum of lies by omission, the next I was a person who couldn't keep my mouth shut to save my life. Once you get a taste of how freeing it is to tell the truth, there isn't any going back.

"I don't need to hear it." She put her hand up to stop me from talking and sighed. I drew a breath in, waiting for her to let me have it. "There is more to life than men and sex. I'm not all that interested in those things anymore. Me and Angel, that's history."

"How can you be so calm about everything? So nice?"

"You expect me to be mad at you when you're mad at yourself enough for the both of us? You don't think I ever slept with someone I didn't have any business sleeping with? You think I'm not a grown woman who can handle two people I care about sleeping with each other?"

"Jesus, can't you see I'm no good?"

"I don't believe that."

"I am. I don't know how anyone could ever love me. I am the fucking worst." I threw my head back in frustration and it slammed hard against the glass again. The pain swelled inside my head and ears. And then something wild inside of me came out. My mouth was open and I heard a noise like a death scream and it was my voice making the noise. Only, it wasn't me. It was some evil thing inside of me that I'd always known existed. It had been there since the time I'd kept my lips sealed about James Dixon finding me in my room at night like only someone with evil inside them can let a thing like that happen. It stayed inside of me and grew. It was the thing that allowed me to kill the baby that had been inside of me. The thing that allowed me to sleep with a man that wasn't my husband. It was making itself known to the world in my death scream—releasing itself into the pickup truck that was too confined to contain such a thing.

My vision rippled and I realized I was crying. My body convulsed like a thing possessed. Howling Woman climbed out of her pickup truck. I didn't care that I was ruining my living situation by screaming into the darkness. I felt a wet breeze slap across my body, hands wrapped around my waist, and then, so much warmth and softness. It was Howling Woman. She had pulled me from the passenger seat and wrapped herself around me. I sobbed into her shoulder and snot dripped down my lips. She petted my head and finally the throbbing in my temples slowed and a pinprick burst the bubble inside my skull.

"Come inside, Buttercup." I felt her hand wrap around mine, and she guided me into the house to my bed and laid me down on top of the covers.

A couple minutes later and Howling Woman was back in front me, holding a cup of coffee out to me. I took it in my hands and stared into it. She sat on the edge of my bed, no longer in leather and torn up jeans. She had on a pair of linen pants and an indigo dyed hoodie with an evil eye printed across the chest. Her hair was pulled back in a floppy bun. She looked like she could be my mother's age. No older than fifty-five. It struck me at that moment that in some ways I had always seen her as somehow ageless, but up close, really looking at her, she had a whole lifetime on me.

"You know, things will get better." She smiled and reached her hand to my thigh, "You need to give yourself time to heal."

"But how?"

"Patience."

"That's not what I mean. Like how. What do you do in time?"

"It's not the same for everyone. I wish I could give you a recipe, but it don't work like that."

I nodded and took a sip of my coffee. It was thick and sweet and coated my tongue with its sugary film.

"What if I can't?"

"Course you can. No one is too broken for la Chupadera." She pointed her index finger up toward the ceiling and swirled it around signaling the vortex.

"You know I don't actually believe that shit, right?"

"You lie."

"No."

"I see you." She stared at me until my eyes met hers. "Always asking about the vortex, looking at that damn mountain like it's a puzzle you can solve. You can't fool me."

"I get everything all messed up with men. I got a husband, and a boyfriend, well, I don't think he's my boyfriend anymore. I mean. Well. I don't know. And then Angel…" I said his name like a whisper, like she might change her mind and be angry and unforgiving like I felt she should be about what had happened.

"Maybe you should try to take a break from all that."

"Do you feel like the vortex has healed you yet?"

"I think healing is a whole life process."

I rested my head on her shoulder and breathed in the palo santo scent of her, "You know, you never finished telling me about how you got your name."

"Sure I did. It was from that night with Bison."

"Yeah, but you didn't tell me what happened."

"Where'd I leave off?"

"Something about him being a creep."

"That's right, though creep hardly does justice to what he is. The details don't matter so much, but you know how the story goes, I was young and a woman and alone. He thought he could take advantage of me and go on and get away with it. Course, I don't think that's any fair."

I waited for her to keep going, but she just petted my head.

"I don't get it."

"What do you mean?"

"How did you get your name? That still doesn't answer my question."

She laughed, and my head bobbed up and down on her chest.

"Well, when I got back at him, he went all hysterical, screaming and crying and such, and in the middle of all his nonsensical yells, I hear him say, *you howling fucking woman, you howling fucking bitch.* I kind of liked the sound of it, so I howled in his face until he looked like he just about seen the dead rise."

I lifted my head off her chest and saw her sitting back in the bed smiling.

"So you got your name from a man?"

"I never thought of it like that, but yeah, I guess so."

"I never would have guessed. Can I ask you something else? Something kinda stupid?"

"Go on."

"Do you think it is possible to escape your history?" I asked.

"Probably not." She petted my hair again and I felt like I wanted to tell her everything. Like somehow she would be able to fix it all. I didn't understand why after all those years the memory of James Dixon had wormed its way into my consciousness like something I couldn't bury. It had been so long ago. A stronger mind than mine would be able to quiet it. Nothing I'd done in all these years had separated me from those nights in my bedroom beneath him. They were always there. In everything I did, even when it wasn't him directly I was thinking of. Nothing could erase him. It didn't seem possible that saying it out loud, releasing it into the world that wasn't just my private space, could somehow be the thing that quieted it. But I'd tried everything else. Running. Marrying someone who'd never fit into my past. Fucking a man I didn't and couldn't love. Running again. And, of course, the drinking. I'd tried everything else. So, why not this? If she could still love me after Angel, if her face hadn't distorted with the knowledge of what I'd done, maybe it wouldn't change if I told her all the parts of me that no longer felt like something I could carry alone.

"Can I tell you something, Howling Woman?"

"Sure, Buttercup."

"You know what you told me last night," I lifted my head off her shoulder and met her eyes, "about your sister Phoebe." Her face twitched below her eyes like she'd been pierced in the back by something sharp.

"Sure."

"I had a stepfather like that." I paused, waiting for her to ask a question or for myself to chicken out, but we just sat there staring at each other. "It was way different obviously. I mean, I am still alive and I never, you know, got pregnant or anything. Fuck, I don't know what I'm trying to say. I guess, you were right."

"Yeah?"

"About the nightmares and the look and all that. I know a thing or two about a bad man. I thought moving to California and marrying David would make the memory of him go away. Like the love of a good man could cover up the hurt from a bad man. It all sounds kind of stupid saying it out loud."

"Hey now, nothing stupid about it. That's how they want you to feel, full of self-doubt. That's what allows them to grow bigger than they actually are. It's what keeps women small. Keeps us quiet. Keeps bad men safe. We do all kinds of crazy things trying to recover from the ways men hurt us—worst of all is blaming ourselves. Tell me more about this stepfather," she said, and so I did, because she asked, because once you break the seal on something, you can't keep it in, because I was sick of trying to make myself small.

TWENTY·FIVE.

I keep thinking I should have read Chekhov. Enough professors quoted the guy that you'd think they would have assigned even one story of his, but no, I had to learn about him through hearsay, his message never settling in the way it does when you learn a thing firsthand. I'm thinking if I'd read Chekhov then I would have done something different about the gun in Howling Woman's truck.

It was the gun in the glove compartment that I should have paid more attention to. Before the gun, I'd been waiting and expecting things to hit rock bottom. To end. To halt me in all my crazy and force me to get my shit together. It hadn't happened yet. No matter how bad things had gotten, I kept moving forward. Life kept happening.

Then, there was the gun. I'd never seen it before. I definitely hadn't seen her put it there, but there it was, bobbing above my knees as we drove down I-25. The only thing separating it from my flesh was a thin piece of plastic and a flimsy latch. I didn't know anything about guns, but it was black and looked like it would fit nicely in her palm.

It had been less than twenty-four hours since I'd cried into Howling Woman's arms, and there I was thinking too much had happened too quickly. It wasn't just the gun and acquiescing to Howling Woman's suggestion we make a little road trip down to my hometown. It was my whole goddamned life. Nearly thirty years of being alive and I'd finally leaned into who I was. Named a part of me I'd tried to pretend didn't exist. Said it out loud. It was like I had uncaged an animal, exposed it to the light, and it wasn't going back into darkness anytime soon.

But I'm getting ahead of myself.

TWENTY·SIX.

It was late the next day when I woke up. Nearly two o'clock and I woke with the strange feeling of newness weighed down by the heavy feeling that comes with crying yourself to sleep. With admitting secrets you'd long kept to yourself. The world looked like a different kind of place. In lots of ways, it was. Howling Woman's house was still so new to me. The life I'd fallen so seamlessly into there—serving drinks at The Whiptail, pretending I hadn't ever been anyone else, but also, naming a part of me I'd never spoken aloud before—made the world look different, like a filter on a photograph that softens the edges and adds a halo of light to everything, rendering the photograph more beautiful, less real than the original.

A hazy light shone through the sheer fabric of the living room curtains and cast itself on the succulents reaching up from their cans and cut-up milk cartons. A path of light across the clay tile floors led directly from the living room to the kitchen, and I could see Howling Woman sitting at the kitchen counter looking at something on her phone.

"Hey," I said, walking into the kitchen.

"Glad you got some rest." She set her phone down on the counter and looked up at me. She was dressed like she planned on going out of the house—light-washed Levi's and a sleeveless burnt-orange button down tucked into the high-waist of her jeans. Her hair was in a long, low braid and you would never have known from looking at her that she'd been up most the night, or that she had put a wild, crying woman to bed.

"Thanks for everything last night. I don't know why now of all times…" I started to say, but then realized I didn't know how to put it into words, especially in the light of day. Maybe saying it once had been enough. "I don't want this to come out weird or anything, but I don't know what I'd do without you."

She took my hand in hers and kissed my knuckles. Her lips were warm and soft on my flesh. It felt like her mouth had penetrated beneath my skin and muscles and bones, right to my nerves. She dropped my hand and brought the coffee to her mouth. The sudden absence of her lips on my knuckles was like my skin being removed.

"And about Angel. . ."

"Nope, I don't want to hear it. That's between the two of you."

"I just want to say I'm sorry."

"No sorries in this house, remember?"

I nodded.

"That's the past, but today is still ahead of us. Go on and get dressed. I want to take you somewhere."

"Where?"

Howling Woman took a deep breath in like she was readying herself to give me some bad news. Shit. This wasn't going to be something good. I imagined us getting in the car and heading west, her returning me to my estranged husband. Had she gotten hold of my mother? David? I'd left my phone to die on my dresser after the call from David. I hadn't wanted to be tempted to reach out to Avery again or answer a surprise call from my husband. Had it still been there when I walked out this morning? It wouldn't have been hard for her to figure out where they were. All she would have to do is charge it and look at my messages. There couldn't be any way she was planning a trip back to California to see David or Avery or the ocean or whatever in some kind of healing journey to closure. I didn't even know if Howling Woman believed in closure.

"I don't want you to freak out when I tell you this."

"Fuck."

"But trust me. Do you trust me?"

"I think so," I said, but I knew I did, even if I couldn't explain why.

"This is something you *have* to do. I've been in your shoes before, you know I have, and I know there is only one real way to get past the types of things you been through."

I stared across the kitchen at her, waiting for her to tell me the answers to overcome something as elusive as violence.

"We are going to Las Cruces."

"No fucking way."

She placed her hands down on the counter in front of her and interlaced her fingers. "You trust me, right?"

"I said I was sorry about Angel. What can I do to make it up to you?"

"This doesn't have anything to do with him. This is about you."

"You're scaring me a little. Why Cruces?"

She stared back at me, her gaze steady. "James Dixon lives there."

I put my hands on the counter to steady myself. "What the hell," I said, my voice low and trembling, "are you talking about, Howling Woman?"

"This is necessary, Sabine."

"How?"

She leaned over her coffee and narrowed her eyes on me, waiting for an explanation.

"How?" I said again, "How did you find him?"

"The internet."

"No." My voice came out loud and clipped. My heart did quickened half-beats in my chest. I'd looked James Dixon up plenty of times throughout the years. Usually when I was drunk and couldn't block his memory from my mind as though seeing him appear in my internet browser could quiet the space he took up in the night. There were so many James Dixons. There was a nature photographer with the same name. Twenty-five plus professionals on LinkedIn. An amateur porn actor. A grip of obituaries. I'd read every one of them a couple years ago, half hoping his face would pop up in one of them, half hoping it wouldn't. I never found him. An article had stood out to me once, though. A domestic dispute that occurred in a rideshare vehicle. There are rarely ever articles published about domestic violence, and as far as I had been able to tell, this one had only made the news because it was part of a larger story about the dangers gig workers face in the field. The passengers had been an unnamed woman and a James Dixon. The man hadn't actually been arrested, but there were no pictures, so it was hard to know, without some serious digging, if the man had been the same James Dixon I'd known. Where had that article been from? I remembered it was somewhere in the Southwest. That was one of the reasons it had stood out to me. Not Las Cruces, that much I was sure of. Could it be possible that he had been there, exactly where my mother still was, all this time? Wouldn't she have known? If she did, I didn't understand how she could have stayed in that town for so long with her abuser, my abuser, less than twenty minutes away by car. It didn't make sense.

"Yes," she said, "that son of a bitch is only a few hours away from here, Sabine."

"I need a cigarette."

I walked over to the table by the back door and grabbed my pack and a lighter. Outside, there was a small window of light cutting through the gray sky. La

Chupadera was a deeper shade of blue from the rain the night before and it looked like another thunderstorm might be brewing. The chickens ran up to greet me, but I shooed them away and sat down on the porch steps. I was dizzy and winded from what Howling Woman was proposing. The wooden step beneath me made my ass wet when I sat, but I didn't care. I lit a cigarette and took a long drag. The patio creaked as Howling Woman stepped beside me and sat down.

"There are some things a person has to do. This is one of them."

"How do you know it's him?"

"Timelines, he works with cars like you said…" and then she produced her phone with a small picture of a blonde man. It was hard to tell because the photograph was so tiny and pixelated, but the blonde hair, the sideways smile, the fact that he was a mechanic—it all added up enough to make my stomach slosh into my esophagus.

"No," I said again, not sure what else to say.

"No, what?"

"No to everything. Whatever it is you have in mind, just no. Forget it."

"So, what. You want to go on like you've been going on?"

"What's the alternative? Some sick road trip where we go confront a man who I haven't seen in nearly twenty years?"

"You have a better plan?"

"Do I need to have a plan? This sounds a little crazy, Howling Woman."

"You just gonna keep goin' on like you've been doing then? Tell me," she slapped the wooden step between us, "how's that been working for you?"

"What do you want me to do? Throw acid on his face?"

She laughed and shook her head. "Someone ought to put the fear of god into that man."

"What does that even mean?"

"It ain't right."

"And what do you suppose seeing him will do?"

"A lot more than you think."

"So what, you want to like kill him? Put signs all over his front lawn warning the neighbors about how bad he is? What?"

"You'll know what to do when you get there. Trust me," she said again, her eyes locking on mine.

"This is fucking crazy."

"No," she said, raising her voice loud like I've never heard, "what is *fucking crazy* is men thinking they got some right to hurt little girls. Enough is enough."

"Hurting him isn't going to change what happened."

"Course it ain't, Sabine. You don't think I know that? Men like that, they don't change. If he's done it once, he's done it a hundred times."

"Do you believe that?"

"Honey, I know it."

"I don't want to see him."

"I'm not asking you to."

"What are you asking then? What's the point of going?" I took a drag of my cigarette and closed my eyes. I thought of my mother, how she was always saying that quote from the Dolores Clairborne film, "Sometimes, being a bitch is all a woman has to hold onto." Was there some truth to it? Isn't being a bitch a form of action? If so, it's more than I'd done up until that point, just willing my memory to dissolve, passive in the act of erasure.

Howling Woman took a breath in, and as she exhaled, her body looked deflated. "All I want is for you to see where he lives. To get a sense of the world with him still in it. He won't disappear simply because you will his memory away."

"I know that."

"Do you?"

I bent my head between my knees and tried to make sense of this. I didn't know how I had gotten to this point in my life. It was hard to believe that the trajectory of my life could all be tied to a single person, to a single period of my life, but if not that, then what? I didn't want to prescribe to a tired trauma narrative of everything being a result of what happened to me as a child, but so many things came back to it. Maybe Howling Woman was right, that if I just saw him, as an adult and not as a helpless child in the dark as he entered my bedroom, maybe then I could reroute my life. I could be in a state of action. I could escape the victim narrative I so vehemently despised. I could do something about it. I could hold onto being a bitch. I could start over.

"Okay," I said, my head still hanging between my knees. I felt Howling Woman's warm palm on my back. It moved in big circular motions like it was activating my heart from the outside in.

TWENTY·SEVEN.

We'd been on the road for a little over an hour when we pulled off the freeway and into the lot of an Eagle Qwik Mart. We needed gas and Howling Woman said a little wine would calm my nerves. My knee bumped into the glove compartment as I leaned over to roll the window down and the latch let it open. That's when I saw it. The gun. I didn't know much about guns, but I knew it was a revolver. I knew it was the kind of gun that was made to fit in the palm of your hand like a missing limb. I slammed the glove compartment shut and pressed my back into the passenger seat creating as much distance from myself and the gun as possible. I didn't want to overreact, for all I knew, the gun could have always been there. I'd never had a reason to open it up and check before, but it didn't change the fact that the air seemed to be sucked from in front of me and my sight narrowed into a spiraling tunnel vision on the closed glove compartment. As much as I was beginning to feel close to Howling Woman, I didn't really know her or what she was capable of or even really why she cared so much about this. About righting this part of my life.

"You look like you seen a ghost," Howling Woman said, pulling open the cab door with two four-packs of mini plastic wine bottles and a thin plastic bag full of corn nuts and airplane size bottles of whiskey. I jumped and looked away from the glove compartment. "You alright?"

"Sure, yeah. I just zoned out for a minute." I reached for one of the small wine bottles and twisted the cap off. I chugged it down in one gulp right from the bottle. The placebo effect hit me instantly and the world took on that gentle blur that made it less dangerous to move through.

"Easy now, these are to calm your nerves, not knock you out."

"Are you sure this is the right thing to do? I mean…" I started to say I think I changed my mind, but she cut me off as she plopped into the driver's seat.

"Sure as scripture on Sunday."

We pulled back onto the road, and dust danced outside the pickup truck and the vast desert sky was heavy with purple clouds like a summer thunderstorm was on its way in. My heart beat heavy and strong in my chest. I could feel the blood flowing through my veins. There was an energy that came with thinking about the rivers of blood inside you, and I was breathing in deep like I could suck in a new life. This was something I had to do. She'd said it. I could feel the wine mixing in with my blood and I swayed a little in my seat, enjoying the way it felt to submit to that chemical I loved so much. I reached for another wine bottle and unscrewed the cap.

TWENTY·EIGHT.

It seemed like it should have been harder than it was for my life to change. Like there should have been more obstacles. More wrong turns. But it turns out it doesn't take much to flip the world. At least not one's perception of it.

I-25 is two lanes heading south and two lanes heading north, both long, flat, black lines without a hill in sight. A petrol window of heat and gas radiated above the asphalt as we continued south. Vultures circled above in the distance. Whole minutes would go by without seeing another car pass by. I kept sipping from the mouth of the little plastic wine bottle. The music was turned up loud, and we drove with the windows down, our hair blowing in the wind, hands dangling out of the truck to ash our cigarettes.

A little over four hours on the road, and there we were, parked in front of what was allegedly James Dixon's house. It was on the outskirts of town, twenty minutes from my mom, but it was impossible to reconcile how close he'd been all that time. I felt a sharp pain in my heart thinking about it—my mother so close to the man that had tormented her. I wondered if she was afraid, or if she knew, or if she had simply moved on. Momentarily, I wished we were closer to one another, that I didn't cringe every time she opened her mouth, that instead of resenting her, I could be a better daughter. That we could share our pain instead of shutting each other out and experiencing it privately.

By the time Howling Woman and I pulled up, the moon was an opaque orb in the sky, the sun casting its final glow across the pink horizon. I'd drunk four of the small plastic wine bottles during the drive and it was hard to grab hold of a clear thought for what to do next. I kept thinking about what I would say to James when

I saw him, but it was hard to believe that I actually would. It all felt so unbelievable. In the past, I'd sometimes thought about what I'd say to him if we ever saw each other again. Stuff like, *you're pathetic* or *I hope you rot in hell*. When I was a teenager, I'd let my mind wander to long daydreams about running into him outside my high school. In my daydreams, I had more friends than I actually did and we were always crossing the street to go smoke weed in someone's car and laughing the way teenagers do in nineties' teen flick montages. It would be easy to tell him what a piece of shit he was with a loyal group of friends backing the happier, more confident self, I existed as in my imagination. But I hadn't seen James since he'd finally stopped banging on the windows outside my mother's house after she'd left him. I'd heard my mom on the phone once saying he'd been arrested, but I hadn't heard for what—something that didn't keep you in long because she'd been saying she was worried about when he'd get out. When he did, he never came back around, at least not that I knew of.

By the time we'd parked across from the house, it was dark and most of the homes around the cul-de-sac had their porch lights on. I reached for one of the airplane bottles of whiskey. My hands shook as I twisted it open and shot it back. The liquid sent spikes of heat down my throat and into my chest. I shook my head as I dropped the empty back into the plastic bag next to the Corn Nuts we never opened. I reached for another bottle of wine and unscrewed the cap. I waited for Howling Woman to say something before I took a sip and chased the remnants of whiskey, but she just sat with her fingers curled around the wheel.

"That one?" I pointed to a single-story adobe style home that looked like a third of the homes in the neighborhood. It was the kind of pre-planned community with three different tract house models you can choose from and then make upgrades and modifications to, like choosing *Sandstone* instead of *Sand* for the paint job. The front yard was all zero-scape and cacti. The little subdivision was out of place in the miles of pecan orchards and onion fields, but the house looked quaint. Not the house of an abuser. Not the house of a person who got off on hurting little girls. It was a newer sect of housing, built after I'd left. An illusion of rural living in desert middle-class suburbia. It was nicer than anything my own mother had ever lived in.

"Yeah, that's the one."

The thought of my mother in her turquoise home with overgrown weeds and walls that perpetually reeked of mildew from the swamp cooler made my breathing quicken. I was clenching my jaw as I looked at the elegant shell-colored curtains in the front window. No blinds that were bent at the ends and tangled with cord from someone fighting with them to lay flat and even. There was a motorcycle in some state of repair on the driveway beside a white minivan. Nothing about this house indicated that a monster lived inside it. I took a swig from the wine, downing half the bottle, and squeezed my eyes shut.

"I know about the gun," I said.

"Aren't you going to go over there?" She sipped the wine she'd opened when we'd parked.

I looked over at the house and saw a silhouette move on the other side of the curtain.

"You should at least go peek in the window or something."

"I don't want to do this."

"We came all this way."

"I don't know what I was thinking."

"Go and take what's yours."

"What the fuck does that mean?"

"Don't get like that with me right now, Sabine. This ain't about me."

"What do you want me to do?"

"Do what you have to do."

"Seriously, what does that mean?"

"This ain't about me. Your anger, that's about the man in that house and what he's done to you, what he has done to other women, what he could do. No one on this whole goddamn earth is deserving of your anger the way he is."

I took the final chug of my wine and threw the empty bottle onto the truck floor. I flung open the truck door and jumped down. The ground beneath my feet sent a sharp bolt up my stiff legs and I stumbled into the truck's side mirror. I had to squint to see straight. The air was swollen and warm like right before a monsoon. I can't remember if I closed the door as I stepped toward the house. All I remember is it swaying with me as I pushed off it. I didn't have a plan, but I thought maybe once I got closer to the house, if I saw him, it would come to me. I would know what I had to do. If it didn't, then at least I would have come, would have proven that I could face this thing, and maybe that would be enough.

I could smell sautéed onions and garlic as I neared the house. A home-cooked dinner. I heard a woman's laugh from inside. There was a small pink bike with glitter tassels hanging from the handlebars that had been leaned up against the side of the house. My bowels liquified inside of me, an ocean of wine and whiskey, as the world seemed to spin a little too fast. My legs were shaky beneath me as I stepped closer to the house. What was I doing here?

Still, my feet moved. Another step forward. Then another. I walked to the side of the house, lava rocks crunching beneath my feet. The kitchen window was small, and its curtains were drawn. There were three of them inside the house. A short woman with wide-set hips in khaki Bermuda shorts and a beige cardigan, a little girl with two French braids and some sort of tablet in her hands, a stocky man with black trousers and a short-sleeved button-down like a mechanic at a tire shop might wear. His slicked back blonde hair. His round, moon face. From where I stood, I could almost see the hook scar on his upper lip. Could almost smell the yeasty scent exuding from his pores. *Daddy*, I heard the little girl say, and he swooped her up into his arms and kissed her brow. My stomach gurgled at the sound. *Daddy*. I narrowed my eyes, not believing that James Dixon could be the father of a girl who looked to be about ten. When I looked, the image before me changed, it was me in his arms, my mother sitting at the table, looking up at where he held me, petting my hair, nuzzling my neck, me taking it in like a grateful daughter, happy to have a father-figure to love her regardless of what happened after night fell. I felt my body collapse in on itself. The air escaped my lungs. Acrid burn. I retched into the succulents beneath the kitchen window.

Everything is out of focus after that. I remember my vision spinning. A little girl in his arms. A wave of his lactic, tobacco scent filling my nostrils. A memory. It feels like acrylic nails have scooped out the lining of my throat. Bile eats at the enamel of my teeth. That is when I hear the sound of metal on metal.

My head shoots up. A slimy stream sticks to the side of my mouth and chin. Howling Woman is in the driveway with an aluminum bat. She is going at the minivan, and I am springing toward her.

"*What the fuck, Howling Woman? What the Fuck?*"

She swings the bat again, not even caring that I am so close to her.

"*Stop it. Please, stop it. I want to go.*"

A door opens. A child cries.

"*What the Fuck are you crazy cunts doing to my car?*" a man screams. It is James Dixon. He sounds the same as the day I saw him drag my mother's flailing body down the hall past my bedroom. From the window, he'd looked almost like a changed man, like I couldn't be sure it was him. A button-down shirt, a wife, a cup of tea in place of his usual bottleneck. *Crazy cunts*. It was him. He was the same man I'd known.

"*I'd watch your mouth if I were you, you sea-monkey prick,*" Howling Woman screams as she drives the bat across the driver's side mirror, shattering it to pieces.

"*Get off my property you fucking crazy bitches.*" He is older, I can tell now that he is closer, but his voice is the same voice that has been stuck in my mind for nearly twenty years. Finally, as he steps off his porch, I can see his face, clear as day, no longer cobwebbed by time in my mind. His gray eyes, the goldish tint of his five o'clock shadow, that scar, the dimple between his eyebrows. It is all so clear. I am nine years old again, trapped beneath the heavy weight of him and his fingers are lifting the band of my underwear. Adult me is grasping for air and running. My lungs burn as I run away from this man. Tears are streaming down my face.

"*No, no, no.*" I am shaking as I hurl myself across the street. Creak of the truck door swinging open. My ears are ringing. Aluminum bat on minivan. Child crying. James Dixon screaming. I hear someone say they are calling the police. His wife? A neighbor? People are coming onto their porches to see what is happening. Something is growing inside of my brain. It cannot be contained within my skull. My body is so full of pressure I am about to burst. This is the moment I will die. I am sure of it. I feel cold metal in my hand. I am out of the truck again. Desert breeze bites at my ankles as I cross the black asphalt across the street.

A cracking sound fills the air. Everything grows quiet. Finally quiet. All I can hear is breathing. Collective, universal breathing. The whole world has inhaled as I return to the yard with the gun. My arm is outstretched before me. A foreign limb. A hand. A gun whose mouth is open. Facing James. His eyes finally meet mine. I am in shock at the stillness, the steadiness of my own hand. Surely it cannot belong to me.

"*That's right. Look at me you fucking pervert.*" There is that word again, *pervert*, like sherbet on my tongue, sweet and soft and puckering.

"*What the fuck is wrong with you, woman?*" he says, his hands in the air, but I can see a smile behind his serious eyes.

"*I want you to look at me. I want you to say my name. I want you to say you're sorry for what you did to me.*" Spittle is forming at the corners of my mouth. I can hear his daughter crying from inside the house. I think I can hear sirens in the distance.

"*You're fucking crazy.*" His voice is steady, like he knows he should take the gun in my hand seriously but like he doesn't think I have it in me to shoot him. His palms are open in front of him, and I can tell something has shifted. Howling Woman has stopped beating on the car with the bat and he is no longer angry and cursing. Somehow, everyone is staring at me like I am the monster, not him, and it makes my insides roar, but I can't really make out the neighbors who have ventured out of their homes to stand on their porches and gawk. I only have so much time to let them know that it is him who is the monster. Not me.

"*Miss, you are about to be in a lot of trouble. I think you should put the gun down.*" His voice is calm, almost placating, and part of me wants to pull the trigger right then. Watch his brain firework across the night sky. It makes me dizzy with pleasure to imagine.

"*Don't you know who I am, you sick son of a bitch?*" My voice is loud, and it shatters the quiet. "*I want you to tell these people who you are. What kind of man you are.*

Look at me. You fucking know me. You know what you did." I am crying so hard the words come out wet, *"You fucking did this. Don't you see? You ruined me, my whole life, everything I ever could have been. I didn't stand a chance because of you."*

He takes a step toward me, his hands still out in front of him, but he doesn't look scared. *"You must have me mistaken with someone else."* And then he does it. He smiles. He looks like he might even laugh, like he just thinks this is all one big fucking joke. My whole life, everything he ever did to me, all the ways it stayed with me over time, it's all just one big joke to him. I'm just another hysterical bitch in the sitcom of his life. Before that moment, I'd spent a long time trying to believe that a person could escape their history, that it was weak to blame your whole miserable life on shitty circumstances, on a single bad person, but looking at him, smiling his smug smile as I cry on his front lawn, I'm just as powerless to will him to be better than I'd been when I was a little girl. No amount of geography or drinking or fucking or self-improvement would give me power over him. The only way to gain power with a man like that is to take every ounce of power they have away from them. I think that's what Howling Woman had intended me to learn. She knows the rules of civilized society aren't enough to deal with bad men. They were designed by men. It isn't right that he should go on haunting me like a phantom all my life. If he wants to be a fucking ghost, I'll turn him into a ghost. I lose it then. A scream emerges from the hollow of my gut, a wild living thing. I pull the trigger. Again and again and again. He is on the ground. The gun is making a clicking sound and my whole body feels like it is catapulting, and I can't tell if it is the gun or the animal inside of me, but it is the best I have ever felt because there is no me. There is only the feeling of release, like everything I ever looked for every time I had the second or eighth shot of whiskey or all the times I raged my naked body against another's, desperate, always desperate, for a release that felt like this. I am looking at James on the lava rocks in his front yard and I cannot actually see him. Not clearly. It is dark outside except for the glow of streetlights and moon. He is a mass of dark shades, one of which is growing darker and spreading out across the sleeve of his shirt. He is writhing on the ground, a hand clutching over the spreading darkness of his arm. He is panting, groaning, saying what the fuck, *what the fuck.* I think, *it's only your arm.* I am hurling myself toward the ground. I am screaming.

"My name is Sabine Barrett, you piece of shit, and you molested me when I was a child. You are the reason I can't get a goddamned thing right to save my life. I did everything I was supposed to and it didn't matter because you planted one giant fucking evil seed inside me and look what I've become! Look what you turned me into. I'm a monster."

I don't remember the exact words I screamed at him as he was lying there in pain, bleeding onto his yard, but I do recall blaming him for the way my life ended up. If there is something I regret, this is it, giving him that much power over what's become of me. I don't honestly think everything that's happened in my life is because of him. After those weeks with Howling Woman, after all the movies and books I've read, I can't help thinking that if it wasn't him, it would have been someone or something else. Women don't make it through this world without it inflicting pain on them. No one does.

I bend down and slam the gun into his face. I hear bone shatter. I slam it again and another crunch and also a wet smacking sound. Later I will learn it was his nose and the ricochet of it splintered his orbital. When I am shown pictures of him by my lawyer, ones that will be shared with the jury, his face is absolutely foreign to me. It holds no power, looks nothing like the one that haunted my memory. His eyes are nearly swollen shut, large black circles shadow them. There are cuts and bruises across his cheekbone. A small portion of his head is shaved to reveal stitches. "This won't do you any favors," my lawyer said as he spread them out before me.

Then I am upright again, my leg drawing back to kick him, but I am being pulled away before it can power toward him.

"Let's get the hell out of here, Sabine." It is Howling Woman, and she is pulling me away, and James is grunting on the ground. He is not so tough. Even in the dark, through my tears, I can see a long dark streak running down the leg of his pants where he has wet himself.

Neighbors are shouting. James Dixon's wife is shouting. It is all just noise lost to sky as Howling Woman drags me back to the truck. I hear someone say *police*, another person keeps shouting *stop*. We don't stop. We are in the pickup truck, it is roaring to life, we are all animals lost to the momentum of violence, we are hurling ourselves into darkness.

TWENTY·NINE.

So there you have it. My confession. The event in question. I did it. I shot James Dixon. I only regret that I got his arm and not his heart. Shooting a gun looks so much easier in the movies, but this isn't fiction. This is my life. The story of how I shot my stepfather. How I only wish I'd done it sooner. Of course, there are people who will deny some of the events in my story, my mother being one of them. She doesn't want anything to do with this case, with the past that it's dredged up. Admitting she knows what happened to me means admitting she knew about it in the first place, that she didn't do something sooner, that she's culpable. I don't hate her for wishing the past wasn't what it is. I tried to do that too. Still, I won't ever forgive her for this. Her refusal to corroborate my past is why I'm terrified of what's to come. Her refusal to admit the truth makes me out to be a liar. It's why it's not likely any of this story will ever make it off these pages. And it is just a story. It's my story. Certainly someone else would see the events differently. I may have lied before, left certain things out, but I'm telling the truth now. I'm not afraid of it anymore. The only thing I'm afraid of is what happens if I keep it inside me without air any longer. But who's to say I'm telling the truth? There are plenty of people who are saying I'm not. Who's to say this isn't all fiction?

THIRTY.

We didn't make it far before we saw the flashing lights. Then, it was all fragments. Doors flinging open. Calloused hands wrapped around my arms. Starch uniform scratching into my bare shoulder blade. A hand over my cheekbone. The other side of my face scraping against the ground. A crunch of boot in gravel. My skin tearing against gravel. Small grains lodging into the flaps of my tissue. It was already a thing of the past even as it was happening.

It feels fitting that we got arrested in New Mexico—two women righting the wrongs of men, pulled over on an abandoned desert highway is the kind of story that has a place in a certain canon. It's in New Mexico that Thelma and Louise are first pulled over. There's a gun at the start of that story, too. Only eight minutes into the movie Thelma pulls out a gun and asks Louise to take care of it for her. "Good lord, Thelma," Louise proclaims, seemingly in disbelief that her friend would bring a gun on what's supposed to be an innocent weekend away. Everyone knows what happens with the gun, or at least they have a sense about it. Less than twenty minutes into the movie a nice enough looking good 'ol boy type named Harlan is with Thelma in the parking lot of a bar. The two of them were dancing in the bar and he thinks he's due to finish what was started on the dance floor. When she rejects his advances, he slaps her, tells her "I said I'm not gonna hurt ya," slaps her some more, slams her down on her stomach on the hood of a car, tells her to shut the fuck up, calls her a goddamned bitch, pulls down her underwear. Just before he can rape her, Louise comes up behind him, puts the gun to his head, says, "You let her go, you fucking asshole, or I'm gonna splatter your ugly face all over this nice car." He concedes. Lets Thelma go. The whole film could have taken a wildly different turn right there, but as Thelma and Louise walk away, Harlan shouts, "Bitch, I should have gone ahead and fucked her." Louise, as played by a young, striking Susan Sarandon, turns around, mouth agape, and asks him to repeat himself. He smiles, says, "Suck my cock." Louise lifts the gun up and shoots him in the chest. The two women speed away in their Ford Thunderbird convertible. Thelma, played by a sweet-faced Geena Davis, wants to go to the police, tell them what happened, but Louise knows better. She says, "Who's gonna believe that? We don't live in that kind of a world, Thelma."

Thirty minutes before the film ends, Thelma and Louise come face-to-face with the law. It's a New Mexico State Trooper, but it'll be another thirty minutes and a different state before an army of law enforcement finally corners the two women. The last shot of the film is an iconic image of them in the blue Thunderbird, top down, hair blowing in the wind, dirt picking up behind them, as they accelerate toward a cliff, toward their death. They know what world they live in.

Thelma left a note for her husband, too. Am I a cliché or just in conversation with other women in history? There's got to be a reason some women know it's best to leave a note—that there isn't any point in trying to say what you want to a person who wants something different.

And what about my ending? Would you call Thelma and Louise's a happy ending? Are the only options death or prison? It's not like I killed a man. I make for a poor outlaw. I never robbed a convenience store or bank or shot another man because I got a taste for power. Does this mean it'll be different for me? Or does it mean I got caught before a different future unfolded before me? James Dixon wasn't the first man Howling Woman ever sought to bring to justice. Who knows what would have happened if we'd made it back to Yu, or if we'd have just kept on driving into a new destiny.

If there's no hope for my freedom, then maybe writing this is an act of salvation. Isn't that what testimony is? Admitting your wrongs to those that bear witness? But in religion it's about getting closer to god, about finding truth through god. The truth isn't what provides salvation. God does that. But I don't know if I believe in god. I don't know if I think what I did was wrong either. Still, this compulsion to tell my story. To let it exist outside of me. Maybe it's the thought that even just one other person will see me as justified the way I saw Thelma and Louise as justified. Maybe Harlan didn't deserve to die, but I can understand why Louise shot him.

THIRTY·ONE.

After we got pulled over, the world kaleidoscoped before me into fractured forms. Time a shattered object and memory a thing pieced together by jagged, incongruous edges. David's face on the morning I left him appeared haloed in my mind as a light flashed in a concrete building. My eyes squinted and I saw The Whiptail on my first night in Yu, Nick's shaking cheeks as he laughed and poured me a shot. My eyes heavy, the world too much to see, as I moved from one set of arms to the next on my way to a jail cell. Aftershave and limes on someone's skin. Angel's face flickering in candlelight. A space too small and one I wasn't meant to be in. I knew this feeling. The world spun and the room was Avery's attic space in an Oakland Victorian, his graying hair damp with sweat between my fingers. The room spun again, and it wasn't any place I'd ever been. It was a jail cell. I closed my eyes and willed it to be something else when I opened them.

The first conscious thought I remember having upon coming to in jail, was *Why the hell did I have my own cell?* At least thinking back on it now, putting the whole thing into a narrative, that's the thought I remember having. I sat curled in a ball on the thin mattress. The metal beneath cold through the foam and fabric. This isn't how I'd ever imagined being arrested might go from the television I'd seen. Where was the drunk tank? Where was Howling Woman? How much trouble was I in and how royally had I fucked up? I slapped my hands over my eyes and felt a sting across my cheek from where my face had crunched the gravel. Had that really been necessary? Being thrown out of the truck? Or had I fallen from the truck? Where was Howling Woman? This question kept interrupting my thoughts, my consciousness something still liquid with wine and whiskey.

I didn't know how much time had passed, though later I would be able to piece it together despite there being no clock. The cell was upstairs in a cement building that lacked air conditioning. The oppressive heat pressed down into me, and I could feel my lungs flattening in my body. Sweat pooled between my breasts, in the divot of my lower back, in my buttcrack, between my thighs. I could smell my rot and the world became overridden by the sensations of my body. Achy. Swollen. Unstable.

Finally, though it had only been a few hours, I was able to call someone. My mind raced as I sat on the low bench and thought about who could help me. I didn't even know what kind of help I needed. None of the officers had spoken to me since I'd been arrested, not more than directional phrases to move me from one place to another. Howling Woman's face came to mind first. I imagined her anti-quated honey-colored phone that hung from the kitchen. Its long cord that could reach across the entire distance of her small house. I didn't even know the number. Not by heart. It didn't matter. She was somewhere in the building with me. It was a gutting feeling to realize there were so few people I could call. Really, there was no one. And so, I called my mother. An instinctual, almost animal longing for her voice and her touch, which I couldn't ever remember having felt but was sure had existed and been good and comforting at some point in my life, flooded me.

"Bean, is that you?"

"Yeah, mom." My voice trembled as I spoke. I was the most tired I'd ever been, and every part of my body radiated with pain. The sound of her voice made my stomach flip. I waited for the comfort of my mother's voice to reassure me, but my heart was racing, like maybe I should have called someone else.

"What the hell have you gotten yourself into?" It came out a flat, quiet question, and she sounded more sober than I'd heard her in as long as I could remember. It was early, and I'd caught her in the small window of hours that existed before she began drinking.

"It's kind of a long story."

"I bet."

"I don't have time to explain it all on the phone."

"Geeze, what the hell?" I heard her reach for something on her end. Glass clinked. The sound of her breath shifted, and I tried to imagine her drinking coffee as she listened.

"I will explain everything to you when I see you." Even as I said it, I knew it was a lie. I didn't have any intention of telling her about James Dixon. I didn't know if there was a way I could keep it from her, but I wanted to suspend the time between knowing and not knowing for as long as possible. I was banking on the fact that I could rely on her being the mother I'd always known, the one who wouldn't ask questions, who would choose ignorance over an uncomfortable conversation—especially one that might lead us down a corridor toward a history I assumed we'd both made a serious effort to forget.

"You gotta be shittin' me."

"No, I'm serious."

"Well no shit, Bean. I heard the damn operator."

"Can you come?" I closed my eyes and I tried to envision her face. I thought of her rubbing her temples in frustration or clenching her fists the way she did when she was anxious or worried. I wanted to picture her reaching out to hold me, or me taking her clenched hands in mine and comforting her. I thought for a moment that I could tell her exactly what had happened, what I'd done, and that she would feel relief knowing someone had finally stood up to the man who had hurt us. But we had never talked about any of what had happened to us.

"Have you called your husband?"

"No, mom. Why would I call David?" I leaned my head against the cement wall and willed her to just make this easy, to help me without question.

"He is your husband."

"Not anymore."

"That's not how these things work, Sabine."

"Mom, please," I whispered, tears finally breaking free from my eyes at the feeling of her name in my mouth. *Mom.* When was the last time I'd said the word? I didn't know what else to say or how to explain this. I knew I didn't have a lot of time, and the truth was I had no idea what my situation was. It felt bad. I felt like a criminal. Being in jail seemed to validate this. What was going to happen to me? How would I explain this in a way that made it so I wasn't a criminal? I'd been a victim, but not necessarily in that moment. I hated that word. *Victim.* Yet another term to add to the list of words and phrases I hate that are so regularly shared among women. I opened my mouth to say something, but the words felt trapped in my throat as it tightened to hold back the sobs I could feel expanding inside me.

"Mom," I said again, the word a cry, a prayer, a plea, "I need you. Please."

"Okay," she said, her voice clipped. I couldn't tell if she was angry with me or if she felt resigned to the task of dealing with the mistakes of her daughter. Twice in a matter of weeks I had reached out to her for help. That was more than I'd asked her my whole life. Didn't she owe me this? It felt greedy to think this way. To think that anyone, even a parent, is emotionally indebted to anyone else.

"I will get this figured out." I could almost hear her shaking her head at me as she said this.

"Thank you, mom," I said, the last word rattling in my throat, and then it happened, my voice cracked open and the tears flooded my face.

THIRTY·TWO.

I didn't expect to see him standing there when I walked into the lobby of the police station, though I probably should have since it was him who was paying for my lawyer. The lawyer who had called me Mrs. Haegan when he reached out his hand to introduce himself to me before sitting down across from me and listing my charges: assault with a deadly weapon; attempted murder; some other tacked on charges I didn't fully comprehend, and which lost their stature in the shadow of the word murder. "Don't worry, Mrs. Haegan, you'll be home soon," the lawyer said, monotone, sitting upright and organizing a file.

"What about Howling Woman?"

"I think it's best you focus on yourself for the time being."

"Is she okay? Can you find out for me?"

"I'll see what I can do, but you have a long road ahead of you, and I think it best you remain in your lane," he said, before letting the guards know we were all finished talking. I didn't see him again until the arraignment, and even then, it was short. He didn't make time to visit me after bail was set, just nodded his head after the judge's statement, like he was proud of a job well done.

It was only another few hours before I was being walked from my cell and into what I presumed was a temporary freedom.

"Hey," David said, his voice soft as one of the officers removed my handcuffs. There he was. For a moment, I felt that all the time apart was swallowed by the present. His sudden proximity a reminder that I had a husband. He was still my husband. It didn't matter how much geography I'd put between us. He was wearing a short-sleeved pale blue button down with little polka dots embroidered on it, a pair of khaki shorts, and his usual ratty New Balances. His curls had grown into a small poof on his head and gray speckled his dark black curls.

"Sabine," he said, when I crossed the painted red line and metal detector to the side of the free. I bit my lip, my mouth quivering at the sound of my name from my husband's mouth. I didn't want to cry in front of him. He didn't deserve to have to deal with my discomfort on top of everything I'd done to him.

"Come here," he said, outstretching his long arms to me, and I did. I dropped my property bag to the ground and let him take me into his arms. When I left California, I hadn't ever imagined being embraced by him again. I didn't think it was a thing I could want, but he smelled familiar, and his grasp around me was tight, promising a certain safety.

"Where's my mom?"

I felt his chin trembling on top of my head. I pulled away from him, my arms still around his waist as I searched his face. "She didn't come?"

"She had to work."

"What about Howling Woman?"

"Who?"

"I need to find out where she is." I hadn't seen her since the night of our arrest. We'd been put into separate police cruisers. Booked without ever crossing paths. I kept thinking I would see her at some point. In a way, I thought more about her than I did myself, as if fixating on her fate could distract me from thinking about my own. Would she be upset with me for letting things get so out of hand? Proud of me? What would this all mean for the future of our friendship? I fantasized about us living out a sort of Thelma and Louise story only with an ending that didn't include driving toward death. The part of the story where they really did just go on a fishing trip. The story that never was, but which would have been a wholesome depiction of a friendship between women. I wanted that part of the story. I closed my eyes and passed the time picturing it was possible.

"What are you talking about, Sabine?"

"Can you give me a second, please?" I said, taking a step away from him.

He sighed and put his hands up, resigned to wait for me as I walked to the circular desk beside where I'd just been released. A middle-aged man with thinning blonde hair cut close to his scalp was holding his smartphone sideways in his hand and I could hear muffled voices coming from whatever video he was watching. When I approached the desk, he sat up in his seat without looking at me and paused his video. He was broad and muscular, but his stomach had a soft mound as though he'd spent years drinking too much light beer after work.

"Excuse me," I said.

"Yes, ma'am." He looked up from his phone.

"I need to find out about the woman I came here with the other night."

"Ms. Haggerty? Or 'Howling Woman' as she calls herself." He said her name with his fingers making air quotes, like it was a joke, something she'd invented upon our arrest. "Yep, she is here alright. Ain't leaving anytime soon."

"But she didn't do anything. It was me that…"

"Sabine," David interrupted, "I think we should talk outside."

"I want to talk to my friend."

"I don't know how well you know this friend of yours, miss, but this isn't 'Howling Woman's' first run-in with the law." He paused for me to say something, but the words caught on my tongue. "Not everyone has a sorry bastard to come bail them out."

"When is she going to be released?"

"Sweetheart, people with murder charges don't just get released. Not unless they have nice men with deep pockets like yourself." He tilted his head toward the desk as if awaiting a dramatic, aghast response from me.

"Murder? What are you…" I stuttered. I didn't know what to say to that.

I felt a hand on my back and flinched. It was David, and his eyes were narrow, his lips a flat, hard line across his face.

"You about ready to go?" David asked, his voice soft near my face.

"Can I talk to her?"

"You should probably go with the nice man, sweetheart."

"Please."

"Visiting hours are over."

"Sabine, we can come back another time. Let's go."

"Wait a second." I stepped away from David, my voice loud in the quiet room, and the deputy stood from his seat and his fingers moved to his hips and rested near his gun as if this was the action he'd been waiting for.

"Now, ma'am, I am going to have to ask you to leave before we have to charge you with assaulting an officer."

"Sorry, sorry," I said, putting my hands up in front of me in apology, "I am sorry. I am just tired and a little confused."

"Well, then you are gonna have to come back during visiting hours." He pointed to his left at a sign screwed to the wall with visiting hours and all sorts of rules listed. "But honey, I gotta tell you, you're probably better off if you don't."

I felt David's fingers wrap around my hand and I took a step back, closer to him. I nodded in agreement. David released an audible sigh as though he could finally breathe normal now that I had agreed to leave the station. I hadn't noticed how rigid his body had been or how out of place he'd looked in the cement room with the scuffed linoleum and bolted down chairs. As we walked toward the exit, David's fingers loosened around mine and he dropped my hand.

THIRTY·THREE.

Outside the jail, the sun was low in the sky and it was nearly dark. There wasn't much around other than dirt and tumbleweeds. I tried to remember the ride to the station or how far we'd gotten from James Dixon's house, but it was all a blur of headlights and blackout.

"Where are we?"

"Jesus Christ, Sabine."

"Cut me some slack, will you? I just got out of jail."

"That's right. You did just get out of jail, and you have no idea where you are." David walked away from me toward a black Honda Civic. "You know," he said, turning back around to face me, "I don't even know who you are. I'm looking at you and you don't look like my wife. I see this woman in front of me who committed a violent crime and is lucky to be out on bail and hasn't even said thank you. All I can think is *This is not my wife. This is not the woman I married.*"

"Actually it is."

"No, you're different."

"I didn't ask you to come get me, you know."

"Well who else was going to come for you?" He turned back toward the car and opened the driver's side door.

"That's fucking low, David."

"Don't talk to me about low, Sabine. Just get in the car."

I did as I was told, not wanting to cause a scene the officer could see, and David walked around to the driver's side door. He got in and turned the keys in the ignition. I knew I should shut my mouth, be apologetic and gracious for how he was helping me, but there was a rage still roiling inside me and he was the only one I could point it towards.

"Where are we going?" I asked.

"Your mother's house."

"No."

"What do you mean, *no*?"

"I mean I don't want to go back there. If she can't even come be here for me, I don't want to go back to that house."

"It's not like you make it easy."

"There's a lot you don't know about me, David."

"And whose fault is that?"

"Can you just drive me home?"

"Home? And where exactly is that?"

"Yu."

"Yu?" He scoffed and I heard something catch in his throat, like he was holding back saying the thing he really wanted to say. He closed his eyes and gripped the steering wheel. I knew I should feel bad or grateful. I did, but they were secondary emotions to my concern for Howling Woman, my desire to get back to where I'd decided to call home. He let go of the steering wheel and pulled out his cellphone and began typing. He waited for something to load on the screen and then he put his phone in the cup holder. A map with directions to Yu glowed. We weren't much more than an hour away. A straight shot after we hit I-25.

"Can I borrow your phone?"

"What for?"

"Please?" I reached for it. He didn't stop me. Just pulled out of the parking lot and onto the frontage road that led to the freeway entrance heading north.

On his phone I typed the name of the jail and in the inmate locator field I typed in the name the deputy had given me. *Haggerty.* There wasn't a mugshot, just a stock photo of an avatar in an orange jumpsuit, but the charges were there.

Name: Chelsea Haggerty

Alias: Howling Woman

Date of Birth: 03/20/1958

Charge: driving under the influence, outstanding warrant, possession of a deadly weapon, murder in the 2nd degree

Howling Woman. *Chelsea Haggerty. Murder.* It didn't seem right. It didn't seem real. Sure, she believed in giving men what they deserved, but *murder*? That didn't add up. She was a good person. Generous. She'd taken me in. Been there for Angel when his mom died. Dressed up as female icons and sang at a fucking dive bar for the fun of it, for the fun of others. But what did I really know about her? Certainly not that she could have committed murder, not in the second degree or any degree. Then again, I never thought I'd shoot a man. Didn't think the only regret I'd have was not killing him. Maybe it doesn't change anything about her, make her any less good or any more bad, that she killed someone.

"Fuck."

"What is it?"

"I can't fucking believe it."

"Sabine, what is it?"

"That deputy wasn't fucking lying. Howling Woman is being held on murder charges. I just, I don't even know what to say." I fumbled in my property bag for my cigarettes and took one out.

"You can't smoke in here, Sabine. It's a rental."

"It's only one. The smell will be gone by the time you return it."

"God dammit, Sabine," David said, his hand in a fist against the steering wheel. "Have you always been this selfish? Have I been blind to it this whole time, or is this a new thing with you?"

"Fine, I won't smoke the fucking cigarette."

"How did you end up hanging out with a woman like that? What even happened the other night?"

"Nothing as bad as you're thinking." He was shaking his head, and I could tell that however he saw me in that moment there was no going back. Whatever I had tricked him into seeing while I was in California—a college student, a smart woman, a kind person—that was all gone now. I was my mother's daughter—selfish, trashy, a magnet for chaos—worse, I was James Dixon's former stepdaughter—broken, violated, vengeful—and there was no hiding it anymore.

"You're telling me she's being held on murder, that you're being charged with assault with a deadly weapon, with attempted murder, but not to worry about it?"

"You think they'd just let me walk free if it was something like that?"

"They didn't let you walk free, Sabine. I paid your bail. You're still going to have to go to court. Even if that man you shot at doesn't change his mind and press charges, this is still going to have some impact on your life. Don't you realize that?"

I could tell then that what he was doing for me, paying for my lawyer, helping me stay out of prison, was out of obligation. Not love. He always did have such good manners. Such a keen sense of do-goodness.

"He's not just any man."

"Who is he then? Why on earth would you hurt someone like that?"

"Don't you think some people deserve it?"

"How can you say that?"

"I am just wondering if you ever think there is a time that violence is the only option."

"I don't believe you think that's true. In your right mind you don't believe you wanted to hurt him."

"I did want to hurt him. I didn't think I was this kind of person either, but I guess I am. Sorry to break it to you."

"What the hell?" His voice cracked as he asked it, and then, almost in a whisper, he asked, "Sabine, were you really trying to kill him?"

He didn't look at me, just kept his eyes on the road, and I could see from his clenched jaw and tight grip on the wheel that he was trying to hold something in, trying not to come undone. I'd done this to him, broken him, and he didn't deserve it.

"You're probably right," I said, though I could feel the lie of it as the words left my mouth, "and I am not living with a murderer. They've got it all wrong. I don't know how to explain it in a way that will make sense to you."

"You're living with this woman?"

"She's my friend."

"You barely met this person, Sabine. You don't even know anything about her."

"I don't think friendships are simply a matter of the math of time."

"She got you arrested."

"If you're so appalled by me, why did you come?"

"You're still my wife, Sabine." He shook his head and let out a sigh.

I leaned my head back against the seat of the car and closed my eyes. It was hard to believe this was true, that I was someone's wife, that someone once loved me enough to promise to spend the rest of their life with me. It all felt so long ago, and I could hardly even remember what it had been like, but then I felt him reach his hand across the center console to my side of the car and take my hand in his and it all came flooding back, how good he'd been to me, how smart, and kind, and unlike any man I'd ever known before. How could someone like that—a professor, an intellectual, a genuinely kind person who was willing to fly with no notice to the middle-of-nowhere, New Mexico to retrieve his runaway philandering bride from jail—possibly ever love a person like me?

"I'm not a very good wife."

He squeezed my hand and then let it go. I looked up and watched him wrap his hand back around the steering wheel. "Why did you leave, Sabine? Was your life with me really so miserable?"

"It wasn't you."

"What about the affair then?" He looked over at me, but I couldn't make out his face in the dark, could only see his eyes searching mine. I shook my head. I didn't know what to say. He turned back to the road.

"I did love you, David. I do love you. I just don't think I know how to be someone's wife."

"Don't you think that's the kind of thing you should figure out before you get married? Why couldn't you talk to me about whatever was going on? We could have worked through it."

"I'm not like you. I didn't grow up like you. You met my mother. That should tell you something."

"She's not so bad."

"She left me to rot in jail."

"You make it all sound so sordid. Was your life so terrible? Were you that messed up?"

And there it was, the judgment I was always afraid of, that my feelings and impulses wouldn't be valid, that I wouldn't be believed, that I was just a hysterical woman unable to control her emotions.

"I don't know how to explain it to you."

"I feel like such an idiot, you know that, Sabine?"

"I'm sorry, David. You don't deserve this."

"There's something we can agree on." He reached for the volume control of the car radio and turned it up. It was a country song and I waited for him to turn it to something else, but he let it play, just kept driving. I wanted him to forgive me, to still love me even though I didn't want us to be together, even though I couldn't wait until we were out of the car and I could be alone. I wanted more than I deserved. I leaned my head against the window and closed my eyes, letting the highway lull me to sleep.

THIRTY·FOUR.

When I opened my eyes again, we were pulling into Yu. The country music station was still playing.

"Hey," I said, my voice breaking from sleep, "Will you turn onto the main drag up here and follow it down to that big building at the end?"

I saw his eyes squinting, trying to make out what I was talking about, but he didn't say anything, just did what I asked. In the car beside David, Yu seemed even more surreal than when I'd first arrived, and part of me felt like it was a dream—any minute I'd wake up and none of the last month or year or decade would have happened, but then what? It's like that science fiction rule—if you change one thing from the past, it's impossible to have any concept of the present— or something like that. That's why it's so hard to distill a life, even part of a life, down to one story. If you leave out one detail or focus on the wrong detail, then it changes the story. Here I am, focusing this story on Yu, on the relationships I built there, but how different would the story be if I'd spent more time writing about California? About my childhood? About the affair or my marriage? About anything else I may have left out?

"Turn into that parking lot on the left."

He craned his neck to look up at the neon sign above the parking lot. "A bar? You have to be kidding me." The car came to a stop in the middle of the road. "No. I am not ferrying you straight from jail to a bar."

"It's where I work."

"That's great, but you're not working tonight obviously, so whatever business you have there you can deal with tomorrow."

"Howling Woman works there too. They'll be worried."

"What's the address to the house?"

"Please, David? This is important. I won't ask for anything else, I swear."

He shook his head, but I felt the car rolling forward and then we were turning into the parking lot of The Whiptail.

The jukebox was playing Journey and the crowd was singing along with the speakers like it wasn't the most cliché thing one could do at a bar. David slowed beside me as we walked in, his eyes scanning the place, taking it all in, the cluttered walls, the singing drunks, the so very small-town America of it all. Nick and Angel were both behind the bar when we walked in, and I caught Angel's eyes right away. He looked at me and then to David and back down to the drink he was pouring for Jesse.

"What the hell are you doing here?" Nick asked, pulling four shot glasses off the shelf as soon as I sat down at the bar in front of him, "Howling Woman said the two of you were going to be on some type of road trip."

"Sabine," Jesse squealed and pulled me into a hug. "Who is this handsome stud you have with you?"

I looked behind me and saw David standing with his arms crossed in front of him.

"This is my husband, David. David, this is Jesse. He lives in town."

Angel looked up and I couldn't tell what he was thinking, but it didn't look good by the way he was locking his jaw and how his eyes kept going back and forth between me and David.

"Oh, of course. She talks about you all the time," Jesse said, his eyebrows nearing his hairline as if to force his face into a blank, stretched canvas.

"Sabine, can you just do what you came here to do so we can get out of here?" David said, ignoring the greeting. Jesse puckered his lips and raised his eyebrows all dramatic, like, *well look at this snob from California.* Then he squinted and moved his face close to mine, the mock-drama vanishing from his expression. "Jesus, honey, what happened to your face?"

Nick tilted his head to get a better look at me too, and everyone's eyes were suddenly on me. "Christ on a cracker, Sabine, you look awful."

I brought my hand to my cheek and felt the cut from when I'd been on the ground after we got pulled over.

"It's a long story, but it's not so bad."

"Honey, it's bad," Jesse said.

"I'm fine. I swear." I looked at Nick and could see he was shifting gears, hearing what I said and tabling his concern to settle back in on being his gregarious bartender self.

"Hey, it's good to meet you, man. I'm Nick, the owner of this fine establishment." He reached out his hand to shake David's, and to my surprise David shook it back.

"David."

"You know I thought she made you up, but look at you, Sabine's husband, in the flesh. Angel, come meet Sabine's husband."

Angel straightened up and stepped down to the edge of the bar where David was standing, "Nice to meet you," he said, but he didn't smile or look at me again and I could feel David looking from me to Angel then.

"Why don't we have a shot to celebrate?" Nick said, already pouring three whiskeys, "Whiskey okay for you, my man?"

"We're not drinking tonight."

Nick and Angel both looked at me then over to Jesse whose eyebrow shot up near off his face.

"I'm going to go pick some songs that aren't as cliché as all get out. Angel, can you get me some quarters?" Jesse stood, "Nice meeting you, hubs. Sabine, call me in the morning, will you?" he said, giving me a once over, and I thought it was strange that he was telling me to call him when I'd never once called him before, and then I realized how I must have looked, fresh out of jail, my face all busted up, my long-lost husband in tow. It was a paint by numbers picture, but they were filling it in all wrong.

"Yeah, sure," I said.

Jesse followed Angel to the side of the bar with the register and I tried not to focus on the two of them leaned in over the bar talking all close.

"Can I get you a soda or something?" Nick asked David.

"Actually," I interrupted, "I came here to tell you something. It's not so good, but here, let's take these first."

"Sabine." David's voice was a whisper, but it was cutting, and I could tell by the way Nick looked away that he'd heard it too.

"It's fine." I reached for a glass and Nick did the same, but his usual smile had faded.

"You are unbelievable," David whispered, "This is a Sisyphean task." David turned and walked away. I slammed my shot back without even clinking it against Nick's.

"Sweetheart," Nick said real serious, putting his undrunk shot back down on the bar, "Are you in trouble?"

Angel looked back over at me and then toward the door where David was walking out. He said something to Jesse and then made his way back down to me and Nick. His face was more concerned than angry this time, like he hadn't considered my husband showing up could mean I was in danger, like he'd only thought it meant we weren't as broken up as I'd let on.

"I'm fine." I reached for the shot Nick had poured David and slammed that one too. "Can I get another?"

Nick looked at Angel like he didn't want to be the one to pour it.

"Are you sure that's a good idea right now?"

"It's fine."

"Why is your husband here?"

"Can I get another shot?"

Angel poured the shot and slid it closer to me.

"Seriously, Sabine, what the hell is going on? Do I need to call the police?" Nick asked.

"Jesus, no. This?" I said, pointing to the cut on my face, "This wasn't David if that's what you're thinking. God, no. He would never. This is from the police."

"What in the hell are you talking about?" Nick asked.

"Howling Woman and I got arrested."

"What the fuck?" Angel said.

Someone at the other end of the bar was tapping their glass on the bar, and we all looked down at him. "Can I get another drink?"

"We're in the middle of something," Nick shouted back. "Fuck it," he muttered, reaching for the cowbell behind the bar, ringing it a couple of times until enough people had quieted down for him to be heard. "Hey, hey, hey, attention up here," Nick shouted over the music, "No one ask me for another drink. Y'all missed last call, but that's it. Night's over. Pack it up. I'm talking to my friend. Mind your own business and find somewhere else to be."

The whole bar groaned, and Angel reached for the remote to the jukebox and cut the music. People booed, but they didn't seem like they were in a rush to finish their drinks.

I took the shot Angel poured me and tried to get the important details out about Howling Woman without getting into everything else that had happened with James Dixon.

"It sounds like it's a charge from a long time ago," I said, getting to the part about how I was released but Howling Woman wasn't. "It seems serious." I looked around to see if anyone was listening, but no one was paying attention to us. "It's a murder charge."

"Fucking hell," Nick said.

"I know. I think it's pretty bad."

"It's got to be some kind of mistake," Angel said, and I felt a flash of jealousy toward Howling Woman, that he was worried for her, wanted to run to her, console her, and I wanted him to do that for me, but I hadn't told him yet about the trouble I was facing.

"I'm going to go see her tomorrow if either of you want to come."

"Yeah, Angel is off. You should go down with her."

"Of course."

"This is fucking crazy," Nick said and poured us each another shot, "and what about you? Are you okay?"

"I don't know. Okay enough," I said. We drank our shots and I felt at least a little bit more leveled out. Not quite right, but like I could make it through another short car ride with my pissed off husband.

"Whatever this shit is, Howling Woman is good people. We got to be there for her," Nick said, and we all nodded.

"Look, I am sorry for coming in like this, but I didn't think it would be right to keep it to myself. I don't even know what to make of it all, but you guys are the closest thing she has to family."

"We all are," Nick said, his face as serious as I'd ever seen it. He walked around to me on the other side of the bar and wrapped his arms around me. He hadn't ever hugged me before, but it felt like the most natural thing, him holding me, resting his face on top of my skull and our chests rising and falling in sync. He was all soft, and he patted my back like I was someone he truly loved. It seemed like the way a dad would hug his daughter. "Your man's waiting out there for you and he don't seem too happy. Why don't you get yourself on outta here before you get in any more trouble. We can talk more tomorrow."

"Yeah," I said, nodding. It was the most level-headed I'd ever heard Nick sound, and it was suddenly easy to imagine that he used to be someone's husband, that he was capable of running a successful business, like maybe the wild side he showed everyone else was only one small part of him, but that the other side he reserved for the more private parts of his life was gentle and calm and fatherly.

"I'll walk you out," Angel said, coming around to me, and before we got to the front door he grabbed my wrist and turned me to face him.

"Tell the truth, your face, was that really the police?"

"I swear."

"If that man..."

"He's not like that. He's the one who picked me up from the station. He's a good guy."

Angel winced. "It looks like it hurts." He let go of my hand and ran his finger across my swollen lips. "How did this even happen?"

"Honestly, if I start talking about it now I might just fall apart."

"You're gonna be okay." He brushed my check with the back of his hand. "Come on," he said, and we walked out the double doors toward the parking lot. I could see David sitting in the Civic, but I couldn't tell if he was looking at us.

"Can you come over when you're done closing?"

"Tonight?"

"Please."

"What about your husband?"

"It's not like that."

"I don't know if that's such a good idea, Sabine. Why don't we meet up tomorrow?"

"I can't be alone tonight."

Angel looked away from me, shaking his head. "I don't know."

"Just to lie with me. Nothing else," I said, stepping closer to him, "Please, Angel? I'm really freaked out."

"Yeah. Okay. I'll come over."

"I'll leave the door unlocked."

When I got to the car, David was looking out the window at Angel taking the flag down from above the front entrance. He put the car in reverse and backed out before I even closed the door all the way.

"Thanks for bringing me."

"Who's the guy?"

"Just a coworker."

"Like Avery was just a coworker?"

"How..." I started to ask, but I didn't want to know. I looked into my lap, waiting for the short car ride to Howling Woman's to be over.

THIRTY·FIVE.

It was after midnight when Angel slipped into bed with me. I'd heard him open the door and close it quietly. I heard him take his shoes off at the front door so he wouldn't make any noise walking across the living room floor to my bed. David was sleeping in Howling Woman's bedroom with the door shut and if he heard Angel come in, he didn't do anything to signal he had. He hadn't wanted to talk anymore after The Whiptail except to tell me he hoped I'd get my shit together.

"Hey," I whispered to Angel.

"Hey," he whispered back.

"Thanks for coming."

He was quiet and I could feel his body turning toward me and mirroring the shape of me. "You scared me tonight."

"I scared myself."

"I don't mean about the arrest stuff." He stroked my back for a second, and then let his hand fall into the space between us.

I turned toward him, so we were facing each other, and he brought his hand up toward my face and ran his fingers through my hair.

"You coming in with your husband. It made me all…"

"Mad at me?"

"No."

"Jealous?"

"No, it was different than that. It's like that feeling you get when you think you might never see someone again and you realize you had all these things you still wanted to do together but will never get the chance to."

I tilted my face up and could feel his hot breath dampening the air between us. I knew I should be thinking about the mess I was in, how Howling Woman was in jail, how my husband was in the room just feet away, but all I could think was how I was grateful that Angel had come. I wanted everything else to disappear. I wanted to be in some other type of story where I really did believe I could start over in a new town and it was as simple as finding another man to love me. I wanted a story that was simpler than the one I'd written for myself.

"I don't know how it's possible, but I just can't imagine my life without you. I didn't even know I felt that way until I saw you in the bar tonight. Is that crazy?" He said.

"No. I feel that way too," I said. I wasn't sure if I believed it, but I know that in that moment I would have been wrecked if he hadn't shown up, if I'd been forced to spend the night alone with my thoughts. I wondered if Angel had really been thinking about his mom when he'd said all this, like maybe the last time he'd felt this way was when his mom was dying, and now he was projecting it onto me. It's possible he was talking about Howling Woman. And then I was thinking that maybe he really meant it and that I felt this way a little bit too. I could feel that my life was on the precipice of having something disappear from it—my husband, Howling Woman, Angel, my freedom? I wasn't sure what exactly, but I knew enough to be uneasy, to want reassurance and comfort to distract from whatever it was I was about to lose.

Angel pressed his face close to mine and kissed me gently, like he hadn't forgotten my lips were still swollen and cracked. When he pulled away, he took my hands in his and kissed them.

"So are you going to tell me what happened with you and Howling Woman?"

"Yeah," I sighed, and was surprised how easy the word had come out of my mouth, "but you have to promise you won't judge me."

"I promise," he said, and in the dark of the living room I couldn't make out his face to see if I could believe him, but I'd told my story once, so maybe it wouldn't be so hard to say again. What else was there to hide? I'd said it once and Howling Woman had believed me. Maybe he would too.

I started from the beginning, with James Dixon, and told him the whole story, all the way through. Maybe that's why I can write this now, why I can try my hand at being honest. I've said it all before, even the parts I didn't think I'd ever say, so what harm was there in saying it over and over again until it became something without power. Writing this all down is only the third time I've ever allowed the story to exist outside of my own memory. I can feel it changing with each retelling. I can't be sure if I am circling closer to the truth of what happened or getting farther from it. There is a sense that words feed on themselves, changing the meaning of the ones that came before them each time there is a new order, a new audience. The darkness of the living room made it easier to put it all together, just like now, showing up to the page when no one else is around looking over my shoulder to tell me I've got it wrong.

In the morning, I woke to the sound of the front door slamming shut and felt my heart racing at the prospect of Angel disappearing without saying goodbye, but he was in bed beside me, his arms wrapped around me, and I knew a better person than myself would have felt worse than I did, but maybe it isn't up to me to decide how I feel. Maybe I'm entitled to let my feelings exist as they are without trying to manipulate them into something I think others might prefer. Right then, the sound of an engine turning over, gravel crunching beneath tires, my husband leaving, I felt relief. Relief that he would be gone when I got up and relief that the other man had stayed.

THIRTY·SIX.

The problem is it's never the whole story. Once you focus on a narrative, tell some details, but not others, it's no longer the truth. It's still just a story. No matter how concerned with confession one might be, it's all a construct. Now, how to end the story when I don't know my own ending? All of this will mean something different depending on the ending. My trial begins in a couple of days. The day after my thirtieth birthday to be exact. How do I write this? How do I assign meaning to the events of my life before others decide who I am and what ending I deserve? I guess all I can do when it comes to ending this confession is bring us as close to the present moment as possible, but it's hard not to think about what comes after this moment, hard not to imagine the end as existing in a larger context of the whole story, as coexisting with the stories of others, their own telling of it contradicting the one I'm writing.

If the story I am trying to get at is the story of healing past trauma, then I should focus on returning to how I felt shooting the man whose memory haunted me all those years. Focus on what it felt like to realize I might have been happier had my aim been better. If this has all been a story about the disintegration of a marriage (which isn't that what most literature is?), then I should focus on how I felt waking up to the sound of David pulling out of Howling Woman's driveway, him leaving divorce papers on the counter next to the jar of coffee beans, the mark of our true end, but this was never a story about our marriage. That was just a de-tail. Maybe this is a love story about looking for love in all the wrong places and finding it when you finally stop looking. But then I think of Chekhov, or rather, what I've heard of Chekhov, and he never seemed to believe finding love was any type of story. It was what came next. And I'm not so sure what Angel and I have is considered love, and what comes next with him won't be the thing that saves me.

Part of me wants this to be a story about female friendship—the way two women together can save each other in a way that isn't possible between women and men. There is something that feels powerful about a story of women who don't need men. Feminist maybe. Superior definitely. But that isn't exactly right either. I don't even know how Howling Woman will fit into the rest of my life now that she's in jail. I imagine if I end up remaining a free woman, then with enough time, Howling Woman, and Yu, and Angel, will all just become minor details of the larger narrative of my life.

I haven't spoken to Howling Woman since Angel and I drove to visit her. She asked us not to come again, my lawyer strongly suggested that I cut off all ties, but I can't help but feel guilty about it. Like I shouldn't have listened to either of them. Like I should have gone back again.

I think back to my visit with Howling Woman. Visitations were limited to fifteen minutes, and Angel and I had waited nearly an hour for the guards to bring Howling Woman in to meet with us.

When they finally brought Howling Woman in to see us, her wrists were handcuffed and linked to a chain that wrapped around her waist. It didn't seem necessary, though she had been charged with murder, and I guess if it was true then that meant she was capable of doing things deemed dangerous.

"Look at the two of you," she said as they sat her down across from us.

"I was getting worried they weren't going to bring you," I said.

"That's what you're worried about?"

I looked at Angel like maybe he could say something that made more sense, but he stared at Howling Woman, a sad look overtaking his face.

"Hey now, mister, if anyone should be looking like that right about now, it's me. Snap out of it."

"Sorry," he said, and she didn't correct his apology.

"We are going to put some money together at the bar to get you a lawyer and get this all fixed," Angel said, which came as a surprise. He hadn't mentioned this to me yet, and I wondered if he and Nick had talked about it at work after I'd left.

"That's real sweet, but I'm not sure how much it will help."

"You can't think like that," Angel said.

Howling Woman smiled, but her face looked pained, like it was hard to hold her lips up like that, and for the first time, I looked at her and could see how old she was. Her hair was pulled back in a long, low braid. Her cheekbones were high, and small wrinkles rivered between them and the bottoms of her eyes. Fifty-four. Her booking report had said she was fifty-four and I could see it.

"I appreciate you both coming down to visit me, but I don't want you wasting your youth on trips to visit an old woman in jail."

"Howling Woman…" Angel started, but she put her palm up to stop him from finishing.

"I love you, Angel, you know that, but lord knows you spent enough of your life making sacrifices for women that get themselves in their own world of trouble."

"It's not a big deal."

"Angel, why don't you give me and Sabine a minute to talk. Do you mind?"

Angel looked at me and then back at Howling Woman.

"Sure, yeah, okay," he said, getting up slowly from the table and walking toward one of the guards.

"How are the girls?"

"The chickens?"

"You feeding them?"

"Of course."

"Good."

"I'm sorry, I got you into this mess," I said.

"Hey," she said putting her finger up in front of me, "Remember what I said? No *sorries*. Not in my book."

I bit my lip to keep from saying it again.

"Hell, it was my idea anyway."

I looked at the clock above her and could feel time running out between us. "Howling Woman," I whispered as I leaned in close to her, "They say you have been charged with murder, that you stabbed a man to death."

"Bison."

"I thought…"

She reached her hands across the table and set them on mine.

"No touching," The guard shouted from across the small visitation room. We both retracted our hands.

"You know, Buttercup, how I told you a certain kind of man never changes?"

I nodded.

"Well, I left so fast back then I always wondered what happened after I'd gone. I guess now I know." She winked at me, and her eyes got glassy. A tear fell in a slow stream down her face. "It was so long ago. With enough time. Enough listening, I'll be free. Men like that make people understand why women do certain things. Then again, it's hard to imagine anyone would ever believe a woman's story over a man's. Why do you think I ran in the first place?"

"It's not fair," I said, my voice cracking, and I felt a tear running down my own face.

"Buttercup, you know as well as I do that life's not fair."

"I don't want to be without you."

"Hey now, don't you start crying. I am the one handcuffed. Remember?" She lifted her hands up as if I couldn't see them on the table between us. I wiped my eyes and tried to put on a smile, but it hurt, and not just because of my swollen lip and cut-up cheek.

"It was self-defense though, right?"

She looked across at me, her face straight. "You tell me. You know what it's like."

And I did. Not exactly, but enough that I knew self-defense wasn't so easily definable. It means something different to everyone, and men like James Dixon, like Bison, like Dick, well, they threaten you even when it isn't so obvious to everyone else. I thought about how she'd thrown acid on her stepfather's face, how she'd blinded him, how she'd put a gun in the glovebox of her car and driven me to face my own stepfather. I knew the answer without her saying it.

"Look, Buttercup, I mean it, I don't want you wasting all your time coming out here to see me. I'm a big girl. I can handle myself. I appreciate what you and the guys want to do, getting me a lawyer and all, but that's good enough for now. I need some time to sit here and think about what's happened, and you need some time to get your own stuff together as far as I see it. Can you promise you'll stay away for a little while?"

I nodded, but I didn't like the idea of her sitting in a jail cell without any visitors.

"Another thing, if you insist on having a man around, and if it's gonna be Angel, then do me a favor and don't go breaking his heart. He's not like us. He doesn't have it in him to go through another heartbreak, so just think about that before you do whatever it is you're thinking about."

"That's time," the guard called, "Inmate, let's go."

Howling Woman stood from the table and smiled down at me, "One more thing."

"Yeah?"

"Get yourself to that damn vortex."

THIRTY·SEVEN.

It smells like rain is coming when I walk out of Howling Woman's house. Angel is parked, waiting for me in the driveway. I don't know how long it will last, and I hardly think he will play the part of loyal bride if I end up serving time. Maybe me getting put away will bring him to his senses and he'll finally leave this town and the chaos it's dealt him. But I don't know what's next for Angel anymore than I know what's next for myself.

When I get into Angel's truck, he stretches over to kiss my cheek. I open the Diet Coke he's brought for me and light a cigarette. He's good like that, bringing me caffeine and cigarettes, driving me to my appointments and telling me it will all be alright. I feel a constant desire to get inside his head, understand why he's doing what he's doing, to see what purpose I serve in his life, to demand he explain it to me so I can work through all the potential narratives of our relationship, but it doesn't seem right when he hasn't demanded anything from me, when I am still not sure what purpose he will have served in mine. After this, I'm done writing, not just here on the page, but in my mind, too. After this, whatever happens, I'm going to just exist, to be in exactly the moment I'm in without trying to see the story of it.

"You look nice," he says, putting his truck in reverse and pulling out of the driveway.

"Thanks," I say, though I know the modest dress I'm wearing, something I pulled from Howling Woman's closet, doesn't do me any favors. That's the point. My lawyer said I should look girlish, innocent. I'm not sure how much it will matter, but he's gotten most of my charges dropped, says he thinks I might even get off with the minimum sentence, so I don't question him too much. I've given up trying to fight for my story to be told in court. I've given up trying to get people to see something in me I want them to see.

"We don't have that much time," Angel says.

"It's important."

"Where?"

"Will you drive us up la Chupadera?"

"We'll be late."

"We've got time, and I could use all the help I can get." Even as I say it I know it sounds ludicrous, thinking a mountain can save me, that a vortex can pull something from me and make me pure. It's not that I believe the vortex has this kind of magic. Belief has nothing to do with it. Belief feels too wrapped up in truth, in a certain knowingness that something is true even if it can't exactly be proven. I'm not sure there is a truth I can believe in. Truth and belief and storytelling all feel manmade—like things designed to explain the unexplainable. Even this writing— my confession, my story, my truth—it all feels insubstantial, like it'll never be able to capture the essence of it all—a whole life. I'm changing even as I write this, not trusting a word I put down because it all belongs to the versions of me that existed before the story. The story is a way to make sense, but how do you make sense of an entire history? All I know is that my body is being beckoned by this force I cannot see and I have to be as close to it as possible before whatever comes next.

"If you insist," Angel says, putting the truck in drive and resting his palm on my thigh. He's shaking his head as he drives, but I see a smile come across his face, and I know he's thinking the town has finally gotten to me, like I'm a real goner now, asking to visit some vortex, to will it to have its way with me before I sit in a room where others will decide my fate. He keeps driving, down the main drag, past The Whiptail, turning onto the long stretch of gravel road that turns to sand and leads up the mountain. I think he gets it, though. None of this makes sense to him—how he ended up here, how he belonged to the mother he was born to, how she left this earth too soon, how he loves Howling Woman, how I came into his life, how he can't seem to leave me alone, how neither of us know what comes next and somehow we've both chosen to stay, to ride it out based on nothing more than a feeling. We could spend our whole lives trying to explain it, but it doesn't change the way it is.

The sky is the stormy violet, pre-sunrise kind of desert sky, and it is marred with dark thunderclouds ready to open. A couple droplets land on the windshield as we head toward the fire trail that leads up the mountain and the smell is distinct. Dust and electricity. Cleansing and filth. I take Angel's hand in mine and hold it tight. Howling Woman was right about him. About everything really. I can still see the moon in the sky even as morning starts to give way. It is full just like Howling Woman said it should be. We are climbing up the mountain, the truck gliding across the deep sand, almost as if we are being pulled by a powerful magnet hidden from sight.

ACKNOWLEDGEMENTS

Writing this novel was a central part of my life for nearly seven years, and it wouldn't exist today without the incredible support of so many people.

First and foremost, I want to express my deep gratitude to my publisher, Patrick Trotti. Your belief in this book came exactly when I needed it most. I will forever be grateful for your encouragement and faith in this project. My thanks also go to David Wojciechowski for his brilliant design work that brought the book to life visually.

To my writing group, Liturgy—Neha Bagchi, Sheila Bare, Nancy Fishman, Ann Guy, Katie Hunter, Jenny McKeel, and Lily Zucker—thank you for reading draft after draft of this novel and providing feedback and support that fueled me for years. Ann, you may not know it, but you especially kept me going. You are the most thoughtful reader and friend. Your voice forever lives in my head as I write and edit.

Thank you also to the writers I admire who took the time to read this book and help me sharpen it: Elizabeth Ellen, Claire Hopple, Rebecca van Laer, and especially Mila Jaroniec, who asked an essential question that guided me to the book's true form.

I am also incredibly grateful to my peers and professors at San Francisco State where this book was started. A special thanks to May-lee Chai and Caro de Robertis for their guidance and mentorship.

The Sou'Wester Residency Program and Virginia Quinan provided me with a much-needed retreat from daily life, allowing me to focus deeply on rewriting. Virginia, your encouragement and kindness over the years have been one of the greatest gifts, and I will cherish our time together forever.

I owe my biggest thanks to my family. Thank you mom for never once telling me that my fantasy of being a writer was insane. Thank you for making me a reader. I am a writer because of you. To Joshua Hinte, you are a hard to please reader and your feedback always makes me strive to be better. Alhelí Harvey, you have been a first reader and my lifelong friend. I couldn't ask for more. And to my husband and stepdaughter, living with a writer is not always easy, and I'm eternally grateful for your love and patience. You've seen me through every stage of this book's creation and have given me purpose beyond the page. Thank you especially to Adelaar, my first reader, my ideal reader, my partner in everything. I will spend the rest of my life writing the books I think you'll want to read. You are my muse, my soulmate, my everything.

Lastly, to you, the reader: If you have read this book to the end, you have given me the greatest gift any writer could ask for. And if you found yourself resonating with the themes of domestic violence or sexual abuse, please know that I wrote this book for you.